Crossing Tracks

A Tale of Rails and Resilience

Terry R Cooper

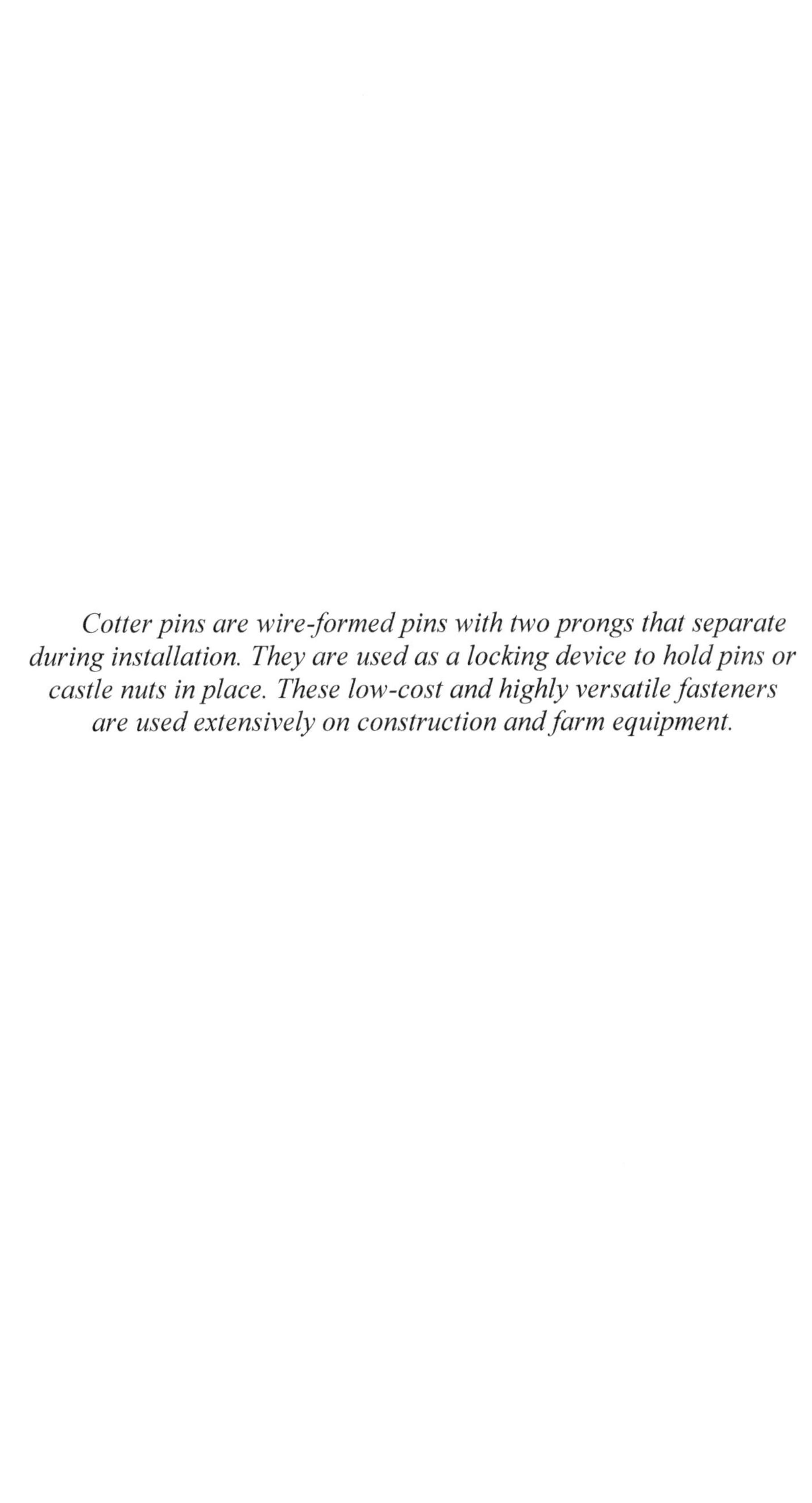

Cotter pins are wire-formed pins with two prongs that separate during installation. They are used as a locking device to hold pins or castle nuts in place. These low-cost and highly versatile fasteners are used extensively on construction and farm equipment.

CHAPTER 1

April 18, 1971, Sardinia, Ohio

I'd watched the Friday morning freight train for the last seven weeks. There'd only been one day when it didn't have a boxcar with an open door. The odds were in my favor. At least for that.

By 5:30 a.m. I crouched among the budding bushes between the south pasture fence and the short gravel slope to the train track. Crickets that had quieted when I climbed over the fence now chirped around me. The eastern sky painted whisps of faint pink. A mosquito buzzed around my head. I shifted the backpack on my shoulders and swatted the biting insect on my neck, feeling satisfaction at the tiny defensive victory. The morning was still cool, but my armpits were sweating. I wondered if black snakes were hunting yet. It was still dark enough that I wouldn't see the creepy Cretaceous survivors if they slithered across my shoes. That wouldn't bother me, but their prey— mice—freaked me out.

Before I had time to worry about that, a train whistle blew in the distance. Dah-dah-dit-dah. The signal for crossing an unmarked highway. Main Street just outside of Sardinia. Two minutes. My mouth was suddenly dry. I reached for my canteen but convinced myself there wasn't enough time. Poking my head around a bush, I could see the locomotive's headlight in the distance across the fields. It had to negotiate two turns before it got to me, so it would be slowed to about twenty mph. Slow for a train but top speed for our farm tractors. Those parameters had played in my head for the last few years, calculating if I could leap into a moving train at that speed.

I stood and looked down the line of the approaching train cars. In the glow of approaching sunrise, there were two open boxcars near the middle and one near the end. I checked the stake I'd driven into the ground ninety feet up the track. The aluminum foil I'd wrapped around the top shone like a star.

Shoving through the bushes, I slid behind my makeshift ramp built from scrap wood. Version three. Over the last year I'd practiced this part. Version one ended up under the crushing wheels of the train, a pile of splinters I later swept away. Version two worked better but slid right back down the slope after I pushed it into place. Two weeks ago, my version-three trial seemed to be a success, at least for the dry-run.

I swallowed and squatted at the base of the ramp. The ground began to tremble. My knees quivered. The locomotive roared by. I grabbed the ramp handles and shoved it up the slope into position next to the track. Two feet between the ramp and whishing train cars. I could jump that easily. Even with thirty pounds on my back. If there was an open door to jump through. If I timed it right. If I didn't slip. If the ramp held.

Backing up against the fence, I looked up the track at the approaching cars. I ran the calculation in my head again. Twenty miles per hour was thirty feet per second. It took me three seconds from my start position to my jump. That meant I should start my run when the door was ninety feet away. Ninety feet was where I'd set my stake four weeks ago. I was good. Unless someone moved my stake. Or the train was going a different speed. Or…I forced myself to stop.

The first car with an open door passed my stake. One-one thousand, two-one thousand, three-one thousand. I twitched. It rumbled by. I looked up the track again. The next car with an open door was already at my stake. Too late. I had to pee. Dad flashed into my mind, his severed head staring up at me. It's been six years and I still try to explain how sorry I am every day.

I squeezed my eyes shut, took a deep breath, and cleared my thoughts. I willed calm and confidence to tamp panic. Here came the last boxcar with an open door. When it got to my stake, I took off, running hard, but not overly hard. It had to be three seconds. Adrenaline could affect my timing. Out of the corner of my eye, I could see the black doorway approaching. Focus. One more step, then jump. I hit the edge of the ramp and jumped hard. The ramp shifted under my weight. If this failed now, there would be no version four of the ramp. I would be bloody splinters. I'd thought a lot about that, too. Maybe I was unfixable, and a swift end was my only relief. But the stars called to me like the trains. There were things I wanted to do. Needed to do. Not just for me, but for…

My foot hit the worn floorboard of the boxcar. Sir Isaac Newton's first law of physics was upon me. I collapsed and rolled, absorbing the force of the train's movement with my roll. Still, a moment later I was in a heap against the far wall of the boxcar. But I was on the train. Moving at twenty mph. No need for ramp version four.

#####

After I clambered through the open door, I lay panting on the floor for several minutes. Years of accumulated stress from planning, guilt, and apprehension evaporated. The clickety-clack of the wheels on the track and the gentle swaying drained my adrenaline away. I dozed off into dreamless sleep for twenty minutes. Then I got to work.

I broke open the seal on the six-pack of spiral-ringed notebooks. Choosing the blue one, I scrawled the number one on the cover and recorded what had happened in the last hour.

It was time to start testing the cathartic value of pouring the horrors of my life onto paper. Talking to a psychologist or psychiatrist might have worked as well. But I'd read a lot about treatment for depression and grief—locking me up, electroconvulsive therapy, or drugging me into catatonia. Not for me. But I had to do something. My life was ebbing away into a sea of nightmares. If I didn't fix it now, I'd never be able to survive college and become who I could be.

Since I was a toddler, the yawning maw of open boxcars has called to me. Half-a-mile away, the rumbling freight trains rattled the house like a tap from God's hand saying, "Pay attention, Tink." Sometimes on moonlit nights I'd crawl out of bed and stand at the window, watching the train cars slide past our lower pasture like a wriggling woolly worm crawling fencepost to fencepost. I always knew that someday I'd be leaving our southern Ohio farm with a scramble and leap into a boxcar's dark unknown.

I hadn't set a departure date, though I'd been packing and re-packing my backpack since Daddy died. But now I was done with high school, had Bobby set up to manage the farm, and needed to turn the page in my life. Desperately. Before the gnawing nightmares and grief permanently wrecked my brain. It had already stolen my adolescence and my sleep. If I didn't stop it, it would steal the rest of my life just like a skid row heroin addict.

The letter arrived in February. It had a NASA logo in the corner and was hand-addressed to me. It was from a female NASA engineer named Morgan who said she had heard about me and my interest in physics and space. She wanted to meet me and offer herself as a coach and mentor. Myself and five other women my age were invited to her ranch near Missoula, Montana, between May 31 and June 13 while she was vacationing from her NASA job. It was as if the combination on a bank vault had just been spun correctly. The gears and levers in my life aligned. The door opened. I had a plan and a timeline. I had to be in Missoula by Memorial Day.

#####

Last night after supper, as it was starting to get dark, Momma took my hand and said, "Let's go look at the cherry tree." We'd had our ups and downs over the last six years, but we carefully tiptoed around what was going on in my head. Our mother-daughter relationship had switched to partners in our farm operation. It was a no-touch kind of thing, too. When she took my hand, it was like a jolt of electricity shot up my arm.

We walked out onto the front porch, leaving my older brother Bobby watching TV. We stood there inhaling the sweet smell, admiring the glinty golden hue of the blossoms in the April setting sun. A train whistle blew in the distance, and in a few minutes we watched it roll by the lower pasture.

Momma put her arm around my waist. "You can always come back, Tink. I'll be here. And your brother. He'll be here after me. It will always be home."

I turned to face her. "What do you mean, Momma?"

She hugged me. "I've known for years, Tink. Ever since you packed that bag. One morning I'd wake up and you'd be gone." She waved towards the train. "It calls you."

Tears filled my eyes. I gripped her in a tight hug. My Momma. She'd always known me, maybe better than I knew myself. At least 'til Daddy died and I shut down like a hibernating groundhog. The NASA letter I'd never shared with her felt warm in my pocket.

"You're a smart one, Tink." She tapped my forehead. "You know up here that you didn't cause your Daddy to die." She tapped my chest. "But you gotta know it here, too. We ain't got the money for them head doctors. Not sure they could fix your heart, anyhow." She looked into my eyes. "*You* gotta do that, Tink."

"That's why I have to leave, Momma."

"You think runnin' away will help?"

"It ain't running away. Riding the train will let me think. I see it as a journey."

"To where?"

"Montana. There's a special NASA seminar for women there. I've been invited."

"That an excuse?"

"No. It's the catalyst."

"The what?"

"Catalyst. The seminar invitation is what brought all the pieces together, made the whole thing work."

"How's that fix your troubles?"

"I gotta do something, Momma. I don't sleep because when I do it's filled with nightmares of Daddy. Nobody talks to me at school. But I don't care. I care about less and less each day. It's just you and Bobby now. It feels like I'm slipping away, draining into the ground like a leaky rain barrel."

CHAPTER 2

I leaned back against the wall of the boxcar. The open door opposite me was a moving window to the passing world. The ride wasn't as smooth as I'd expected. It was more like a high-gear tractor running across a pasture field. Except I was sitting on a solid wooden floor. I pulled a gray sweatshirt out of my pack and folded it under my butt. A few days on this train and I'd have butt bruises.

The train was slowing. I listened for the whistle to tell me why. Nothing. A faint ding-ding-ding of a crossing sounded somewhere up ahead. I was afraid I'd be spotted if I stuck my head out. The laws about hitching a train ride varied a lot, depending on which state or county you were in. The train workers were unpredictable. Some could care less. Others reported you or tried to chase you off on their own. I intended to avoid them all.

At eighteen, I'd already built a mental encyclopedia of train travel. There's a hobo camp about twenty miles east, near Peebles in Adams County. Hobo camps were common during the 1930's Depression. But during the late 1960's the sights and sounds of the Vietnam War and related protests on TVs in every home demoted hobos to background noise. Drugs, long hair, and burning flags were the hot topics. Hobos become invisible and, to most, didn't exist. But they were still there in the shadows, moving around on the trains as they had for decades.

Ten years ago, as Dad drove us to buy a calf in Adams County, I'd spotted several men in tattered clothes squatted around a campfire. "Who are those men in the woods, Dad?"

He glanced out the window where I pointed. "Probably hobos. Not many left. Train track runs right by there."

"I've read about them. They ride the trains. It's called 'train hopping.'"

"Well, they're dangerous. Lot of drugs and crazies in that group."

"Know how to tell the difference between a hobo, a tramp, and a bum?"

Dad glanced at me. "Where'd you hear those names?"

"They were in a history book about World War I. Said the hobos were migrant workers; a tramp travels but doesn't work; and a bum does neither." I gazed out the window as the camp disappeared around a bend. "I bet the bums are the ones doing drugs."

"You left out hippies. They hang out with that group, too."

I wasn't sure I believed that. According to what I'd read, the politics of the hobos was nothing like the left-wing ideals of the hippies.

That camp stuck in my mind. Every chance I got I'd checked to see if they were still there. When I turned sixteen and got my license, it was one of my first solo drives. I came to think of it as Trainhop University.

I spent a lot of summer Sundays there the last couple of years. They didn't trust me at first, but the smell of fried chicken in my basket loosened tongues after a few weeks. Pretty soon they were nodding and grunting a greeting when I arrived.

Bobby warned me about going to the camp alone. He said it was dangerous. Sheriff cars cruised by frequently. One time, before I'd won over the more onery hobos, a new guy showed up. He sat on a dirty Army blanket under an oak tree and stared at me for a while. He finally got up from his blanket and came over to the picnic table where four of the guys and I were sitting. He grabbed my chicken basket and turned, carrying it off.

"Hey," I said as I jumped up. "That's not yours."

He turned and smirked at me. "It is now, mutt."

I started to grab him but one of the guys at the table snagged my sleeve. When I turned to look at him, he shook his head and pulled me back to the table. Confused and fuming, I watched the new guy sit down facing us with his back against the tree trunk. He pawed through the basket and started gnawing a drumstick.

"Look at me," said Herb, the hobo across the table from me.

"What?"

"Look at me."

"Why?"

"You don't want to see nothin'."

"What do you mean?"

He grabbed my sleeve across the table, pulled me towards him, and hissed, "Even if it don't turn your stomach, it'll turn your dreams. Forever."

I was perplexed. Some of these guys talked gibberish, but Herb was always coherent and pleasant, even if he did smell like a wet dog.

He released my arm. I leaned back on the bench and glanced at the other three men down the table. They were all looking the other way. It made me think of what Momma said many times. Mostly in the kitchen. It usually included her pointing at me with a wooden spoon or spatula. "Tink, you always swim upstream. Gonna bring trouble if you're not careful."

Herb said, "You best git on home."

"Why?"

"'Cause you don't wanna be here when the cops come through."

I didn't know what he was talking about, but I was on his turf. I stood and turned to retrieve my chicken basket.

"Shit! I told you not to look. Git outta here now, boy."

The guy who'd stolen the chicken still sat with his back to the tree. His head lolled to one side. A huge red gash splayed under his chin. His shirt was covered in red. Someone had slit his throat.

I swallowed, feeling my stomach rumble. A thousand thoughts raced through my head. I'd seen death before. Gruesome death. Bloody. Haunting. But Herb was right. I didn't want to be connected to this murder. I needed to erase any evidence that I was here.

Rushing towards the guy, I grabbed my basket and pulled it away. It smelled like the rusty steel fenceposts around the chicken coop. It was obvious how he died. They wouldn't waste taxpayers' money on an autopsy, so no one would discover my chicken in his belly. I dumped the pool of blood in the basket on the ground between his legs where it joined the rest of his life ebbing back into the dirt.

On the way home, I stopped at the end of our lane and filled the basket with rocks. Then I tossed the whole thing into the pond next to the lane. It didn't float. There were some bubbles at first. The blood swirled around in the green water, but in a couple of minutes, it disappeared altogether.

I don't think the hobos thought I'd be back. But they didn't know me yet. The next Sunday, I brought more fried chicken and some candy bars. Seven of them crowded around the table in silence while they chowed on chicken. I dumped the bag of candy bars on the table. They quickly disappeared into pockets without a word. No grumbling about who got how many, and no one tried to take more than their share. These guys were counting on each other in a weird cross between friends and brothers.

In the ensuing weeks, I asked a lot of questions and wrote the answers in my black spiral-ringed notebook. In trip preparation, I read through that tattered notebook every month since then. It's committed to memory now. I learned the train signals, how to snag food and water, and how to stay hidden. They also taught me what to do if I get caught. I don't plan to need that information.

#####

The train jolted to a stop. Out my open door, I saw farmland. I glanced at my watch. We'd been rolling along for about ninety minutes. Maybe sixty miles.

I stood up and stretched, creeping carefully towards the door. When the sun was bright, like it was now, the dimness of the boxcar made it impossible to see anyone inside. The hobos understood this well. But I looked it up in the library anyhow. It's the way the eyeball protects itself and manages the light exposure to the retina. In bright light, the pupil shrinks so the retina doesn't get burned by too much bright light. As a result, it doesn't let in enough light to see inside the gloom of a dark space. Like a boxcar. But after a few seconds in dimmer light, the pupil opens, and you can see inside. The same book said it's not related to photokeratitis, which is "snow blind," or sunburning your eyeball. But years of eyeball exposure like that will probably cause you to have cataracts. That's why I have sunglasses in an outer pocket of my backpack.

Anyhow, I looked out the door. Another track ran right next to us. The boxcar floor began to vibrate with a growing rumble. I realized we'd pulled over to a "passing siding" to let another train go by. The blast of air knocked me down as the locomotive rushed by. It must have been doing sixty mph. It was a passenger train with less than a dozen cars. The silhouettes of people on the train were like the black cutouts of Bobby and me that Momma had hanging in the hallway.

We began to move again, slowly picking up speed, and in a minute I felt us clank over the switch connecting us to the main track. It wouldn't be long until we were in the suburbs of Cincinnati, then to the Queensgate railyard along Mill Creek. Before we got to the yard, I'd have to get off. Even if they didn't inspect this car, I had no idea where it was going. I needed to find a train headed north towards Chicago. My hobo buddies said track nine *usually* went that way.

I stared aimlessly out the door for a while before we got to the suburban towns and buildings began dominating the landscape. I saw a sign that said "Batavia" something or other, so I knew we were on the east side, twenty miles or so from the yard. The train would slow through the city. As it got to the yard, it would slow more so it could traverse the multiple switches to get on the correct arrival track. Being back this far in the train from the locomotive when it navigated those switches would give me a good combination of slowest speed and safe distance not to be noticed. That's when I'd jump.

I'd practiced this with Bobby driving the tractor and me standing on a flatbed wagon. He thought I was crazy, but I told him it was for a school project. I borrowed a stopwatch from Mr. Pitzer, the science teacher at school. Bobby drove by a stake I set up in the pasture. I timed how long it took us to pass the stake from the front of the wagon to the end, twenty feet. From there I could calculate our speed accurately. Jumping off the wagon always took the same time to hit the ground, regardless of the speed. Two point one seconds. That was from a height of thirty-two inches. The box car was forty-eight inches from the ground. I used my physics book and more of Mr. Newton's laws to arrive at a jump time of two point eight seconds from the boxcar. I built a curve where I plotted the distance I'd travel during my jump time for a given train speed. It was linear so I only needed two points. I plotted four to be sure.

#####

Six years ago, on a frozen Saturday morning in February, my alarm clock clanged. It was 6:30 a.m. I clubbed the clock into quiet and cracked open an eye. Frost on the window blurred the glow outside. It had snowed overnight.

Dad called to me from the stairwell. "Tink, ten minutes."

I pulled the covers back and padded to the bathroom. Ten minutes later, I clomped down the stairs and shrugged on my coat over my insulated coveralls. Momma handed me a strawberry Pop-Tart as I dashed out the door. Dad sat in the idling pickup, a 1952 greenish International Harvester. I climbed in and stashed my Pop-Tart on the dash while I pulled on my gloves and toboggan hat.

The snow was only an inch or so deep, but it gave definition to the term "hushed silence." All the noise in the world was muffled. Except the road noise coming through the rusted-out floorboards of the pickup. My Pop-Tart slid off the dash and I snagged it before it fell through the floor and became Kellogg roadkill.

I ripped open the package and took a big bite. "Where is this sale?"

"This side of Ripley. It's Wayne Martin's place." He glanced at me. "You remember him? He bought Bobby's steer at the county fair last fall."

I nodded. "Straw hat and glasses. Big ears. Why's he having a sale?"

"He died about a month ago."

"From?"

"Heart attack. Was building fence all day. Came in, sat down to supper, and keeled over on the floor."

"His wife is having the sale?"

"Yeah. Typical when a farmer dies. Wife can't run the place herself. Sells off equipment and livestock. Then sells the farm and moves to town. Or Florida."

"What are we buying?'

"Maybe a combine. This cold weather will keep a lot of people away. Prices will probably be low."

"That's not good for Mrs. Martin."

Dad shrugged. "Way of the world."

I thought about Mom. If something happened to Dad, would she have a sale? I'd make sure it wasn't in the winter on a cold day.

When we got to the Martin place, Dad led us to a concession trailer selling coffee. He bought us each a cup. I didn't much like the taste of coffee, but it kept my hands warm for a while.

The equipment was spread out on the grassy areas between the house and barn. A man with a John Deere flapped cap was going from one piece to the next sweeping off the snow. There were three tractors and numerous pieces of equipment that could attach to them. I counted four flatbed wagons, and three gravity wagons for grain. The combine was in the back sitting beside the barn. Dad wandered through the rows of equipment and took some time examining each tractor.

He kicked the tire on the big Ford tractor, knocking off snow and mud from his boot.

"How come you're looking at all of this other stuff if you're only interested in the combine?"

He turned to me and whispered, "There'll be one bidder in the crowd who works for the auctioneer. His job is to not let anything sell too cheap. If he knows you really want to buy something, he'll push the bids as high as he can. We need to make him think we might be here to buy just about anything."

Nodding, I kicked the tractor tire and knocked off some snow and mud from my boots.

Dad moved on. I wandered towards the barn, hoping to get out of the cold wind. I dumped my coffee and tossed the cup into a fifty-gallon drum being used as a trash can.

Inside the barn, the familiar smell of cows and hay thawed the frost in my nostrils. Outside, the auctioneer had set up on a flatbed wagon and began to bellow out the rules and procedures for the auction. No refunds. Cash or check only. Full payment before removing the equipment. I tuned him out.

A window on the side of the barn faced the combine. I climbed over a gate and pulled myself up to the window. The combine was a Gleaner. It said so on the paper taped on the side. "1964 Gleaner Baldwin Model A-2." It was tin colored except for the orange wheel hubs. I didn't see much rust and wondered what they had done to prevent the galvanized sheet metal from rusting. Mr. Pitzer, my science teacher, might know.

A black three-step ladder over the front wheel allowed the operator to climb up to the platform. Uncovered pulleys and sprockets dotted the front of the combine. Belts and chains sewed them together. I figured the Gleaner would make an awful racket when it was running.

Someone started the big Ford tractor and revved the engine a few times. In a moment, its throbbing bass was joined by the Massey-Ferguson tenor. The Farmall Cub hum completed the trio's chorus. When they all shut down together, my ears throbbed for a few moments in the silence.

One of the tractor people climbed up the ladder on the Gleaner, and in a few seconds its engine began to rumble. The guy was in gray insulated coveralls like mine and had a red corduroy cap pulled down with the flaps covering his ears. He twisted a knob, pushed a lever, and the header reel began to turn. The noise level doubled as the beast thrashed non-existent grain.

After a moment, he turned it off, shut down the engine, and climbed down. The auctioneer was bellowing again about the next item for sale. I hopped down from the window and made my way outside. A knot of a dozen farmers gathered around the auctioneer as he sing-songed the bids on a red three-bottom plow.

I walked to the side of the barn and climbed up on the Gleaner. It had a single operator seat and a safety rail that kept you from falling into the header in the front. The grain bin, where the thrashed grain collected, was directly behind the seat. The controls looked a lot like most tractors, except there were a few extra gauges and knobs, and two extra levers. In a few minutes, I'd worked out what they all did and how it was controlled from the operator platform.

I wandered back into the barn to wait for the auctioneer to reach the Gleaner. It wasn't warmer in the barn, but it did block the wind. Perched up on the rail by the window, I barely heard the barn door open. When I turned to look, an elderly woman stepped into the barn and closed the door. She was wrapped up in a long black coat and had a bandana tied over her long gray locks. She stamped her feet a few times and blew on her cupped hands.

Mrs. Martin. I'd seen her at the fair with her husband. Maybe I wasn't supposed to be in the barn. Like a hobo hiding out. I didn't want to startle her, but I didn't want to seem to be hiding. "Pretty cold today."

She snapped her head in my direction, her piercing dark eyes squinting. "Sure is. Creeps into my old bones more than you, I expect."

I nodded.

She stared at me, blowing on her cupped hands again. "You Will Truesdale's girl?"

"Yes, ma'am. Tink."

"Tink. Funny name, ain't it?"

"Better than the one on my birth certificate."

"'Spect so." She rubbed her hands together. "What's Will plannin' to buy?"

"I think that's supposed to be secret so he can buy it at a lower price."

Mrs. Martin laughed. "Don't worry. I ain't biddin'."

She seemed like a nice lady. Probably lonely because she'd lost her husband. I didn't think they had any children. I jerked my thumb towards the window. "The Gleaner."

She nodded. "I figured. He about talked Glen's ear off at the fair last year. Knew he was keen on this new way of farmin'."

"I'm sorry about Mr. Martin."

She looked at the ground for a moment, her lips pursed. "Thank you." She took a few steps into the barn, looking around. "He was proud of this farm. What we built. How we took care of it." She turned towards me. "Now…now I wonder."

She didn't speak for a couple of minutes—just kept looking around the barn while the auctioneer's banter wailed in the distance.

I slid down from my perch and picked up a loose piece of straw from the floor, twirling it around my finger. "What do you wonder about, Mrs. Martin?"

She looked at me, blinking her dark eyes like a hoot owl. A tear escaped one eye and trailed down her cheek. I walked to her and wrapped my arms around her. She leaned into me and began sobbing. I wasn't sure what to do or say. Even though I was only thirteen, I was still an inch or two taller than her. Her hair smelled of Prell shampoo. Like Mom. We stood there for what seemed like hours, her sobbing, me patting her back. Finally, she calmed, stepped back, and pulled a handkerchief from her coat pocket and blew her nose.

"I'm sorry. You're just a child. You shouldn't have to worry about adult problems. Don't pay no mind to me. Just a crazy ol' woman."

I took her hand. "You're not crazy. You're sad. And missing your husband. Do you have other family?"

She shook her head and seemed to be struggling to stifle another cry. "We couldn't have children. My family's all gone, 'cept for a drunk brother. Wayne had a brother, but he died a few years back. There's only a niece, but she lives out west." She looked up and smiled at me. "Ellyson. We call her Ellie. She came for the funeral. Brought her hippie boyfriend. They both smelled like marijuana the whole time they were here." I tried not to giggle. Her hand flew to her mouth. "I shouldn't be telling you this. You're just a child. I'm so sorry." She turned towards the barn door.

She was lonely. And alone. A strong woman devasted by the loss of her husband. And here she was walking among the vultures picking apart her life at bargain prices. It must be awful for her. There was a knot in my stomach and I felt a little nauseous, but for some reason I was desperate to help her. "Mrs. Martin, I'm thirteen, but I read a lot."

"What?"

"At the school library mostly. And the town library. I read a lot of science and math books. Have you ever heard the story about Sir Isaac Newton and the apple falling from the tree?"

She frowned. "Maybe."

"Well, I've read all his papers. Einstein's books. Max Planck." Mrs. Martin's eyes seemed to be glazing over. I took a different tack. "What I mean is I'm smart about physics, math, mechanical things…like the Gleaner. I'm hoping Dad will buy it so I can take it apart."

Her eyes flew wide. "Why on earth would you do that?"

"To figure out how it works." I smiled. "And I'll put it back together. But my point is I don't have many friends. Kids at school think I'm weird. An egghead. But I could be your friend. Someone you can talk to. Do you bake?"

She stared at me for a moment. I think she was trying to decide if I was joking. "Of course."

"Maybe you could teach me to make some of your specialties some time."

She continued to stare like I had just gotten off a spaceship and had little antennae sticking out of my head. "Thirteen, you say?" She shook her head, and then took my hand. "Dear, Tink, I'm an old lonely woman. You don't want to waste your time listening to me prattle on about the way it was fifty years ago."

I squeezed her hand. "There's so much you could teach me. I'm a quick learner and a good listener. I could stop by your house when we leave and give you my phone number."

She nodded and drifted out the door.

Somehow, I was drawn to Mrs. Martin and her grief. I wanted to help her, even though I didn't know how. I had no experience with grief except for my own, and I sure didn't know how to overcome it. But when I looked at Mrs. Martin, I could see Momma. I'd never thought of it before, but what would happen to her if Bobby and I moved away, and something happened to Daddy? She'd be another Mrs. Martin. I hoped someone would be kind to Momma. Maybe as a kind of repayment for me helping Mrs. Martin.

It was another two hours before the auctioneer got to the Gleaner. From my perch back in the barn, I watched through the window. There were only five farmers left, counting Daddy. A sixth guy I recognized from the John Deere dealership followed the knot of farmers and the auctioneer. The auctioneer's helper held up a manual with a picture of the Gleaner.

The auctioneer said, "This here is a 1964 Gleaner Baldwin combine. It has a fifty-bushel bin, rear steering, and an Allis Chalmers G-230 gasoline engine. It has a twelve-foot grain header and a three-row corn header." He clapped his gloved hands together and smiled. "All right, boys, let's get Mrs. Martin a nice price for this near-new combine. Then we'll all go get warm. What am I bid?"

The bids started at eight hundred dollars. One farmer and the John Deere guy bid. It got up to eleven-fifty and the auctioneer got to "going twice" before Dad bid eleven-seventy-five.

The John Deere guy glanced at Dad and frowned. "Twelve hundred."

The auctioneer got to "going twice" again before Dad bid twelve-ten. The John Deere guy shook his head. A minute later, we owned the Gleaner.

I followed Dad to the cashier. She was working from the side window of the concession trailer where they had a heater. The warmth felt good on my face. I pulled off my gloves and leaned on the counter, hanging my hands towards the heater.

A minute later Dad counted out twelve hundred-dollar bills, and then put an Alexander Hamilton on top of the pile. He signed a piece of paper. The lady gave him the carbon copy, a rusty key, and the combine owner's manual. Dad handed the dogeared manual to me. The cover was worn and had several grease and oil stains dotting the picture of the Gleaner. I unzipped my coat and slid it under my coveralls.

Dad stepped around the trailer corner and said, "You still got hotdogs?"

"Sure do. Still hot, too." The lady fished two hotdogs out of a pot of steaming water, slid them onto a bun, and set them on the counter.

"Give me a couple of Cokes, too."

The lady smiled. "Don't need no ice to keep these cold today." She popped the caps of the bottles and set them next to the hotdogs. "Seventy cents."

Dad paid her while I studied the Coke bottle. I held one up to the light, smiling. The neck of the bottle was now filled with slushy brown liquid.

"What are you looking at?" said Dad.

"Ice. Coke ice. When she popped the cap, the pressure lowered and some of the liquid froze." I took a swig of Coke and sucked in some of the ice. I grimaced because it made my teeth hurt.

The lady said, "You got a smart one there."

Dad nodded. "Gets it from my wife, I expect."

I helped Dad hitch together the two gravity wagons I didn't realize he had bought. We hooked them to the truck one behind the other for the trek home.

As we started out the driveway, I said, "Could we stop at the house for a minute, please? I have to give Mrs. Martin our phone number."

"What for?"

"She might need someone to talk to." Dad stopped and I hopped out, running up to the front door. Mrs. Martin, with paper and pencil in hand, answered after one knock. I gave her my number. "Please call me later today or tomorrow. I'll bet you bake cookies, too."

She smiled. "You're right about that. Thank you, dear. I'll be seeing you."

I climbed back into the truck. Dad looked at me for a moment, and then we took off. Top speed with the wagons in tow was about twenty mph. It took us a full hour.

Dad pulled around beside the barn and unhooked the wagons from the truck. When he climbed back in, he said, "We'll deal with those on a warmer day. But we have to get the combine tomorrow. You coming with me?"

"Sure. Maybe Mom can have some hot chili when we get home 'cause we'll be pretty frozen."

Dad smiled. "You mean like today?'

I didn't respond, but I was thinking of my face on that open combine ride. Somehow, I'd have to protect it or get frostbitten. Dad too.

Inside the house, Mom had chicken noodle soup with Ritz crackers. It was the Campbell's kind that you add water to. But it was hot and tasted wonderful.

That night I memorized the Gleaner operator's manual. There were forty-five pages with twenty-five adjustment procedures, belt and chain diagrams, and a lubrication schedule. I learned where to order the service manual and parts catalog but fell asleep. When I awoke to my alarm the next morning, the manual was still in my hand.

CHAPTER 3

On July 8th of that year, Daddy did a small trial run of wheat cutting. As his tomboy sidekick, I rode on the operator platform with him and mentally recorded all the adjustments he made to adjust tension on belts, tighten chains, and adjust blowers for wheat. That one acre of former tobacco ground yielded a half-full bin of wheat—nearly forty bushels. Bobby, whose seventeenth birthday was the next day, pulled the gravity wagon alongside and Dad tripped the auger to transfer the wheat to the wagon.

It was glorious to see the golden stream of grain pouring out of the pipe and into that wagon. I thought the Gleaner combine was a marvelous invention. And complex. I already knew it well because I'd taken it apart and re-assembled it in the spring. Just for fun. And to learn how it all worked. The Gleaner was mine.

By mid-morning the next day, we had combined a third of the twenty-nine-acre wheat field. Dad seemed happy with the yield and was probably calculating if the sale of his wheat would cover the cost of the Gleaner. He was concerned about the onions in the wheat field, though. He scooped a handful of the wheat out of the Gleaner bin and smelled it. He offered me a sniff, too. "If the mill smells onions on the wheat, they'll dock our price. We're better off leaving the onion patches than ruining the whole harvest."

I nodded conspiratorially. He leaned into the bin and stuck his arm deep into the wheat, presumably for another sniff. But when he tried to stand up, the strap of his bibbed overalls caught on the shaft of a spinning auger. He yelled at me to stop the combine. I stomped on the clutch and the beast stopped rolling forward. But the auger continued to twist his strap tighter. He reached into his pocket for his knife and hacked at his overalls, trying to cut himself free. His scream cinched into a croak as the ever-tightening strap began to choke him.

I lunged to turn the ignition key, but he was flailing now and kicked me in the face. I slammed into the railing and nearly fell into the churning combine header. I scrambled under the operator seat and twisted the key. The engine died. But the Gleaner had flywheels and mechanically advantaged belts and chains. It was a self-propelled momentum monster. It would take fifteen or twenty seconds for everything to completely stop, including that auger shaft. Dad's feet no longer touched the platform. He was draped over the edge of the bin, face down with his shoulders and head in the bin.

"Dad!" I screamed as I scrambled up beside him and began clawing at the overall strap where it was caught on the auger shaft. I dug into the strap, ripping and pulling with everything I had. Something in the auger shaft snagged my index finger and ripped part of it off. I didn't notice.

The Gleaner went silent.

I pulled myself up to look over the edge of the bin as Dad's severed head fell into the wheat.

I stared at his head for what seemed like hours. I knew he was dead, but my fourteen-year-old brain couldn't process it. Wheat dotted the skin of his face. His faded John Deere cap was half-buried beside his head. His mouth was stretched open in mid-gasp. His eyes, still bulging open, were red with burst blood vessels. I looked at the neck of his now lifeless body. His overall straps were a twisted mass of bloodied denim and crushed neck parts. It was an effective tourniquet for the rest of his body. But he was dead.

A shriek from Bobby broke my trance. "Dad!" He clambered up the ladder to the operator platform and grabbed Dad's feet, trying to pull him out of the bin. Unyielding, Bobby lunged over the bin side and met Dad's severed head. He screamed, then puked down the outside of the bin onto the ground. He began to cry. I hugged him. We slid to the platform floor, hugging each other like we had never hugged before. He sobbed. I held him.

Ten minutes later he gathered himself and pulled away. He rubbed the snot from his face with his shirt sleeve. "What happened?"

"He got his bibs caught on that auger shaft. I couldn't get it stopped fast enough."

Bobby pointed. "What happened to your face?"

I felt my right cheekbone and discovered a dent just below my eye. It was throbbing, but I hadn't noticed the pain. "I guess it's where he kicked me. He was thrashing about while I was trying to get to the ignition."

He eyed me. I knew the question. Why didn't you turn it off faster?

"It kept going after I turned it off. For a long time." I glanced at Dad's feet still dangling in the air. "Too long."

He looked at me and nodded, and then started to climb down.

"Where you goin'?"

"We gotta get help. Call the sheriff." He pursed his lips. "Tell Mom." He got to the bottom of the ladder and said, "Come on. We gotta go."

I shook my head. "No, I'll stay here. You go get help."

"I can't leave you here, Tink." His face softened. "Come on. You can't help Dad. He's...he's gone. And you got a busted face."

I glared at him. Dad was dead. I hadn't decided if it was my fault. Maybe I could have turned off the Gleaner faster and he'd still be alive. But I wasn't going to leave him alone now. No, I had to stay until they could get him out.

"Okay." He climbed onto the tractor and raced off towards the house.

I sat on the platform floor and looked across the golden wheat field. The sun was high in the mid-summer sky, and shadows were short. My cheek throbbed. I could feel a big dent just under my eye. When I moved my jaw, the pain was excruciating. But I ignored it. In a twisted way I felt it was punishment for letting Dad die. Or at least for not being faster to get it turned off.

I finally looked at my hands. Several fingers were bleeding. Most of my nails were broken or ripped where I'd clawed at the strap. Blood dribbled from the gash in my index finger. But it didn't hurt. I watched my blood run onto the platform and across to the corner. Dad's open pocketknife lay there. Maybe it had some answers. I grabbed it and began to hack at the bib strap where it was twisted around the auger shaft. Something in there had caught my finger and ripped part of it off. And it was probably the same thing that caught Dad's bib strap. The strap was so tightly wound around the shaft that the blade parted the fibers quickly. As soon as I cut away the first layer, I could see an unbent cotter pin leg standing straight out from the shaft. It held the main pin in the shaft that connected it to the auger. Both cotter pin legs were supposed to be bent over, not sticking straight out. I'd had this whole thing apart on a tarp in the barn. And I reassembled it. I missed bending over that cotter pin leg. That's what caught Dad's strap and my finger. My mistake killed him.

CHAPTER 4

I heard and felt the train lurch over another switch. This one was big. We were crossing multiple tracks. A new exit strategy had unfolded in my head while I was writing down the part about buying the Gleaner. If I sat on the boxcar floor at the door with my legs dangling, I'd be jumping less than two feet. Of course, the gravel sloped away from the tracks so it might be a few more inches. Still, it would be much less risky than a standing jump all the way from the boxcar floor. On the other hand, I'd risk detection with my legs hanging out the boxcar door. I figured I would be quick and only put my legs out when I was ready to jump. Apparently, that time was approaching rapidly.

There were two tracks to the left of us now. Freight cars of various sizes and types sat on the far one. A locomotive went by the other way on the adjacent track. It wasn't going that fast, but our respective speeds added together to make the difference somewhere north of 40 mph. I thought of a new risk I hadn't accounted for. Jumping off the lumbering boxcar into the gravel, brush, and weeds in the countryside was one thing. I'd practiced a lot of landing rolls off the wagon. But now with the adjacent track, I had to drop down without rolling beyond the fifty-six inches between the two boxcars. Though the tracks were another two feet away, a landing roll might end up with me on the other track. I couldn't risk that. Even if I didn't hit the track, a boxcar or flatcar going the other way could clip me and toss me back into my own train tracks.

Another switch crossing shook the boxcar. We'd be in the railyard soon. I snatched up all my gear and stuffed it into my pack. I had to get off now or risk getting caught in the yard.

#####

As I scooted forward and dangled my legs out the boxcar door, Mr. Pitzer's voice echoed in my head. "Even the most elaborate experiments and simulations may omit unforeseen elements of the real world that are ultimately fatal." I had practiced jumping off the wagon, but not with a thirty-pound backpack. I scooted forward to drop to the ground only a few feet, but my backpack hung on the edge of the boxcar floor and tipped me over. My feet swung under the boxcar, and I landed flat on my face. Instead of the short sideways roll I had planned, the front of my body absorbed all the impact. The momentum rolled me sideways, but only a half-roll. The backpack stopped my roll and I skidded to a stop on my side. I jerked my knees up to my chest. Daring to squint open an eye, I checked to make sure my feet were still there. Looking up, I realized I had landed half-way under the overhang of the boxcar. My feet were no more than eight inches from the rails and the huge steel wheels rumbling past. Before I pulled my feet in, they must have been only a couple of inches from the track.

I crawled toward the center space between the two tracks and stood up. My knees were shaking, and my right palm was scraped and bleeding. I wiped it on my pants and started jogging along the track towards the rear end of the train I had been on. As soon as the last car passed, I checked for approaching trains and raced across five tracks into the weeds along a fence. It was a rusty six-foot "hurricane" wire fence like many train boundary fences. I shoved my backpack over the top, and then climbed up and over. Anyone spotting me wouldn't care because I was exiting, not entering the railyard.

The ground sloped away from the tracks, giving way to backyards and a dirt path through the weeds. To the left was a park that flanked the bulk of the main railyard as far as I could see. Train whistles sounded frequently in the yard.

I followed the dirt path for a hundred yards or so towards an Esso gas station sign I could see over the tops of the houses. The path intersected with a tree-lined street. New green leaves of the oak trees were starting to blanket the branches.

I hung back in the weeds, watching the gas station for a few minutes. I didn't want to attract attention (a lesson from my hobo friends) and I wanted to make sure the restroom wasn't in use. No customers appeared.

Leaving my pack here had its risks but carrying it would scream hobo or tramp to anyone who saw me. Herb had talked about this dilemma several times. His advice: get good at hiding your pack. I left it in the weeds, off the path near the fence so it wouldn't be spotted, and then sauntered towards the station carrying only my canteens. In the restroom, I locked the door and relieved myself. I washed my face and hands and filled both canteens. When I went into the station, a thirtyish, bearded guy behind the counter eyed me all the way to the candy rack. I picked up a candy bar. When I turned back towards the counter, he glanced away. The bell sounded, announcing a car pulling into the gas pump. We both glanced outside at a white '59 Chevy. A guy with shoulder-length hair got out of the car and lifted the hood.

The guy behind the counter muttered something but the only word I caught was "hippies." I laid the candy bar on the counter and fished in my pocket for some coins.

"Nickle," said the guy.

I counted five pennies onto the counter and picked up the candy bar. As I turned to head out, he said. "I shoulda done that, too."

I paused, looking back. "What?"

"Head to Canada. Been better than this." He raised his left arm and I saw that the sleeve was pinned together at the elbow.

I nodded. He thought I was a draft dodger headed to Canada. "How long you been back?"

"Little over a year."

"You dream about it?"

He nodded. "Even when I'm not asleep."

"Thank you for fighting for my freedom. I'm sorry about your arm."

He nodded again. "Me, too."

I went out the door and slid around the side towards the path. The guy had seen or sensed something about me that made me memorable. That was bad. I needed to figure out what it was and fix it. My hobo friends had convinced me that survival depended on being unremembered if not unnoticed altogether.

I retrieved my pack and retraced my steps along the dirt path. There was no way to determine which train was going where, but Herb said most of the north- and west-bound ones left from this side of the Queensgate yard via the far entrance. After twenty minutes along the path, I spotted the other trainyard entrance ahead. Trains were moving both in and out. The inbound trains used more of the middle tracks and the outbound ones were on the outer tracks on either side of the yard. I waded through the weeds and crouched next to the fence, watching for an hour or so. A lot of the departing train cars were tanker cars or flat cars, but almost every train had at least one open boxcar. I waited another forty minutes until a locomotive rumbled by on the nearest track. It had nine flatcars with lumber. A few minutes later, a row of tankers was pushed up behind the flatcars and connected. I stood and looked down the track. No boxcars. I squatted back down and waited. At least it was early enough in the spring that bugs weren't crawling all over me.

Shortly, a loud bang startled me. I recognized it as more cars being pushed into the line. I stood and looked again. There were three boxcars together after the tanker cars and more flatcars behind them. None of the boxcar doors were open. Scrambling over the fence, I threaded my way along the weeds to the boxcars. The doors were latched shut. I laid my pack down and darted over to one of the cars, trying to lever the latch open. It wouldn't budge, and from the looks of the rust on it, it hadn't been opened in quite a while. Only one thing to do. I retrieved my pack, crawled under the boxcar, and tossed my pack across the tracks under the car. Crouching, I crab-walked across the tracks to the other side. I grabbed my pack. The doors were latched on this side, too. But there was another train moving slowly to my right, outbound, two tracks over. An open boxcar was only four or five cars away. I glanced both ways to make sure I wasn't stepping into an oncoming train, then ran for it as hard as I could, lugging my pack in my hands. I got there just in time, tossed my pack through the open doorway, and swerved to my right, running to keep up with the accelerating train. I grabbed the trailing edge of the door with both hands and tried to pull myself up. I got one arm up onto the floor, but my legs were flailing under the boxcar. I couldn't find any leverage to hoist myself up. I was about to slip off. And lose my pack. My trip was going to end before it got started. I was going to end up under the wheels of this boxcar.

At first, I thought I had already died and was floating to heaven, but then I realized a hand had grabbed the back of my coat and was pulling me up into the boxcar. I rolled over onto my back and looked up at a hulk of a man standing over me. "You gonna get yourself killed, boy."

I sat up. "Thanks for the help." I pulled off my hat and ran a shaking hand through my hair. "Guess I have a lot to learn."

A chorus of chuckles echoed in the afternoon dimness. I looked around and counted five smiling sets of white teeth among a shapeless group of black men, all dressed in dark clothes. They blended into the shadows so well that I had missed them altogether.

"What you doin' out here by yourself, boy?"

I looked toward the voice, but still couldn't make out a face. "Traveling. To Montana."

"Why?"

I shrugged. "Cause it's there, I guess."

"What's there?"

"Whatever I'm looking for, I hope."

"You already got hope, boy. You on this train. What is it that you hopin' for?"

The train whistle sounded, and I looked out the door at the passing houses. I was on this train because it called to me. It offered me hope. Relief. Freedom. Freedom from nightmares. Relief from the stone in my chest. Opportunity to get away from all of those who stared at me, knowing I killed my dad. The sad looks from every classmate. They all knew my secret. Maybe that was it. I was running away from people who knew me. And my secret. I wanted to disappear into the darkness of the boxcar where no one knew. And I didn't have to bear the weight of them knowing. I wanted relief and freedom.

"A new start, I guess." That's what my hobo friends told me to say when asked.

"Shoot, boy, you ain't old enough to have started the first time. How come you wanna start again?"

Someone tossed my pack down next to me. I pulled my knees up to my chest and wrapped my arms around them. "Guess I started early."

"Well, you gonna trainhop, you best learn how."

I looked up at the big guy who had hoisted me aboard. "How'd you learn?"

He glanced at the others. "Mostly our pappy."

"Maybe you could teach me. Please."

The big fellow laughed. "You a Yankee for sure. Asking black men all nice with 'please.'"

I felt my face redden. Dealing with strangers was a lot harder than I expected. "I'm sorry if I offended you. My momma taught me to be polite to everyone."

Except for the wheels clicking rhythmically on the track, it was silent for a moment. A new voice spoke from the darkness. "Our momma taught us not to trust whites."

I didn't know much about racial prejudice, but the news was full of ongoing racial struggles, mostly in the south. Between Vietnam, Nixon, and race, the news wasn't much else except some sports squeezed in.

My eyes had adjusted to the gloom. These guys had been in this boxcar a while. They had blankets laid out, and several brown grocery bags sat at the end of the car. I stood up. I didn't know these men or how they thought, but one of them had saved me. Maybe to get my pack or worse, but for whatever his reason, the big guy had saved me.

I shrugged. "I got a lot to learn. Just trying to get to Montana." I waved a hand towards the door. "You can throw me out anytime." I picked up my pack and moved to the other end of the car where I sat down. Rummaging in the outside pocket, I dug out the candy bar from the Esso station and started eating. Four of the men spread out around their end of the car. The fifth, a skinny kid not much older than me, moved to the center of the car and sat down on a one-legged stool, staring out the door.

I finished my candy bar, drank some water, and watched the kid for a while. He was a stone statue somehow balancing on that one leg, leaning into the curves, and always staring out the door. He was like a lookout, but for what I didn't know. To the group in general, I said, "What's he looking for?"

"Danger."

I recognized the voice as the big guy.

"I'm Tink. What's your name?"

There were some mumbles and quiet laughter. "You can call me Hoss."

I smiled and started to ask if he meant like the big guy on *Bonanza*. Then I realized these guys might not have watched that TV show. They might not have had a TV at all. I thought about my hometown, Sardinia, and the kids in my class at Eastern High School. We were poor, but we never went hungry. Not like some. Now that I thought about it, most of those hungry kids were black. In my class of forty-two, there were nine black kids and one Mexican. I realized all were poorer than me. They mostly stuck to themselves, too. I never socialized with anyone at school but my one friend, Susie. She lived a couple of miles from us in a trailer. I'd known her before school because her dad used to help us baling hay. At least he did when we were little. Now he drove a truck. One of those big semi-rigs. *Long-haul*, Susie called it. He was gone for weeks at a time.

Susie was a social magnet. With dirty blonde hair and blue eyes, the chubby sixth grader had blossomed into a curvy young woman that Momma graciously called "voluptuous." She was a self-proclaimed slut and wore the badge proudly. Her current mission in life was to have sex with the lone basketball team hold-out, a slight little Jewish guy who was a dribbling magician. He'd told Susie his first time couldn't be with a *shiksa*. Slut was a close-enough translation.

It was mostly quiet in the boxcar, although I could hear whispering and low voices on the other end of the car. I wondered if they were talking about me and if I should be afraid of them. An hour or so later, a different guy replaced the skinny kid lookout. This one was skinny, too, and had lopped-sided, Afro-style hair that bounced with the train motion. He stared at me for a moment before he sat down on the one-legged stool and took up his vigil.

I took a swig of water. "Hoss, do you know where this train is headed?"

"West."

I'd already worked that out by the mid-afternoon shadow angles from the telephone poles along the tracks. "Do you know what city?"

"Indy's probably the next stop."

"Thanks."

Hoss paused, and then said, "Come here, kid." He moved over to the door on my side of the car. I got up, wondering if he was going to toss me out now. He seemed relaxed and casual. I didn't feel threatened, but I didn't want to be surprised. I took a step towards him. An alarm went off in my head. *Never turn your back on your pack.* The hobo education had been drilled into me more than I realized. I stopped and looked down at my pack.

Hoss laughed. "Somebody tried to give you trainhoppin' schooling, Tink. I ain't gonna push you out. And your pack'll be fine."

I smiled and walked over to him.

He pointed at the door frame on the opposite side of the opening. "See that latch handle at the bottom—that's what you gotta grab to get on. You best get ahead of the car and grab it as it goes by. That'll swing your legs out, and you roll in the door. It's like mountin' a horse." He looked at me. "You ever ride a horse?"

"Yeah. A few times." I wanted to practice. Train-hopping mistakes were often fatal. I looked at Hoss. He weighed close to 300, well north of six feet. "You're a big guy, Hoss. That work for you, too?"

He smiled. "Don't let my size fool you." He jerked a thumb over his shoulder. "I can outrun all my brothers."

I stared out the door at the latch handle. It was a thick iron lever, like the handle of a hammer. A little over a foot long, it was bolted to the bottom of the door. A curved hook, like the claw of a hammer, completed the other end of the lever. I'd never noticed them but saw how the hook part would slide into the cleat on the other door and snug it closed when the handle was rotated.

"I wish I could practice," I said absently.

"Wait for a time when we stop at night, so you don't get spotted."

"What about when the boxcar is going the other way? The handle will be on the other side of the door."

"I 'spect you can work that out." Hoss moved away from the door.

I slid up to the side of the door and stuck my head out enough to get a better look at the latch hook on this side. It was about six inches wide, like a small ladder rung. I looked at my hands, and then at Hoss's. "That'll work for me because I have small hands."

He smiled at me. "I hafta use one hand. But I can use the other to grab the side of the door and help swing me inside. It's easier on this side for me. But the boys sometimes need help, too."

I glanced at the boys. They lay on the floor ignoring us. The chance that all five of these men could grab a door and swing into the same boxcar in series was low. If one got hung up even for a couple of seconds, the next one would be blocked and couldn't grab the handle. This group didn't mount the boxcar when it was moving.

"You don't do this when the train is moving, do you?"

Hoss laughed. "You brighter than I thought. Nah, we try to get on when it's stopped. Only hit a moving train when we bein' chased. Sometimes have to hop whatever car there is. Tankers. Flatcars. Then we work our way back together. Ain't lost none yet."

"Who chases you?"

Hoss put his hand on my shoulder. "When you black, most ever body just one step from chasing you. For a white boy like you, ain't nobody gonna care too much. By yourself, they think you ain't gonna cause much trouble. But us—we trouble 'cause we there. People send all kinds of cops after us just 'cause."

The black kids in my town had more than their share of interaction with the local and county police. Front-page articles about some "negro" being arrested often appeared in the weekly newspaper. The only time the town cheered for the black boys was when they won a basketball game. Even then, a lot of people didn't like the blacks using the same locker room as the whites. I recalled several fights around that issue. The blacks were always the ones blamed and punished.

Prejudice was a concept I never considered for the folks around me in Sardinia, but that's what Hoss was describing. Racial prejudice. Racism. Everything he said clicked together with what I'd witnessed in my community. Were they racist, too? Maybe not overtly like the Klu Klux Klan. But there were a lot of folks, mostly older, who subtly treated the black boys differently. Even teachers. They made the black kids sit in the back of the classroom. Or those kids were so used to it that they naturally sat there. Conditioning. I knew about that. Like Pavlov's dog.

It was as if Hoss had drawn a curtain back and I could see my world a little more clearly. Or differently. Or maybe it was a little of seeing things through Hoss's eyes. Or all of those.

"What are you thinkin' about, boy?"

I'd been staring out the door at the moving scene. Suburban houses drifted farther apart. Soon, fields and trees were dotted with farmhouses and barns. I glanced at Hoss, and then at the group of men crouched in the dimness. "Racism. I was thinking about racism." I shook my head. "Is it really everywhere, just more or less obvious?"

"It ain't a disease only the whites got. Blacks got it, too." He jerked a thumb over his shoulder. "They'd a pushed you out the door just 'cause you're white."

My heart raced and I glanced back at those men. His brothers. "But you didn't. You saved me."

"Nah. I just give you a little help. I figure the only cure is one person at a time. Dr. King, he thought you could convert the people all at once. Way I see it, everybody gotta get the vaccination. Like polio or smallpox.'Cept that racism vaccination ain't the same for everybody. From the look in your eyes, maybe you got yours. I got mine in 'Nam. When people shootin' at you, it don't matter what color skin you got. Those that came back ain't got much prejudice now. They all brothers. Blood brothers, like the old Indian stories."

Another train whooshed by the door, the swirling wind blowing dust into the car. I pulled my cap tighter.

Hoss pointed out the door. "Looks like we got the right train. Indy be the next stop. Two, maybe three, hours." He joined his brothers and slid down to the floor.

If racism and prejudice was a disease, maybe it could be cured. But not by the medical folks. The treatment would have to be social, like Hoss said. I didn't know I had it. And I wasn't cured. But at least now I could look at myself and see the symptoms.

I thought back about Sammy Washington. He'd been in my seventh-grade class. They said he stole a candy bar from the drugstore. He ran, the cops chased, and he jumped a fence on the edge of town. Maybe the angus bull that gored him in the back wasn't what killed him. Maybe it was racism that led to his death. They didn't print that in the paper.

#####

Two lookouts later, we clacked across several track switches and the train slowed. Houses were getting closer together and we soon entered the suburbs of Indianapolis. We all stood and looked out the door, not close enough to be seen from outside, but so we could get a better view and tell when we were getting to the railyard.

"You gettin' off here, Tink?" asked Hoss.

"Yeah. Can't travel at night by myself."

Hoss smiled. "You gonna do alright, boy." He stuck out his hand.

I grabbed his massive paw and shook it. "Thanks." I wanted to say more, but the words stuck in my chalky throat.

"Maybe we'll see you in Montana someday."

"Where you headed?"

"Colorado Springs. Government's building a new section to their underground missile base. We figure our coal mining experience'll get us a job."

I'd read about that in *Aviation* magazine. Cheyenne Mountain. A missile control complex in case the Russians nuked us. We'd nuke them in retaliation. It was crazy to everyone but the politicians.

We clacked across a few more switches. The railyard fence was just a few tracks over. I shouldered my pack, moved to the door, and stuck my head out to look for trains on the adjacent track. I nodded to Hoss and jumped, rolling a few times on the grass next to the track to absorb my inertia. When I stood up, I could see Hoss leaning out the door and waving. I waved back, and then ran across the track towards the fence. The weeds hadn't grown tall yet this spring, so I had little cover here. I tossed my pack over and scrambled to the other side into a thicket of briars and brambles. I was getting scratched up, but at least I was hidden.

CHAPTER 5

I squatted in the thicket for a few minutes, listening to the sounds around me. The working locomotives and moving train cars sang a rumble-bang melody punctuated with whistle signal solos.

Tuning that out, I could hear a few birds in different directions. Glancing at the sun, I realized the fence ran east/west. We'd arrived at the east end of the railyard. To the west, I could see some wispy smoke floating my way on the breeze.

Using my pack as a battering ram, I worked my way out of the thicket with minimal damage. A scratch on my left cheek bled for a couple of minutes, but that seemed to be the worst of it. I made my way through the weeds, winding around briars, and following a worn path likely made by smaller animals. I had to duck down to get through the holes in the brambles. Dogs, raccoons, or coyotes probably traveled through here. It wasn't big enough for deer. Or people.

I caught a whiff of a wood fire up ahead. Something was cooking. My stomach growled. Staying low, I inched forward. A depression in the ground ahead hid whoever built the fire. The low murmur of voices danced on the breeze with the promise of a bubbling pot of stew. I crawled closer, dragging my pack, inching up behind a low evergreen. Peeking through the branches, I spotted three ragged men hunched around a fire. Small rocks encircled the fire and a shallow pan sat on the rocks. One of the men used a stick to stir something in the pan. I couldn't make out what they were saying, but I knew these men. They were hobos. They were my brothers.

I stood up so they could see me, but remained there, unmoving. It was up to them to invite me to join them. Or not. It was hobo etiquette. Violators were often beaten or killed.

The one stirring the pot saw me first and pointed towards me with his stick. The three stood, all staring at me for a moment. They whispered among themselves, never taking their eyes off me. I slung my pack on one shoulder, ready to run if they gave chase. But the one with the stick waved me in. I'd passed their test. If my hobo friends in Peebles could see me now, they would be cheering.

I walked down the slope towards the fire. The men eyed me. I dropped my pack and squatted next to the fire, warming my hands.

The one with the stick grunted. "What happened to your face?"

I wiped my hand across my cheek and felt dried blood along the scratch. "Briar."

The three laughed. "You got blood all over your face, boy. Looks like you's in a fight with a weasel."

I poured a little water from my canteen onto my hands and wiped my face. The water turned pink. After the third time, it stayed clear, and I dried my face with my sleeve.

The guy pointed the stick at me again. "You got anything for the stew?"

I fished in my pack and pulled out one of my three potatoes. The men smiled. The guy with the stick snatched it out of my hand. A knife materialized, and he sliced it into pieces, dropping it into the "pan." I recognized the pan as one of those moon-shaped hubcaps like Bobby had on his 50's Chrysler.

No one spoke for a while as we stared at the stew. Glancing around, I didn't see any packs or other belongings. These guys traveled light. The guy with the stick kept looking at my pack when he thought I wasn't noticing.

After a while, one of the other guys said, "Good enough. Let's eat 'fore the cops show up."

I dug out one of my notebooks with a plastic coating on the front, figuring it could serve as a plate for a couple of minutes without too much damage. The other three pulled out folded pieces of stained cardboard.

I snagged three packets of salt from my pack and handed one to each guy. They looked surprised, but as the stick man scooped out half-a-cup of stew to each of us, they dumped their salt onto their portion.

It wasn't the worst thing I'd ever eaten. Bobby's cooking held that honor with burned hamburger helper and spoiled venison. After the first awful bite of that, I realized he'd cooked the maggots in the meat.

This stew was mostly water with a few shreds of some unknown meat and my potato chunks half-cooked. It was hot, though, and felt good in my stomach. A lot of lip smacking and cardboard licking went on before they stamped out the fire and stood up. The three of them stared at me. I tried to read their intentions. So far, they'd been hobo cordial. I'd contributed to their stew, so they shared it with me. Otherwise, I wouldn't have had a portion. But my pack drew their attention. Whatever they had, it was in their pockets. And stick man had a knife readily available. Most hobos did.

I fished out three packs of sugar and handed one to each guy. For a tense moment, they eyed the little white packet and glanced back and forth at my pack.

I hitched up my pack onto both shoulders. "Thanks for the stew. Be seeing you." I turned and walked off to the west. One of three things could happen now. They could tackle me from behind, cut my pack off, and leave me there. Or, they could add a knife into my kidney and leave me there to bleed to death. Or they could let me walk away. With each step, the latter option got more likely.

"Boy," called stick man.

I stopped and turned. "You doin' good, hobo. But watch out for tramps down that way." He waved his stick in my direction.

"Thanks." I turned and walked on. In a few minutes I found the game trail, such that it was, and continued my trek along the side of the railyard. Thirty minutes later, two- and three-story buildings began to line the railyard fence. Eventually, the trail became an alley between the buildings and the fence. It was late afternoon, I guessed about six. Long shadows filled the alley, though sunset was an hour away. I didn't want to go into that alley. It didn't feel safe. The warning about tramps might have spooked me, but intuition was a precious talent in hobodom.

Taking to the streets would make me more of a target. Not just to the tramps, but to the cops and any other nosy folks on the lookout for those who didn't belong there. I thought about what Hoss had said. Nobody cares much about a white boy. But if I was black, or worse yet, a group of blacks, walking down the street with a pack on my back, I wouldn't make it three blocks.

I could also hop the railyard fence now, not knowing how far I was from the western gate. Unless I got on a train quickly, I'd be spotted there, too.

I decided to hole up in some bushes until it got dark. Then I'd hop the railyard fence and take my chances there. As I settled down and listened more intently, the songs of the railyard played in the background. After a few minutes, I could separate the east sounds from the west sounds. The west sounded closer, so maybe I'd be lucky and get an exit train quickly.

The crickets resumed their chirping around me and before I knew it, I'd drifted off to sleep.

When I awoke, it was dark. Not twilight dark. Ink black. I'd slept longer than I intended. Over the background noise of the railyard, I could hear a few dogs barking. Something hit my foot and I raised my head to see a person standing at my feet.

She said, "You best move on 'fore others find you. They don't take kindly to you bums." The shepherd at the end of her leash growled.

I pulled my feet under me, then stood up, shouldering my pack. The woman turned and walked away, pulling at the leash as the shepherd kept trying to look back at me. I moved along the fence to a clearing, and then climbed over. Keeping low, I ran along the fence in what I hoped was a westerly direction. After fifteen minutes, my back was aching from my crouched run. I stopped to catch my breath and stood up straight, stretching.

A flashlight beam swept over me. I dropped to the ground. Someone was walking towards me along the second track over. They had a flashlight and swept it along the track, and then along the fence. I doubted they had seen me yet. My pack originally had four reflective patches that were easy to spot at night. I'd removed them six months before starting this trip. Another lesson from my hobo friends: at night, you need to be even more invisible.

While the flashlight guy was illuminating the track in front of him, I shrugged off the pack and army-crawled six feet closer to the fence. The short weeds here provided some camouflage. I hoped my pack would be mistaken for a rock. Face down, I kept my head turned enough to see through the few weeds and keep an eye on the flashlight. The guy was only thirty feet away now.

Before I could react, a panting dog trotted right up to my head. I could see it was a beagle with a wagging tail. I considered running, jumping the fence. But my pack was six feet in the other direction. Flashlight guy might have a gun. He'd surely sound the alarm. Who knew how many would give chase then?

But the beagle didn't bark. He lifted his leg and peed right on my head and shoulder. I ducked my face, but he soaked my hat. Then he trotted over to my pack and relieved himself on it. Dog piss ran down my neck. I shuddered but remained there on the ground. I could survive this. I'd had a lot worse.

Flashlight man and his dog continued down the track behind me. Beagle wasn't a guard dog. He was just a hound dog, and flashlight man was out walking him so beagle could pee. Flashlight man might not be a rail employee but a neighbor who routinely used the yard to walk his dog.

I pulled off my hat and retrieved my pack. Using one of my tee shirts and canteen water, I washed up as best I could. My hat and coat smelled awful. So did my pack. I stuffed the hat into a coat pocket, shouldered the pack, and walked westward.

CHAPTER 6

An hour later, I watched the yard build a train four tracks over. It didn't have many cars yet, but you could never tell when they were done. There were two open boxcars twenty cars back from the locomotive. There were no cars on the other tracks between the fence and the boxcars, so I had no cover. But it was still dark, near midnight I guessed. I needed rest and someplace safe to hide out. The boxcar was as good as anyplace.

Hopping over the tracks on a dark night isn't easy. The footing is uneven with lots of fist-sized rocks to roll an ankle. But I made it to the open door without incident and climbed up into the dark space. I shined my little flashlight around to make sure I was alone, and then moved to the rear of the car. As soon as I felt the train start moving, I fell asleep.

#####

The train stopped. It was already bright daylight. I'd slept at least six hours. Maybe more. I hadn't anticipated how conducive to sleeping the train would be. Maybe it was the motion or the clickety-clack syncopation of the wheels on the track. In any case, I learned I could fall asleep about anytime on a train. But that didn't stop the nightmares.

Scrubby trees filled the view out the boxcar doorway. I pulled on my shoes and repacked my bag for a quick getaway if needed. Drawing closer to the door, I could see a track next to us. I could see for miles across the vast flat farmland of Illinois. Except there was nothing to see. No buildings, no grain silos, no sign of civilization. Just dirt for miles and miles. Except for a bubbly creek rushing below a bridge not far from my boxcar. To the north, the creek was a blue-green pool that flowed over a rocky barrier. A gnarled tangle of rotted logs and branches caught there. I looked at the hat in my hand—the one the beagle pissed on.

A low rumble signaled a passing train was coming. I stuck my head out the door just as the locomotive raced by with nine passenger cars. Then it was gone. I glanced at the creek again. Fresh water and a bath with no one around were probably rare train hopping luxuries. I looked at my hat again. I couldn't even smell the stench, probably because I smelled the same. My pack did, too.

I jumped down from the boxcar. This train would soon leave, abandoning me out here in the middle of some cornfield. But there would be more trains, some of which would stop on this sidetrack to let other trains pass. Maybe later today. Maybe tomorrow. Maybe next week. I had at least four days of food, plus my emergency two-day pack.

Peeking between the cars in the other direction, I saw miles of dirt. No buildings, no farmhouses, no signs of civilization. This wasn't a place to be stranded. It was at least a full day's hike to people.

I looked back at the open door of the boxcar. It wasn't calling to me. Grabbing my pack, I turned and ran across the other track and down the short embankment to the fence. A willow tree grew on the left side of the pool, and I made my way to it through the weeds and brush. Graceful branches swayed in the soft breeze like lazy fairies swaying to their unheard song. Part of the branches danced over the water's edge, occasionally tickling the surface.

I slid between the dangling tendrils and dropped my pack on a flat rock. Back on the farm, a willow stood next to our pond. Dad said it was there when he moved to the farm after the war. As children, Bobby and I often used the willow as our fort. It's inner sanctum, wrapped in dangling branches, gave the illusion that you could see out, but no one could see in. That wasn't exactly true, but it was close enough for a child's imagination. Today, a warm sense of safety swelled from this little piece of earth under the stream's willow.

The train whistle sounded in the distance. I looked towards the track and could see the tops of the train cars start moving to the right. I watched until they all disappeared and man-made sounds ceased.

Someone had been under this willow before. There were several flat rocks here that had been rolled or carried in. Judging from their size, I guessed it would take at least two strong men to carry one of these. A gang of kids or teenagers could have rolled them in, too. I smiled, wondering if this was a make-out nest for teens. I ran a hand over a flat rock, wondering how many bare butts had sat there. I looked at my hand. It was time to wash up.

Thirty minutes later, my hat, coat, and empty pack lay drying in the morning sun. The clothes I'd been wearing lay next to them. I'd only been on the trek for a day, but they were plenty dirty and smelled of beagle piss. I didn't know how often I'd get a chance like this, so I washed my clothes and swam around naked for a while. Momma's voice rang in my ears. "You don't wash nothing else, you make sure you get your pits and lady bits."

My pack had no room for a towel, but I had a small blanket rolled up and strapped to the outside. I spread it out under the willow and lay back to drip dry. The sun shone on the willows now and the light danced inside my fort like the mirrored ball they hung in the gym for the prom. I lay there for at least an hour, not sleeping, but in a dreamy state. The noises of the creek and surrounding trees became distinct so I could pick out animal noises, too.

Another train roared by on the track, breaking my reverie. I pulled on my other set of clothes and went to retrieve my drying stuff. When I picked up my pack, I noticed it felt heavier than I expected. I should have dropped it. But I didn't. Instead, I opened the flap to see what was inside. A snake darted out and bit my wrist. I twisted away and dropped the pack. The snake slithered out of the pack towards the creek and disappeared. I grabbed the bite wound with my other hand. That was a natural reaction whenever you stepped on a nail or cut yourself. But this was a snake bite. A first. All the stories about cutting the bite marks, sucking out the venom, or applying a tourniquet ran through my head. I recalled an article by Southernland—no, that wasn't his name, but it was close. He suggested that none of those were effective, and I should wrap the bite area tightly until I could get medical treatment.

With my good hand, I dumped the pack to make sure nothing else was lurking inside. Grabbing my drying clothes, I moved back to my willow fort. So much for protecting me. My wrist was starting to swell. What kind of snake bit me? I thought back about what I'd seen of it. I didn't have an eidetic memory, but it was as good as anyone I'd ever met. In the biology class on reptiles, venomous snakes like the water moccasins had large blocky heads. All I could remember was it looked huge latching onto my wrist. My wrist throbbed in agreement. Little droplets of blood seeped from the two punctures. I squeezed around them to make it bleed a little more, hoping some of the venom might leak out.

I sat down and drank some water, trying to keep calm. If it was a water moccasin, I was going to die here. I'd already seen that it was a full-day hike to people. That meant medical help was too far away to get anti-venom in time to save me. There had to be some ironic epitaph for my tombstone about the protective willow tree. There is a ton of folklore about it, much of it depressing and linked to various religions. That led me to recall reading about willow bark and the discovery of aspirin. I couldn't recall the details, but I sliced off a chuck of soft branch bark and began chewing it. It might help stop blood clotting from the venom and maybe ease some of the wrist pain.

If this was a common water snake, my wrist, hand, and arm were going to be sore and swollen for a few days. All I could do was treat the bite like any other wound and try to keep it from getting infected.

After chewing a dozen bark chunks, I dug out a big band-aid and taped it over the bite. My bowels growled and I wondered if I was going to get the shits from the bark. Or was it the venom?

I stuffed everything back into my pack, closed the flap, and set it against the tree trunk. Taking my canteens, I started walking upstream along the pool bank. Here and there, I threw in a rock to see how deep the pool was out in the middle. It was a marshy, flat area and the pool was large but not more than six or seven feet deep at most. The rock barrier that dammed up the creek and made the pool was probably man-made back when they built the train track a century ago. Catfish likely lived in this pool. At the head of the pool, the creek flowed rapidly and had a lot of volume, so the pool wouldn't freeze completely, even in the coldest winter. Plus, the trees protected the pool from the winds and provided plenty of detritus to make the pool rich with fish food. The bottom-feeding catfish could have a good life here.

My head was pounding, and I felt feverish. Where the water ran clear at the head of the pool, I refilled my canteens. I fumbled with the screw-on tops and realized I must be a little delirious. Heading back to my willow camp grew more difficult with each step. I staggered and tripped on weeds and sticks. Finally, I fell flat on my face. I struggled to all fours and stared across the twenty feet toward my willow camp. Someone was in there watching me. Light danced through the willow tendrils, shifting the shadows like an old black and white movie. I blinked. I must be hallucinating. A water snake bite surely wouldn't cause a reaction this severe. So it was a cotton mouth after all. I was going to die here, alone, maybe to be eaten by whatever predators came by. I rolled over onto my back, staring at the darkening sky. Several vultures circled. They were coming for me. They'd pick my eyes out first like they always did to dead animals. I dragged an arm across my face, trying to shield my eyes from them. My short journey, though documented, would probably never be read. No one would ever know me or my life. They'd never see my torture, the hell I lived in after Daddy's death. No one would ever care. And Momma would always wonder about me. Was I dead or coming back some day? This was it, Momma, here on a creek bank in the middle of Illinois-nowhere. Maybe the teens would discover my half-eaten body and bury it here. A couple of dead branches tied into a cross stuck into the ground.

Something pulled on my wounded hand. I slid my arm off my face and turned toward the willow. Whoever was in there was motioning for me to come to them. Maybe it was the devil, and I was going to hell, not that I ever believed in heaven or hell. But it didn't matter. I had nothing much to do now but die. Might as well crawl over there and see who it was.

I rolled onto my belly and began an arduously slow slither toward the willow. It was only twenty feet but seemed to be miles away. I kept it up, one limb after another crawling like a cat stalking its prey. It was hard to keep my head up. I dragged my mouth through dirt and dead leaves several times. When I spit it out my sputtering sounded like a distant motorboat. That made me laugh, at least inside my head. It reminded me of that kids' rhyme about a motorboat that ran out of gas. Like me. I put my head down and closed my eyes. The sounds around me stopped. I was falling into eternal blackness, bottomless and thick. My brain quit.

CHAPTER 7

Saying that I awoke with a jolt would be literally accurate. I don't know if I died or something closer to passing out, but my body now tingled and twitched everywhere. I was wet. Soaked. It was pouring rain.

I raised my head and looked at the willow in the waning twilight. It was cleaved in half, part falling into the creek, the other part still standing and whipping in the driving wind and rain. Smoke spewed from the smoldering trunk laying half in the creek.

My thoughts were jumbled, and I struggled to understand what I was seeing. Somewhere in my head, I knew, but I couldn't grasp those thoughts and concentrate enough to bring it to full consciousness.

I sat up. My head pounded, but I laughed out loud. The snake wasn't a cotton mouth after all. I stared at the willow, only five or six feet away. It had been struck by lightning. That's why I awoke tingling and twitching. Wet and flat on the ground, I made a good contact and got a jolt from the lightning. The palms of my hands were red and burned. When I pulled up my shirt, my belly was red, too, but there were no blisters. I'd been struck by lightning. And I was alive. I wanted to ponder how and why, but right now I was shivering and needed to get out of this storm. Plus, I needed to get to higher ground before the rain caused this creek to flood and wash me away.

As I stood up, I heard a roar behind me. I turned to look. A seven-foot wall of water slammed into me. It drove me right past the willow. Tumbling under water, I scrambled to grasp anything I could find. If it slammed me into that rock dam, I'd break bones for sure, if I didn't drown.

I couldn't tell up from down. But I knew if I hit something solid that would have to be down. I was flailing, rolling in the leading edge of the flash flood swell. Some branches lashed my arms as the water pushed me past some shoreline bushes. I grabbed one and it held for a second before whipping my body downstream. Now I knew where up was and I kicked and paddled with everything I had. Just as I thought my lungs would burst, my head popped to the surface. I gasped in some wet precious air, kicking and paddling to stay on the surface.

Ahead, the dam loomed across my path. I tried to swim towards the shore, trying to get out of the racing wall of water before it bashed me into the rocks. But it was too late. I hit the rocks broadside. I was at the top of the water wall, though, so the water rolled me over and over across the top of the dam. It pushed me over the dam instead of into the rocks lower down. With only a foot of flowing water, it couldn't drag me along anymore. Bruised, scraped, and freezing, I sat up. After a moment of continued pelting from branches and debris, I stood up and waded to the shoreline behind the dam. An inventory of my body revealed nothing broken. There were dozens of tender spots, but everything seemed to be working except my little finger on my left hand. It stuck out at a ninety-degree angle to the rest of my hand. Dislocated. Pain was screaming at me but was lost in the sea of sensory input flooding my recently electrocuted brain.

Bobby had dislocated fingers before, mostly playing baseball. He'd always come to me instead of Momma. I don't know why he thought I knew what to do. All I could think of was to put it back. So that's what I did to Bobby's fingers. Swiftly, in one motion, with solid force. I did that now to my finger. It hurt like a bitch for a moment, and then subsided. It could join my other myriad of bruises and swelling. I needed more willow bark.

My pack. I'd lost my pack. It was almost full dark now and I could barely see to navigate back upstream around the flooded creek toward the willow. Three feet of muddy, swirling water covered the rocks that had been at its base. The lightning-severed half of the trunk was gone now, washed somewhere downstream. The half-willow stood naked on the creek bank, the flood water clutching its dangling branches, trying to pull the willow over. I didn't know what to do. I had to find my pack. After all I'd been through in the last twelve hours, surely this couldn't happen. It could be downstream, swept over the dam, miles away by now. But I didn't think my pack would float. It was waterproof and the current might push it around, but I convinced myself it wouldn't float high enough to go over the dam. It was here, somewhere in this pool. I had to find it.

But right now, my teeth were chattering. I trudged away from the creek into the woods, trying to locate some bushes I could use as a wind break. It was completely dark, and I moved by feel until I ran into some kind of bush that didn't have thorns. I stripped off my soaked clothes and spread them across the bush hoping they didn't blow away. I curled into a ball on the ground, shivering for a few minutes. Then my stomach lurched, and I rolled over, puking the creek water. If I didn't die of hypothermia, the water I'd swallowed probably seethed with a cocktail of bacteria, parasites, and germs that, at best, would give me the shits for days. I curled up again and tried to conserve my body heat.

The rain had stopped but the wind still swirled. The bushes flailed their branches, torturing my refuge with their thrashing din. I wondered if I was lying fully naked in a bed of poison oak. After all that had happened, I was certain of it. Hobo karma. Most of them believed in it. They talked about it all the time. Story after story. It was their folklore, embellished a hundred-fold, but with some shred of truth in each story, some cause that drew the first effect.

I felt my hand where the snake bit me. It was sore to the touch. The two punctures were obviously swollen and warm. So much for trying to keep them from getting infected.

I curled tighter with my knees to my chest. The shivering had mostly subsided. I wondered if parts of me had turned blue. I tucked my hands under my armpits and buried my face in my knees.

Sometime later, I awoke to the hoot of an owl nearby. The sky had cleared, and the moon cast a silver glow like light snow. I paused for a moment to make sure it wasn't snow—what else could go wrong?

Fumbling around, I found my clothes except for my socks. The clothes were damp when I pulled them on. My boots were still squishy, but I couldn't walk around in the dark barefoot. I'd find the socks when it got daylight. I curled back up, wishing I had something to eat and some clean water. But I didn't, so I pushed that out of my mind and went to sleep.

#####

The sun rose and quickly turned up the humidity around the creek. My shoes were still wet, but I did find my socks. They were still wet, too, so they wouldn't be useful in my wet shoes. My feet weren't going to last long without getting blisters.

I made my way back to the willow. It was a sad mess. The flood water had receded, but the last couple feet of dangling branches were covered in mud. Lightening had split the trunk, leaving a charred remains that was missing one whole side. The tree would surely die by the end of the year. It would die alone, without me. I'd be long gone. If I could find my pack.

I made my way downstream to the dam. Water spilled over it, ten times more than when I'd arrived. The part of the willow tree that had been split off was hung up on the dam. Its jagged trunk jutted out over the dam downstream with its branches half submerged upstream like they were hanging on, fighting to not let the water carry it over. Most of the other debris and branches were gone, washed over the dam and on to some river a hundred miles away.

After searching around for a few minutes, I found an eight-foot stick I could use to probe the water. I removed my shoes and rolled up my pantlegs, wading carefully across the dam toward the willow. I couldn't see the rocks in the murky water, so I had to be cautious, feeling each step with my foot, sometimes balancing with my stick. I poked and probed the water in front of the dam, hoping to find my pack.

When I reached the willow, I realized it was teetering, barely hanging on. I poked at it with my stick and the trunk dipped, branches mostly rising out of the water. I poked again. It tipped more, only two branches still submerged in the water. They were taunt, though, the last hope for the willow to not be swept away.

Then I saw it. My pack. Those two branches were tangled in my pack's straps. The weight of the pack was all that was keeping the willow on the dam.

Using my stick for balance, I waded my way into the water fronting the dam and grabbed the pack. As I heaved it out of the water, the willow flew into the air and slid down the dam's face. It floated downstream and disappeared around a bend behind the train trestle.

A train rumbled by on the track. It was time for me to get out of here.

CHAPTER 8

By noon I was in the weeds on the far side of the train track, waiting for my ride to arrive. It didn't come today. I had a pocket full of willow bark branches I chewed. I ate one of my emergency candy bars, too. The snake bite was odd. One of the punctures was still red and a little swollen, but the other one was a mess. By late afternoon, I could see a red streak running a couple inches up my arm from the bite. I knew that wasn't good, chastising myself for not reading a few books on first aid before I started this trek. I'd become friends with the school librarian, Chuck, a stick-of-a-man with a crewcut from the fifties. He used to stamp my card each time I borrowed books until one day I chose Newton's *Principia*. His eyes twinkled and his lips curled into a slight grin as he stamped my card. When I checked out Einstein's *Relativity* a few days later, Chuck said, "You understand these books?"

"Mostly."

"Why this one?"

I shrugged. "I want to learn the basics so aerodynamics and orbital mechanics will be a lot easier."

Chuck stared at me for a moment. "How old are you?"

"Twelve. I'm in seventh grade."

Chuck stared some more. He picked up my library card and read my name, then looked back at me. He tore my library card into four pieces and dropped them into a trashcan beside his desk.

I gasped. "Why'd you do that? What did I do?"

Smiling, he stood and rounded his desk to stand next to me. He put his hand on my shoulder. "You don't need a card here, Tink. These books are yours. Read them all if you want. Any time you want. You stop by to see me tomorrow, okay?"

I was confused, but I nodded and shoved Einstein into my bookbag.

When I returned three days later and set Einstein on the returns cart, Chuck smiled at me from his desk. He motioned me over. "What did you think?"

I'd never discussed my technical reading with anyone. I figured they'd make fun of me. In school, I was careful to hide my books. Bobby thought I was a little crazy. Mom never commented.

I glanced at the book on the cart. "Apparently his theory of gravity is accurate," I said, "because we put men on the moon and got them home. But I'm not so sure about his special theory of relativity. It's fine for low velocities, but someday we might have to revise it."

Chuck's mouth fell open. "Hmmm…well, I hope you find a reason for revision." He reached into his pocket and pulled out a silver key. "Here. This will get you into the building and into the library." He glanced around nervously. "It would be better if you kept this between us."

I took the key and looked at it, thinking of all the times on weekends and nights when I'd wished I could have gotten another book. I had worked out a balance between books for my classes and my reading so that I could still carry my bookbag. The lane to our house where the school bus dropped us was a half-mile long. With an overloaded book bag, I'd often had to stop and rest. This would allow me to drive my reading rate through the roof and not have to lug a haybale-sized bookbag.

"Thanks. I'll take good care of it and keep it quiet."

By my senior year, there weren't any technical books left in the library I hadn't read. With a little help from my math teacher, I got Chuck to purchase Knuth's *The Art of Computer Programming* three-book set. I devoured them over Thanksgiving break. But two weeks later I was still ruminating on the whole new realms of technology those books revealed. I could see the Jetsons and Star Trek becoming reality. And Chuck had received a news clipping from his friend, Larry Roberts. The four-node ARPANET was soon to be expanded to fifteen nodes. Wright Patterson Air Force Base, fifty miles away—practically next door—was on the consideration list as a new node. The most stunning part was they were planning to add a Terminal node, called a TIP, which would allow any dumb terminal with a modem to dial into the network. With the right credentials, I could connect to some of the most powerful computers in the world from any location with a telephone line.

I was dazed. The possibilities were endless. I had to find out how to apply for access. I was sure I could get Chuck to buy the dumb terminal and modem. I could see myself practically living at the library. Bobby was already taking over the farm. I was almost giddy.

As I floated down the hallway to my next class, my elation burst into despair. Susie slipped me a note. *Chuck is fucked*!

I had no idea what she meant but cornered her in the backseat of the bus on the ride home.

"The school board found out he's gay. They're firing him at the end of the semester."

"Why?"

"They're prejudiced and ignorant to the core. They think homosexuality is a communicable disease."

I stared at her for a moment. She nodded. "Not kidding. My dad told me they discussed it at the board meeting. Randall King said he didn't want his kids catching no queer germs. He wanted to disinfect the whole library."

I was astounded. Yes, at King's comment. But more so at how ignorant and biased people still were. The 60's riots and demonstrations about the Vietnam war, racism, socialism…were those efforts wasted? Had nothing changed? I admired people for standing up for what they believed and standing up for others who couldn't stand up for themselves. There were rumors that Congress was going to lower the voting age to eighteen. I sure hoped so. I wanted a voice in who was making our decisions, and Nixon, for one, wasn't going to get my vote.

The next day during lunch I went by the library. It was locked. I used my key and went inside. Chuck was packing.

He looked up. "Hi, Tink. I guess you heard."

"Yeah. Lot of ignorant people in powerful places."

"You reading political science now?"

I smiled. Chuck was the smartest teacher in our school. Other than Mr. Pitzer, I didn't talk with other teachers. They were doing their jobs, trying to get the basketball players to pass and keep the cheerleaders from getting pregnant.

"I'm hopeful it's going to change," I said. "But not right now, I guess."

He pointed at me. "You make a difference, Tink."

"Haven't seen any evidence of that so far."

"You made a difference to me." His eyes welled with tears, and he sniffed. He waved his arm in the air. "How many books have you read from here? Couple thousand? Maybe more. And most of those, Tink—you're the only one who ever read them. They won't be touched again for decades. *The Principia!* You're the reason I've hung on here, Tink. It was a race against time. Eventually, the community would shun me, but I hoped it wouldn't be until after you'd graduated. I've had a part in your real education, so I could make a difference through you and what you're going to do with your life."

I shrugged and looked at the floor. Deep down, I knew what I was doing and why. I thought that was my darkest secret I could never share, not even with Susie. But I wondered if Chuck had figured it out. I glanced back at him. A sad smile tugged at his face. He spread his arms. I stepped into his hug. Something broke in me. I sobbed into his shirt.

When I quieted, he patted me on the back. "It wasn't your fault, Tink. Nothing you could do. It was an accident that couldn't be stopped once your dad leaned into that grain bin."

I nodded and glanced out the window. Snow had begun to fall, wrapping everything in a quiet white blanket. "Intellectually, I know that. But the emotional sea, it keeps trying to drown me. So I keep trying to build a better boat. Trying to stay afloat."

"I know. But you need to find a way to drain that emotional sea or you're still going to drown. Your boat is already as good as it can get."

I shook my head. "I have a lot more to learn, Chuck."

"I agree. But it's not in these books. Look at you. Perfect grades. Perfect SAT score. Who does that, Tink?"

"Lots of people. Everyone who gets into MIT, Caltech, Harvard."

"But still, you struggle with your emotions. Somehow, you need to find emotional education, or at least a salve. I don't know if it's counseling or what, but you need better balance. Or that perfect boat isn't going to stay afloat."

"I don't know where to look."

Chuck shrugged. "It's different for everyone. Look at me. I'm forty-three and still trying to find out who I am and where I fit." He smiled. "Apparently, it's not Sardinia. At least not anymore."

I hugged him again and turned to leave when I remembered my key. "Do you need the key back?"

"No. You keep it. O'Dell will keep our secret. But find a new section to devour, okay?"

O'Dell was the school janitor. I'd run across him many times on weekends when I slipped into the school library for a few hours. He never said a word, but always winked at me.

I nodded. "Thanks, Chuck. Write when you get a chance."

"You, too. They say writing can be cathartic."

CHAPTER 9

Alongside the track, I slept fitfully that night with alternating sweats and shivers. A few trains rolled by, waking me momentarily. I dreamed crazy stuff, mostly about the creek and Chuck, but I couldn't remember details when I awoke at sunrise.

My hand was throbbing. I rolled up my sleeve and examined the puncture wound. It was red and swollen with red streaks running half-way up my arm now. I chewed the last of my willow bark and ate another candy bar, staring across the flat fields that drained to the marshy creek area.

I heard it before I could see it. The tracks began a slow low frequency hum. I scanned both ways, up and down the track. Finally, there in the far east, a black mark near the horizon was crawling towards me. Ten minutes later when it pulled onto the sidetrack, I nearly jumped up and cheered. I thought I might be delirious when an open boxcar stopped right in front of me. I poked my head out of the weeds, looking for train employees who might be out stretching their legs. As I was about to stand, a passenger train raced by on the other track. I grabbed my pack and scrabbled up the embankment to the train. As I tossed my pack in the waiting door, the train began to move. I grabbed that handle Hoss had showed me and swung myself inside, landing on the hand with the snake bite. The puncture wound exploded onto the floor. White pus and blood pooled on the dirty wooden planks. The pain was already excruciating, but I gritted my teeth and squeezed the area around the wound, hoping to drain out as much infection as possible. I'd have to get off at the next town and find a drugstore before this became serious trouble.

Providence, or maybe chance, was with me. An hour later the train entered a small town. I stuck my head out the door and decided it was big enough to have a drugstore. This time I tossed my pack out the door on its own as I jumped. My landing was perfect, just as I'd practiced back home from the hay wagon. I rolled a couple of times, scrambled up, and retrieved my pack. Not far ahead I could see a sign for a diner, so I trudged off that way along the tracks.

The Open Door Diner was intended to be a hip place, but set here along the tracks, its clientele were mostly workers from the grain bins across the tracks. It was painted bright yellow inside and a Rolling Stones' tune drifted from a jukebox near the door. A couple of guys sat at the counter drinking coffee and puffing cigarettes.

I took a corner table with my back to a wall. In thirty minutes, I had my fill of eggs and bacon. Following the waitress's directions, I headed down Main Street a few blocks to the Route 40 intersection. To the left was Kremer Pharmacy.

When I showed my hand to the druggist, his face paled. "You need antibiotics." He pointed across the street. "Go over to Doc Franz's office and have him look at it. He'll give you a prescription. Bring it back here."

"Can't I buy the antibiotics from you now and skip the doc?" Remain invisible or at least unremarkable. Plus, this could be a big hit on my finances. I had thirty-some dollars in my pocket and inside my pack I had five twenties and three hundred dollars in traveler's checks.

"No. Law says you need a prescription." He threw his hands up.

Doc Franz was a red-headed hippie. He wore a tie-dyed coat that surely was white when he got it. His long hair was tied back in a ponytail, and he had a matching red goatee. When I showed him my hand, he frowned. "Snake bite, huh? Not a cotton mouth, but this infection could kill you." He pulled up my sleeve and made pen marks on my arm where the red streaks ended. "In twenty-four hours, if those streaks are farther up your arm, you go to the hospital. Or come back here. But get medical help quickly."

I nodded, wondering if I should stay in this little town, Altamont, until my snake bite was resolved.

He called in his nurse who gave me an injection of antibiotics in my other arm. Ten minutes later the druggist handed me a bottle of pills and I headed back up Main Street towards the tracks. The doc and the pills drained my thirty dollars, but finances weren't my main worry right now. I had plenty of time and needed to make sure this snake bite didn't completely derail me.

I spotted a U.S. flag off a street to the left. As I expected, it was a post office. I pulled a pen and a pre-addressed/stamped postcard from my pack and jotted a note to Momma. *You'll never believe this, but I got snakebit! I'm fine and headed to St. Louis.*

I realized this street was at a forty-five-degree angle to Main Street and intersected the tracks. In that direction, I could see several huge grain bins and some grain cars that were being loaded on a service track. When I got to the tracks, I found another diner on the corner. It was too soon to eat again, but I had to kill some time and remain invisible while I watched my red streaks. I wandered around the corner and back down Main Street where I'd seen a grocery store. Although my food supplies were in plastic bags, some had leaked and all of them smelled of the dirty creek water.

It took forty minutes to wander down every aisle evaluating products against my needs, space, and weight capacity. In addition to the replacement food supplies, I added a pound of bologna for tonight and tomorrow. In the end, I added some foot blister pads, two pairs of heavy socks, and a cheap pair of cotton gloves. I also bought a plastic canteen that was half the weight of my metal one.

By the time I'd paced myself through another diner meal, it was late afternoon. I headed west along the tracks out of town. I'd only walked a few minutes when a second track from the north joined my path. Dual tracks out here in nowhere meant heavy train traffic for some reason. Or there used to be when the tracks were built.

I walked on for a couple of hours and no trains went by in either direction. It was clear that the land was laid off in one-mile squares, and the roads mostly stuck to this grid. In the early evening, a freight train went by in my direction, but it was going too fast to board. I walked on.

The sun wasn't far from setting when I made it to County Road 100E. They didn't name the roads out here; they gave them a number. But my hopes for a ride shot up because a spur track split off to the right. A ditch separated the main track and the spur. I chose the spur. Somewhere ahead railcars were likely being loaded or unloaded and those cars would be stopped.

The sun was nudging the horizon, casting long shadows and a golden glow across the mostly baren fields. In the distance, I could see a dozen little smoke streams dotting the farmland. Apparently, that thunderstorm that tried to drown me didn't reach this far because the farmers were plowing their ground for the coming season. The northwesterly breeze carried the dank smell of newly turned earth—a smell that repulsed me since the day we buried Daddy in that same dirt.

CHAPTER 10

Several trains on the main tracks across the ditch passed through in the night. As soon as the sun rose, I chewed off a piece of bologna and swallowed it with my antibiotic, adhering to the pharmacist instructions to take it with food. Rolling up my sleeve, I examined my snake wound. The bite mark still seeped a bloody white pus onto the gauze the doc had taped over it. I replaced it with a band-aid and pulled my sleeve higher to examine the red streaks. They were a couple of inches short of the marks the doc had made yesterday. The antibiotics were working.

I shouldered my pack and walked on along the spur. It paralleled the main track as far as I could see. Although I was in good shape when I started a few days ago, I hadn't anticipated how much walking I'd have to do with this pack on my back. My legs ached some, but I could tell they were getting stronger each day. I suspected my shoulders were developing callouses where the pack straps were, too.

A freight train went by westward on the main track. It had the usual mix of tanker, flat, and boxcars. I watched as it went by, looking for open boxcar doors. There were three. Through one, I could make out a couple of shapes standing back from the doorway. Friend or foe? My hobo training said to always opt for going it alone if you could. It was the least dangerous path. I thought about Hoss and how his brothers might have reacted to me if he hadn't been there.

The last train car passed, and I watched it recede down the track. I walked on.

By noon, I could see some cars on the spur ahead. All of them were hopper cars. I took off my hat and wiped the sweat from my face. Hopper cars. Grain hauling. I scanned the fields to the right for a grain elevator where they store farmers' grain before loading onto trains. I didn't find one and walked on. If this was a spur for a grain elevator, I wasn't going to get a ride here. It was the wrong season. Grain mostly moves in fall and early winter. This was planting season. Those hopper cars ahead may have been there for months.

As it turned out, I was right. The hopper car wheels were rusty. It could have been a few weeks, but it felt like longer since they'd been rolling. The track turned to the left, and the trees in the ditch that had been blocking my view fell away. The elevator complex was far ahead, maybe two miles, and comprised of at least a dozen smaller bins. Most elevators had one or more tall bins you could see from far away across these plains. These were smaller, maybe built more recently, one at a time as the operator made enough money to expand. I felt an eerie camaraderie with the nameless owner—that's how I'd grown our farm operation, too.

I passed twenty-some empty hopper cars. As I neared the elevator, another spur turned off towards the bins. There were no cars or trucks I could see, no one working there. I was on an industry line, not a spur. This probably joined the main track somewhere ahead. In the season, this was a busy place with hundreds of hopper cars coming and going. I was at the right place, but at the wrong time.

I walked on. I could see another town not far ahead. The industry line would rejoin the main track soon. There'd be some switches where trains had to slow. Every time a train went by this morning on the main track, they were going too fast to board anyhow. With each one passing, I felt my hopes diminish. My bologna was gone. I had one canteen of water.

Ahead, I spotted several signal posts. The industry line joined the rightmost main track. A little further on, the main tracks joined into one. I'd hit the jackpot of train hopping boarding spots. Not a hundred yards farther, a track split off to the south. Three switches within five hundred yards.

My hobo training kicked in. If this was a great place to board trains, I wasn't the only one to spot it. There might be a hobo camp nearby. You never could tell about the hobos in a camp. They might be mean, deranged, or both. Or they might be lukewarm, at best. I was their competition. For food, travel space, and information. For the most part, I planned to skirt these camps and take my chances on my own.

I smelled smoke and glanced around. If the smoke hadn't alerted me, I'd have missed a knot of men standing around a small campfire in the trees across the track to the north.

One of them called to me. "Hey! Boy! What you doin' out here?"

Alone was safer. I could use some more supplies, so I waved and walked on. The little town was only a few hundred yards ahead.

CHAPTER 11

Early that spring after we brought the Gleaner home, Daddy attended a four-session night class in Georgetown, the county seat. The Farm Bureau class was billed as *Modern Farming*, and covered topics like crop rotation, yield increases, and grain finance. He brought home a workbook, some brochures, and references to several related books. With some help from Chuck and the inter-library loan system, I'd soon read all those books.

Visits from seed companies occurred regularly for a week in late March. Despite their pitches, Daddy chose DeKalb because the salesman was the son of Daddy's high school classmate. We had a half-dozen yellow signs along the road announcing that our corn was DeKalb 805.

Daddy focused his time on buying the best fertilizer for our fields. Samples of the dirt were sent off to Ohio State's extension service. A week later, Daddy received a report characterizing the relative needs of nitrogen, phosphorus, and potassium. It also specified how much lime he needed to add to the soil so that the acidity was ideal for corn. There were different reports for both wheat and soybeans.

I spent most of my time absorbing the Gleaner. Daddy came into the barn one evening in early April.

"Time for supper, Tink." He looked around at the parts scattered about. "We're gonna need this space in a week to store the seed and fertilizer. Think you can put it back together by then?"

I gave him a disgusted look. He raised his hands in defense. "Okay, just making sure you know the timetable."

I waved a crescent wrench to one side. "We need a new pair of auger bearings. Otherwise, everything works okay."

"You better get on up to the house and wash up. Momma'll kill me if you come to the table with grease on your face."

When I got home from school the next day, Daddy handed me a box with two new auger bearings. "Had to drive to Hillsboro to get 'em."

He went with me to the barn that afternoon. By the time Momma called us for supper, a good part of the Gleaner was back together. Three days later, I drove it over to the shed where it would sit until harvest time in October.

The next afternoon Jake Cluxton showed up with a twenty-four-foot flatbed truck loaded with twenty tons of fertilizer in 500 eighty-pound bags. Jake expertly backed the truck into the barn. He was a wizened old man at the age of fifty. Daddy referred to him as a "hauler." He had trucks of every kind to haul gravel, livestock, equipment, and obviously fertilizer. I'd seen Jake a few times a year since I could remember. He was always dressed in dirty bibbed overalls with the sides only partially buttoned. Apparently, Jake never wore underwear, which was both embarrassing and a curiosity to me. I didn't understand that decision, nor did I ask about it either.

Daddy laid a tarp on the ground so none of the bags drew moisture from the dirt. If the paper bags got wet, they would dissolve and break open. If the seed corn got wet, it would sprout in the bag and be ruined.

Jake pulled the tarp off the load, and I scrambled up on top. Daddy, Bobby, and Jake carried the bags from the truck to a stack in the middle of the barn driveway. I couldn't yet carry eighty pounds, but I could drag the bags to the edge of the truck bed so they could grab them. I was a skinny five-foot-four, a couple inches shorter than Jake. I vowed to carry those bags next year.

The next day Jake returned with a load of seed corn in thirty-five-pound bags. I carried my share, except Jake and Daddy carried two bags at a time.

The following day Jake returned with a load of lime. It was in fifty-pound bags. The barn driveway was filling up so the walk with the bags was shorter. I struggled but managed to carry a dozen or so to the stack. Jake and Daddy only carried one bag at a time that day. The seed corn was in burlap bags and easier to carry than the fertilizer and lime which were in heavy paper bags.

Over the next two days, Dad emptied the barn of lime, spreading it over the 120-acre cornfield while we were in school. The next day, Saturday, two men in a truck arrived from Kentucky loaded with a sprayer that unfolded like a bird. Its wings were eighty feet across.

They pumped water from the pond into a tank on the truck, added some chemicals, and filled the sprayer tank from the truck. Dad pulled the sprayer with our tractor, one of the men riding with him, and they sprayed the cornfield.

At supper that night, I said, "Won't those chemicals kill the corn when it comes up?"

Dad chewed on the roast for a minute and shook his head. "Only works on contact and wears off in twenty-four hours."

I thought about that for a few minutes. By afternoon, you could see the weeds in the cornfield already curling up and withering. "What about you? Is it dangerous to get on your skin or breathe it in?"

He shrugged. "Not supposed to be. But I washed off and changed clothes just the same."

"How about the planter? It can't dig into the unplowed ground. How's that going to work?"

"They're bringing a special planter tomorrow. The Young brothers in Kentucky been doing this for a few years now. We're using their planter. It's called 'no-till.' The guys at OSU say it will be the only way in a few years. No more plowing. Save a lot of erosion and get better yield."

Momma said, "I'll miss the smell of the earth. It was always spring when you could smell it all around."

"You mean like the smell of manure?" said Bobby.

Momma slapped his hand. "No! Not like manure, Bobby Lee. Like earth. Dirt. That was always the smell of real farming."

"Times change," said Dad. "Supposed to increase yield by twenty percent. Less work. Faster. Lots of wins for us."

Momma stabbed a sole lima bean on her plate. "I suppose so. But I worry about being the first." She pointed her fork at Dad. "You be careful, Will. It may be better, but it's new. Don't you go gettin' careless. And these kids, too." She waved the fork between us. "You make sure they stay safe, you wanna keep sleepin' in this house."

Bobby and I looked at each other, trying not to laugh. Momma didn't say much, but we knew who ruled the roost in this house. Always had.

That night Dad came into my room and sat down on the side of the bed. He usually said goodnight from the doorway and turned off the light. But tonight, Momma had apparently stirred him up.

He swiped my hair out of my eyes. "You'd make a great farmer, Tink. You know more about it than me or any man in Brown County. But I know you're too smart for that. You're gonna do somthin' special, I know. So don't you ever fret about staying on the farm. You find what suits you. Okay?"

"Okay. Thanks, Dad."

"But while you're here, I'm countin' on you to use that big ol' brain of yours to help me squeeze this farm for every drop of profit we can find. But mind what your momma says and make sure you stay safe."

"What about Bobby?"

Dad frowned. "He's an ox and he'll do whatever you tell him. But he'll never figure out what to do on his own. He knows that. Just don't rub it in his face. He'll do what you ask."

I'd known this for a long time. Bobby was self-aware of his major shortcoming, his mediocre intelligence. He got average grades and would have made a great football player, if our school had football. His lineman body type didn't excel at our two main sports, baseball and basketball. But he was a gentle giant in the high school hallways. Everyone knew him and joked with him, even some of the teachers. He was the quintessential good old boy from Sardinia.

The next day, the same two men arrived with a different truck and unloaded a complicated looking corn planter. Bobby and I loaded bags of seed corn and fertilizer on a flatbed wagon and met Dad and the men in the field each time the planter needed to be refilled. We used the old John Deere B to pull the wagon. It had a hand clutch and two cylinders, which caused the putt-putt noise as it pulled the loaded wagon across the field. I loved that tractor. In my childhood brain, I'd grown up thinking the B was a cousin to the train locomotives rumbling by the south pasture. Momma said my imagination would get me into trouble someday.

On the second Saturday in September, I backed the Gleaner out of the shed and into the barn. We pulled the grain header and attached the three-row corn header. I greased all the fittings again, checked the engine's fluids, and declared it ready for harvest.

On Sunday, Dad and Bobby drove to Jake Cluxton's and borrowed a truck to haul the shelled corn. It was only a few weeks after Bobby got his driver's license, but Dad let Bobby drive Jake's truck. Before they left, I overhead Daddy tell Momma, "He's gonna have to drive it around the farm to unload the corn from the Gleaner. May as well learn now."

Momma handed him a small, worn paper bag. "You best make sure the kids use these." She turned and walked away.

With me standing on the platform behind him, Dad drove the Gleaner down the road to the gate into the cornfield. He stopped and fished the paper bag out of his coat pocket. He reached in, pulled out a little box, and handed it to me. "Put these in your ears."

The box, once white, was yellowed. Faded blue lettering on the end read, "Ear Warden V-51R."

"Where'd these come from?"

"Your grandpa was on an artillery crew in WWII. I guess your momma kept them." He looked at me. "Ain't gonna hurt to save your hearing. She's right."

"What about you?"

"I probably done enough damage already. At least I can't hear that loud rock music kids are blasting out of their cars these days."

I thought of Bobby's endeavor to put an 8-track player in our old Ford. He finally asked me for help in wiring it up, but he'd blown out the dash speaker playing The Rolling Stones' "Satisfaction."

We pulled through the gate and stopped. Dad idled the engine, and then pushed the control clutch to the right, engaging the harvester. It made quite a racket. I was glad I had the earplugs.

Dad slowly increased the throttle to full and released the clutch. The Gleaner crawled forward chewing off corn, spitting the kernels into the bin and the threshed fodder out the back. The noise was deafening. In second gear, we rounded the field in thirty minutes. The bin was half-full. Another round and we were full. We stopped at the gate and Dad motioned to Bobby. He pulled one of the gravity wagons behind the B and lined it up with the unloader tube. When Dad nodded, I stepped on the unloader lever where I stood near the steps. In a few seconds, yellow corn kernels spewed from the tube into the gravity wagon. It was a yellow stream of gold, pouring money into our pocket and a visible measure of our crop's success.

Dad grinned and hugged me. He yelled into my ear, "Damn pretty, ain't it."

I nodded. Even Bobby had a broad smile that day.

Dad let me drive the Gleaner on the next two loops around the field. I guess he knew I knew more about this machine than he ever would, and he trusted me to operate it. I used the separator clutch to adjust our ground speed, slowing where the corn was heaviest, and then speeding up where it thinned out. The same lever was used to raise and lower the header as we crossed the ditches in the field.

Before we unloaded the second time, Dad ran his hand through the bin. "Dry enough. You two are stayin' out of school tomorrow. It's gonna rain on Tuesday."

Fear struck me. I didn't miss school. Never. It was like a religion. On the other hand, I was in seventh grade. Who would care if I missed one day, a whole day out here on the Gleaner? Momma would care. But Momma was a farm wife and understood how the saying, "making hay while the sun shines" applied to our lives. We tracked the weather relentlessly, always calculating how and when to get the farm work done around mother nature's meteorological tantrums. If the corn was dry enough to harvest, it had to be done before rain made the ground too wet for the Gleaner to get through the field.

Dad left me driving the Gleaner while he and Bobby shuffled the gravity wagons and transferred the corn to Jake's truck. Momma brought out some sandwiches around sundown and we all ate on the run, never stopping the harvesting. Just before midnight, Dad called a halt.

We unloaded the bin and I shut the Gleaner down. When we got back to the barn, Dad pulled the loaded gravity wagon into the barn and shut down the B.

"You kids go wash up and get some sleep. We'll start again at seven tomorrow."

My alarm sounded at six. I pulled on yesterday's clothes, grabbed a Pop-Tart, and dumped the oil, grease, and grease guns into the back of the pickup. By the time Dad pulled up to the Gleaner on the B, I'd completed the lubrication and had begun filling the fuel tank from the pickup supply tank.

"You're up early, Tink."

"Yup. Takes a while to get the Gleaner greased up. Cleaned the air filter and breather cap, too."

Dad smiled and looked at me for a minute while I continued turning the crank on the fuel transfer pump. "She use any oil?"

"No. Transmission and coolant are good, too. Had some fodder stuck on the straw walker. Belt and chain tension is good."

I finished fueling and stowed the transfer hose on the tank in the pickup. As I turned to climb up the Gleaner ladder, Dad handed me a paper bag and a water jug. "Momma sent you a fried egg sandwich. Better eat it while it's warm."

I nodded. "Thanks."

Dad wrapped his arms around me and hugged me for a long time. Hugs weren't that unusual from him, but I couldn't remember one this long. When he stepped back, I saw that his eyes were blinking back tears. It scared me. My Dad never cried.

Before I could ask what was wrong, he said, "Tink, you're one of a kind. I'm so blessed to have a child like you." He pointed at me. "You be careful now. And put those ear plugs in so Momma don't skin both of us." He climbed into the pickup and drove off toward the house.

It was a moment I remember clearly. One of the few emotional moments with Dad. He was mostly a no-whine, all-business kind of guy. I wondered how he and Momma could have two kids so different. Bobby was a slow-minded gentle giant. I was a skinny egg-headed blabbermouth who had learned to keep her mouth shut. But I was growing fast. I'd put on fifteen pounds over last summer and grown as tall as Bobby. I had two thirty-pound burlap bags of leftover seed corn I hefted around in the barn each day. Still, my strongest muscle was my brain.

CHAPTER 12

The sun was casting long shadows by the time I got back to the train switches. I kept to the south side of the track, trying to use the berm of the track to shield me from the hobo camp view. I had more bologna and cheese in my pack and my canteen was full. I'd eaten a bowl of chili at a diner. It tasted great going down, but my stomach was still growling after two bouts of diarrhea. I hoped it was the spices and not something spoiled in the chili.

The headlight of a train coming from the south caught my attention. The track began to hum. I crouched down short of where the northbound track merged with the eastern track. Some of the hobos slipped out of the woods and stood waiting on the other side. Remaining motionless and in the shadow of a mulberry tree, I didn't think they had spotted me.

The train rolled by, slowing to twenty miles per hour to cross the switch. About forty cars back, a few open boxcars passed by, and the hobos moved closer to the track in the dimming light. There were five of them. Two stood facing each other right next to the car's path. They grabbed each other's hands and crouched, making a kind of step up to the boxcar. As the second car passed, the other three men ran in a single-file line, bouncing off the human step and through the door in quick succession. The two men on the ground turned and walked back toward the camp in the trees.

Cooperation among hobos wasn't common. Maybe the guys on the train had paid the two ground guys for help in boarding. Or maybe the three who boarded were coming back with something of value for those remaining here. Whatever their arrangement, it was clear they were working together for some reason or purpose. I wanted to steer clear of them. I was definitely an outsider to them.

A few minutes after that train had cleared, another train came by from the western track. It blocked my view of the hobo camp, so I didn't know if anyone had boarded or gotten off. While they couldn't see me, I moved into the bushes against the town perimeter fence and hunkered down as twilight gave way to darkness. It was a good thing, too.

After the eastbound train passed, two men ran across the track towards me. They looked around, maybe searching for me. I shrunk lower into the bushes, my head against a wooden fencepost. The snakebite on my hand itched something fierce, but I refused to move.

A voiced called from across the track. "You see him?"

One of the nearby men yelled back, "Looks like he's gone. You sure you seen him here?"

The other one swatted the talker's arm and hissed, "You best not challenge Elmore."

"You two stay there. See if he crawls out of his hidey hole."

Three trains went by in different directions while the two sentries sat on the track berm and whispered, occasionally looking around. I remained motionless. My butt unavoidably was getting wet from sitting on the ground. It was full-on dark now and the moon hadn't risen. But the starlight in the country paints a dark gray landscape where movement is readily apparent. The light from the nearby town washed out some of the stars, but it wasn't close enough to light up anything near the tracks. The fence row where I sat was an irregular black swath to anyone looking this way. The two men couldn't see me as long as I stayed still. The snake bite itch had subsided thanks to me slowly rolling my wrist back and forth in my sleeve.

A stick cracked behind me on the other side of the fence. I didn't have much cover from that direction with my back against the fencepost. If someone on that side of the fence looked closely enough, they'd spot me.

The two sentries had heard the stick snap, too. They stood up and walked a few paces toward my fence. A shadow walked around the end of the fence near the track. "You boys are shitty lookouts."

"Elmore, we ain't seen nothin'."

"Course you ain't, sitting on your ass. Go get some sticks from camp. We gonna beat the bushes to find that boy."

"Why do you care about him? It's just one boy."

"'Cause I rule this here trainhopping station! You start lettin' one or two slip by, pretty soon ain't no one paying." I could see the one called Elmore pointing at them. "And that means you don't eat. Now get them sticks."

They scrambled up the berm on a run towards the camp. Elmore stood unmoving like a statue. I needed to get out of here quickly. A train light shone in the distance and the track began to hum. Elmore turned toward the train, and then yelled across the track towards the camp. "Hurry up."

I could see several men moving about quickly in the campfire glow. It didn't matter which way this train was going, I had to hop it. But Elmore stood between me and the tracks. Either way, west or south, he'd grab me before I could get by and to the track. He knew where to stand to block me either way. He'd done this before, and that made my skin crawl. He'd have a hell of a time catching me if I could get a step or two on him, pack or no pack. It could be a run for my life.

The two men ran across the track, each with a six-foot stick in hand. Elmore pointed. "You start down that way and work your way back." One of the men shuffled off down the fencerow. I could hear the second one move to a corner of the fence fifty feet away. He started whacking and poking the bushes, trying to flush me out.

While they were making noise and looking in that direction, I shifted to a squatting position. I had to start quickly when I ran but I had to have someplace to go. First, I needed to know which track this train was going to be on, west or south. And then I needed a train car I could grab onto, or they would push me into the wheels and that would be it.

My legs were trembling. I reminded myself this wasn't my first life-or-death situation. I'd had several. This train-hopping life was full of danger, and I'd known that before I started. Even that first leap into the first boxcar three days ago could have been a disaster. But it felt like months ago. I was seasoned now. I had real hobo experience, not just the picnic table education I'd gotten at the camp in Peebles. My legs calmed but my hands were sweating.

The approaching locomotive was loud, masking the noise of the guy with the stick near me. But I sensed he was getting close. The locomotive reached the switch. It went south. To my right. The stick whacked a bush ten feet away. It was fully dark, and the hobos had no flashlights, no visual advantage. He whacked six feet away. The train roared by on the track sixty feet away. The stick struck three feet away. I tensed my legs. The stick came down to the left of me. I grabbed it with both hands and pulled hard. The guy with the stick fell forward crashing into the bushes next to me. Keeping the stick, I sprinted directly at Elmore who was outlined by the faint campfire across the tracks. When I slammed the end of the stick into his chest like a jousting lance, he cried out and fell over backwards, rolling. He wouldn't be down long.

I wheeled to my right up the slope towards the passing train. The guy I pulled into the bushes was yelling. "He's runnin' for the train, Jerry. Get him!"

I presumed Jerry was the other guy with a stick. He could cut me off if he could see me. I certainly couldn't see him coming. The train itself was a shadow in the blackness. I reached the gravel next to the tracks, the whoosh of passing cars washing over me. I ran alongside, trying to find something to grab and at the same time figure out what kind of car was next to me. I knew Jerry couldn't hear me running because the train noise masked that. But if Jerry had a brain he'd stand right alongside the cars and wait for me. And he did.

I was about to grab what I thought was a ladder rung at the end of a tank car when I rammed into Jerry and went sprawling. My face slammed into the gravel, raking across my forehead and nose. My left knee skidded across a railroad tie and into the gravel, ripping my pants. Jerry's hands were flailing, trying to grab me. I rolled to my right, away from the train. But Jerry had snagged my pack strap. I could feel him standing and pulling me back. I could dump the pack and get loose, but I'd lose everything that was keeping me alive. That wasn't an option. Yet.

"I got 'im," yelled Jerry as he dragged me down the slope.

The other two would be here in a few seconds. Whatever I was going to do to escape had to be done now. I remembered that neither of the stick guys were big, so I had a fighting chance. Jerry was dragging me by the pack. I unclipped the pack strap, rolled to my knees, and got my feet under me. I leaped at Jerry, wrapping an arm around his neck, and driving him to the ground. He went down easily. Much easier than Bobby when he was teaching me to defend myself. He wrestled in school and taught me that a lightweight could take out a moose with a proper choke hold. But Momma caught us one day and forever forbade wrestling in the house again.

While I had Jerry in a choke hold, I realized he was downright scrawny. He was, after all, a hobo who was probably hungry more often than not. Hanging with Elmore gave him a better chance at filling his belly occasionally.

He went limp in four or five seconds. I felt around and found my pack, then raced for the train. I could tell from the sound that most of the train had passed. The last car wasn't too far behind me. If I couldn't catch on to one of these passing now, I'd be stuck here.

By the time I got to the track, the last train car was next to me. It was an empty flat car. There were no steps, loops, or hooks to grab. But it was the only option. I slung my pack up on the flat car and used what momentum I got from the throw to launch my shoulder up over the edge. I tried to claw and pull my way up but couldn't find a place to grab onto the smooth floor.

My right foot banged against something hard under the edge of the car. It wasn't a wheel, or it would have pulled me down. But I could hear the wheels roaring. I was right next to them. Clinging to the car, I tapped my foot towards whatever I had hit before. It felt like some part of the wheel frame or axle, but it wasn't turning. My hands were starting to slide off the floor. I couldn't hold myself here much longer.

I slid my leg toward whatever was under the car and as soon as I made contact, kicked out, rolling my body as best I could up over the edge of the flat car. I rested there for a moment, and then wriggled fully onto the bed. My feet dangled over the end of the flatcar. Another couple of feet and I'd have missed the train altogether.

And then I felt the train slowing. In another minute, we crossed a switch and the train stopped. It had pulled over to allow another train to pass. I looked back up the track toward the hobo camp. We hadn't gone more than a quarter mile. Three dots of light bobbed along the side of the track, coming towards me. Elmore and his buddies had known this train would stop here. They had flashlights now and were coming for me.

CHAPTER 13

That first year of no-till corn yielded better than Dad had expected. To celebrate, he took us to Cincinnati for the weekend during Christmas break. It was my first trip to Cincinnati or any other city. In fact, it was the first night Bobby or I had slept anywhere but our house. They were restless nights with the four of us sharing a pair of full-sized beds in a Bond Hill motel. We went shopping at Mabley & Carew department store, a two-floor store in Swifton Shopping Center offering more products than I knew existed. We spent hours walking around the store, mesmerized by everything from sewing machines to tuxedos and evening gowns. It had a beauty salon where Momma got her hair done before we ate lunch in the Tea Room.

On the first night, we went to Cincinnati Gardens and saw the final Ice Capades show. It was a spectacle of lights, glitter, and glamour on ice. Bobby and I grinned at each other, comparing this to our winter skating parties on our frozen pond where we burned old car tires to stay warm.

The second night we returned to Cincinnati Gardens and saw the opening show of the Harlem Globetrotters. Our cheeks and ribs were sore for days afterwards from the endless laughing and smiling. I ate more chocolate and drank more soda that weekend than I think I had the entirety of 1964. It was a special time for our family, one I remember as our happiest time and one that opened the door to my wanderlust. And Bobby's love life.

The importance of good crops and making a profit became crystal clear. And real. We made unplanned extra profits on the corn, so Dad shared and took us on a weekend trip. I got some new clothes and three new books from that trip, in addition to the truly enjoyable time with my family. Bobby, always whining when he had to get off his butt, was enthralled and was recharged when we got home. Secretly, or so he thought, he'd bought a trinket-like pendant for some girl at school. He was friendly and chatty with everyone at school. Everyone except his classmate Janet Nilsen. He never spoke of or to her. Whenever her name came up, Bobby's red face did, too. Her family lived ten miles away on the outskirts of Mowrystown. She had four siblings in school, including James in my class. All of them had names that began with J, and they were all Nordic blonde, blue-eyed, and shy. According to Susie, Janet didn't date, and the boys had labeled her a prude. But that didn't stop them from ogling her and her tight-sweatered breasts. According to Susie, those tight sweaters were hand-me-downs and too small. But what could Janet do? Like half the kids in our school, the only new clothes we got were made by our mothers, grandmothers, or aunts. Momma said the junk clothes from K-Mart might be fashionable, but they didn't last on the farm.

A week later I spotted Janet in the cafeteria. She wore an off-white turtleneck sweater with Bobby's pendant hanging from a delicate gold chain. I wanted to tease Bobby on the school bus ride home, but I didn't have the heart for it. He was my brother and he'd somehow found the courage to proffer his gift to her. But Susie pulled me into the seat next to her and started whispering in my ear. She had the scoop.

Yesterday, Bobbie had sworn Susie to secrecy and threatened to reveal her budding slut reputation to her father if she ever told. He'd given Susie the pendant and had her pass it to Janet as a present from a secret admirer. Susie cornered Janet in the girl's restroom. She handed Janet the box. "It's from a secret admirer. I'm just the messenger."

Janet smiled and opened the box. "Thanks, Susie." She closed the box and slipped it into her purse. "Is he going to ask me to prom?"

Susie blinked and her mouth fell open. "I don't know," she stammered. "Should he?"

"I don't think I'm going to get a better offer, do you?"

"Well, no, I mean, I don't know." She looked at the floor. "He's a nice guy, Janet, but he's so shy."

"I know. I've been in class with him for ten years and he never makes eye contact with me or says anything to me."

Susie's eyes flew wide. "Wait. I didn't tell you who it is."

"You didn't have to."

Susie stared at her. I'm sure she wondered if the whupping her daddy was gonna lay on her would leave bruises. She'd never get out of her house again. Her daddy would nail her bedroom window shut and lock her door. Her future was ruined.

She grabbed Janet's hand. "You gotta tell him that, Janet. If he thinks I told you, then I'm gonna be in big trouble. Really big trouble. With my daddy."

Janet frowned. "You don't need to get in trouble, Susie. I'll make sure of that. Isn't my little brother James in your class?"

Susie nodded.

"He'll have a note from me tomorrow. You pass it on to this 'secret admirer.' Okay?"

And that's what Susie did today, right before boarding the bus. Bobby sat staring out the window. The bus stopped at the end of our lane. He didn't get up. I had to nudge him to get off. As we walked up the gravel lane, side-stepping the puddles and trying to avoid the mud, I said, "You got a big-ass smile on your face, Bobby."

"Hey, you watch your mouth, Tink. Ain't no way for a twelve-year-old to be talkin'."

"Maybe. But you still got a smile I haven't seen before."

"Shut up, you hear? You keep your mouth shut or I'll shut it for you."

"Big ol' mean Bobby. Not foolin' me. You're a softie at heart." He stopped and wheeled on me. I held up my hands. "It's okay. I ain't telling nobody. You're my brother. But you ought to know Susie don't keep secrets from me."

We walked on. "Besides," I said, "that pendant is pretty. And she's smart. I like her. And Susie says the boys call her a prude 'cause she won't let 'em paw her."

"They better not, either. Or I'll beat the crap out of 'em."

We walked into the house. "I don't think you'll ever need to do that."

"To do what?" said Momma.

I glanced at Bobby. "Worry about flunking any classes."

"You flunking classes, Bobby Lee?"

"No, Momma." Bobby glanced at me. "I'm gettin' help when I need it."

I stifled a laugh all the way to my room. Bobby was gonna get himself a girlfriend. She'd make sure he didn't flunk any classes. All because that corn crop had been good enough to fund our little family trip. Funny how one crop can change your life's direction.

CHAPTER 14

I sat on the Gleaner platform, staring out across the wheat field. It seemed like a lifetime passed before Bobby returned. Momma was driving the tractor, but Bobby wouldn't let her climb up the ladder and see the nightmare in the bin. She called to me. "Tink, come on down here."

I glanced at the Gleaner header and wondered if it would have been better to have just fallen in when Daddy kicked me.

"Come on. I need to look at your face."

I wiped my nose on my shirt and climbed down. Momma poked around my cheek and eye for a minute.

"Open your mouth."

I winced.

"That hurt?"

I nodded.

A siren sounded in the distance. We turned towards the highway and saw a flashing red light on a vehicle approaching from Sardinia. Probably the local police headed our way.

I climbed back up the ladder and took my position on the platform floor. The red-winged blackbirds were swooping over the wheat field, diving and soaring back up into the air. I wanted to be one of them. Flying so freely, looking down on everything. I wondered if they could fly to the clouds.

Men and vehicles came and removed Daddy while I watched the birds.

Momma called me again. "Tink, come down here and let the doctor look at your face."

I climbed down. A man in a suit poked at my eye. He took a bright flashlight out of his black bag and moved it around while shining it into my eyes. He had me follow his finger as he waved it in the air.

"I think she has an orbital fracture, but it's not severe enough to require surgery. Put an ice pack on it for a few days. If the pain doesn't subside, then come in to see me." He turned away and started closing his bag.

Momma looked at my shirt. "Tink, is all that blood…your daddy's?"

I looked at my blood-covered shirt. My pants too, particularly my right leg. I held up my hands. "I tried to get him out."

Momma threw a hand over her mouth, then started to cry. She grabbed both of my hands by the wrists and held them up, tears running down her cheeks.

"It'll be okay, Momma."

She started to hug me but noticed my torn index finger.

"Dr. Franz, maybe you should look at this."

The doctor set his black bag down and looked closely at each finger on both hands. He twisted up his mouth. "Just that index finger. Big chuck of flesh torn off. Can't stitch it very well but I'll disinfect and bandage it. The others will heal." He looked at me. "You need some band-aids on those other fingers?"

"No. I'll just wear my gloves till they heal."

"You're a tough one, young lady."

Ten minutes later he was on his way with his black bag. Momma walked with him back towards the house. Bobby stood with his hands in his pockets, leaning back against the tractor, staring at the ground. I pulled my gloves out of my hip pocket and worked them onto my hands. My index finger was inflexible due to the bandage, but I made it fit into the glove.

"Bobby, go get a gravity wagon so we can unload this wheat."

He looked at me. I knew his heart was broken. He was as lost as I was, but there were things to be done.

"Now?"

"Yup. We need to finish. Ain't gonna cut itself."

He nodded and climbed onto the tractor.

"I love you, Bobby."

He sat there crying for a minute, and then said, "This ain't right, Trudy."

"If you don't want me to pull you off that tractor and kick your ass right here in this wheat field, you will not use that name."

He stared at me for a minute, and then started laughing. He started the tractor and drove off toward the barn.

I grabbed the grease gun from the Gleaner toolbox and gave each of the twenty-seven fittings a shot of grease. By then, Bobby had returned with the gravity wagon, and we unloaded the half-full bin into it.

"Dump it on the ground back by the chicken house."

"Why can't we just put it in the storage bin with the rest?"

"No. It's…it has blood in it. Somebody might be weird about making bread out of that. Or they might dock our price for blood. I don't know. Just dump it. The chickens will eat it."

"What are you gonna do?"

"Cut the rest of this wheat."

CHAPTER 15

We finished just before sunset. By the time we washed up, Momma had supper on the table. She'd set a place for Daddy, too. We ate in silence for ten minutes. I knew we were on an emotional roller coaster, operating on adrenalin, consumed with grief and shock, but we didn't have time to wallow in our sorrow.

"Momma, I have something to say."

"'Spect so."

"Bobby's sixteen. He can drive a car and handle equipment okay, but he doesn't know how to run a farm. Far as I know, you don't either."

"What makes you say that, Tink?"

"First time I saw you drive a tractor was today."

Momma stared at her plate. "I 'spose we sell the farm and move to town."

I slammed my fist on the table. That was a mistake. My bandaged index finger woke up and sizzled my brain with a jolt of pain for a moment. "No. That isn't what we're doing. I can run the farm. With Bobby's help."

Momma said, "What make you think you know how?"

"Sitting here, right now, I don't know how. But you know I'm smart. I read and learn better than anyone you know. I'll figure it out. We will not be selling the farm. You will not be another widow Martin."

"Tink, you're fourteen years old. And you're a girl. You can't possibly run this farm, even if Bobby was the best help in the world." She pointed at me with her fork. "It ain't possible."

It was too much for her right now. I needed a bite-sized chunk she could swallow and ease her into a new day. "Tell you what, give me until the end of the year. See where we are then. If I'm looney toons, we'll all know it by then."

She shook her head and spooned some beans into her mouth.

"Momma," said Bobby, "Tink's smarter than everybody at school. Includin' the teachers. And they know it. You've seen the stuff she's been readin' from the library. I say give her a chance."

Momma said, "They wanted you to skip grades. Fourth and sixth. Your daddy and I didn't want it. You've always been smart, way smart. But you're just a fourteen-year-old girl. And you just come of age a year or so ago. How could you possibly run a farm?" She stopped for a moment and looked at the ceiling. "This is crazy talk. You can't do this, Tink."

I was pissed that they never talked to me about skipping grades. I might have graduated and been in college by now if they'd let me. Still, I was using the time to self-educate, devouring the library. No sense worrying about it now.

"Momma, please give me a chance. I've never failed at anything I tried."

"'cept today." Her hand flew over her mouth. "I'm sorry. I didn't mean that, Tink."

My stomach contents revolted. I jumped up from the table and ran outside, heaving over the porch rail onto the day lilies. In a moment, I heard the screen door open behind me, but I ignored it. I ran down the steps and out to the barn, climbing up onto the Gleaner's seat. I leaned on the steering wheel with both arms, head down, staring at nothing.

My mistake had caused Daddy to be beheaded. In gruesome fashion. But it wasn't just the cotter pin. I didn't get the Gleaner turned off in time to save him either. It was my fault any way you look at it.

The voices in my head were a din over my throbbing cheek and pounding headache. I couldn't tell if it was one voice bouncing from thought to thought, or if I had acquired a cadre of voices all bombarding me simultaneously. I couldn't seem to focus on one thing. Between the pain and the din, I had lost control.

I stood and leaned over the rail, looking down at the Gleaner header. When Daddy kicked me, I'd barely been able to grab the rail to keep from falling to certain death. What would it have felt like to be crushed in the Gleaner, ripped apart as the thing tried to sort wheat from chaff? Probably wasn't painless but it would be quick. Whatever was going on in my head now was a tortuous nightmare set on replay. Daddy's severed head screamed at me to turn it off. But I moved in slow motion, like I was under water. Straining against the invisible force, I clawed forward to the Gleaner ignition. Even after I turned it off, the pulleys spun and chains clattered as the Gleaner severed the final sinews of Daddy's neck.

I took some deep breaths and tried to think of something calm and peaceful. The shearing of sheep at the county fair came to mind. All the wool spooled from the sheep into a soft sea of white fleece. The sheep scampered away afterward, seemingly refreshed from carrying that blanket around all year. It was a kind of metamorphosis, like the Monarch butterfly life cycle every kid learned about in grade school.

I couldn't bring Daddy back. And I didn't know how to end the grisly replay in my head without ending me. Momma and Bobby needed me to save the farm and get them past their own grief. I could do that. I could endure. Save the farm. For them. But I'd have to become a cocoon, wrap myself tight and focus on my one task. I had to remove the distractions, shut out the world, and do what needed to be done.

If I didn't succeed, I could die later.

And if I was going to run the farm, I needed to look the part. No one would take a fourteen-year-old girl seriously.

The moon was just rising when I returned to the house. I went upstairs to the bathroom and got out a comb and scissors. In ten minutes, I had trimmed my black hair to a two-inch uniform length that looked a little like Paul McCartney.

I felt a little giddy and grinned at my new look in the mirror. Maybe this was how the shorn sheep felt at the fair. Until they became lamb chops.

I rifled through my closet, piling my dresses and skirts on my bed. I added any top that looked remotely feminine. It really wasn't that much, but I carried it out to a spot on the gravel driveway between the house and barn. Another trip returned shoes, ribbons, lipstick, and anything else I could find that signaled female. Dousing the pile with a cup of gasoline from the farm tank, I lit a match and watched until only wisps of ash marked the spot where I was once a girl.

CHAPTER 16

The trio of bobbing lights heading my way were bouncing wildly. They were running. Because another train was coming. The train I was on would move on as soon as the other train went by.

I rolled over to the side of the flatcar and looked up the track. A single beacon of light, the oncoming locomotive's headlight, shone in the distance. Eight or ten minutes before it would pass and we took off.

These hobos coming for me knew at least as many hobo tricks as I did. I was still an amateur, counseled by the experienced hobos in Peebles. But still an amateur. I needed to use my non-hobo brain to elude them.

I could jump the fence and probably get away, but I'd lose my train ride. Plus, the open plowed field in that direction had no cover. They still might spot me. I could loop back toward the town, but that would just put me closer to these hobos in pursuit. And I'd have to hop a train near them at some point.

I rolled off the flatcar on the fence side. I couldn't risk a light, but I had to get past the locomotive before the hobos spotted me. I ran alongside the train as fast as I dared, with my pack in my hands in front of me to break my fall when I tripped.

On the third fall, I looked over my shoulder. One of the hobos was shining a light on a boxcar. They were closing the doors. As I scrambled up and ran ahead, I smiled. They were buttoning up the boxcars. I'd have no access to board. Just like the railroad folks did to keep hobos out.

I kept running as best I could. I had a lead on the hobos, and they had to look over, under, and inside every open car. I was gaining distance from them and had just passed eighty-three cars when I saw a man jump down from the locomotive four cars ahead. I dove into the weeds. He flicked on a spotlight and shined it back down along the track.

"Hey! What are you fellows doing?" he called.

He'd spotted the lights of the pursuing hobos and saw they were closing the doors. Their lights went out.

The approaching train locomotive rumbled by on the other track. The locomotive on my train let out a short whistle blast. A few seconds later, I could feel it power up and ease ahead, taking the slack of each car's connection and notifying the hobos chasing me that the train was about to take off.

I eased my head above the weeds and saw the train guy with the spotlight climb up a ladder into the locomotive. He leaned out and kept the spotlight shining down the track, looking for the hobos. My plan to get ahead of the train hadn't work. The spotlight had me trapped.

I slid my pack on and crawled through the weeds to the fence. It was a good thing I looked up and down on the other side of the fence before I slid over. One of the hobos was in the plowed field running towards me with his flashlight pointed at the ground. I shrunk back into the weeds. Can't go left, can't go right, can't go back. Only one way to go: forward. I split the weeds between the fence and the train and started to crawl on all fours. It wasn't as fast as the hobo was running, but he'd have to stop soon, and I didn't have far to go.

By the time I got well ahead of the locomotive, the other train had passed. I glanced over the fence. No sign of my pursuer. I crawled out of the weeds next to the gravel that led up to the track. I was fifty feet ahead of where the layover joined the main track, a few feet beyond the signal post.

As soon as the locomotive rumbled by, I sprinted back the hundred feet to where the two tracks joined. I'd spotted a boxcar with an open hatch. Car number twenty-one. If I could get on top of the train now, I could get to that hatch and climb inside the boxcar. The hobos would never know I'd holed up in a boxcar they'd already checked and closed.

My boxcar, number twenty-one, didn't have a ladder on the front. But number nineteen did. It was the one I had to grab. I counted the cars. Twelve. Thirteen. Shouting came from the other side of the train and lights played under the cars twenty feet away. I must have lost count because when I got to nineteen, it had no ladder. None on twenty or twenty-one. Twenty-two was a box car. No ladder on the front. The next car was a hopper. I had to take some chances now. I ran alongside the train and tried to grab the ladder on the back of twenty-two. No ladder there. But the hopper car behind it had a step-up. I grabbed it and pulled myself up on the open frame. A ladder ran to the top of this car, but it was on the other side, the side where the hobos were. Lights flashing all around on that side of the train.

The end of the hopper car bed sloped towards the center, leaving a wedge-shape open space supported by an angle-iron frame. I shoved my pack through an opening in the angle iron and wedged myself into a pocket between uprights. If they were looking for someone clinging to a ladder, they'd probably miss me here. A few seconds later a pair of flashlights played over the space between the cars. I held my breath.

The train picked up speed. The flashlights fell behind. I was about to crawl out and make my way to the hatch from the top of the boxcar in front of me when a light flashed across the end of the boxcar. A shadow leaped from the hopper to the boxcar roof. At least one of the hobos had boarded and was still looking for me.

I couldn't cling here forever, straddling a few pieces of angle iron spaced a couple of feet apart. As the speed increased, the ride became rougher. My foot could easily slip off and I'd fall to the track. I had to get inside a box car.

I slid out of the pocket and pulled on my pack. Although the moon hadn't risen yet, the sky was clear, and the starlight provided enough light to see the ladder on the left side of the boxcar in front of me. I climbed up a few steps and glanced at the sky. We were headed south, away from Montana. Maybe I should have taken to the plowed field, but I had to move forward with the decisions I'd made, good or bad.

I stuck my head above the boxcar just enough to see what was on top. It was clear. As far as I could see, about five cars forward, no one camped on a roof. The same was true behind me.

I crawled onto the roof, doing an army crawl mostly to hang on. The car rocked a lot up this high and the fifty-mph wind was blasting me in the face. I wasn't sure if this was car twenty-two or maybe twenty-three. In any case, the roof hatch was locked. When I got to the gap between this car and the next, I hesitated. It was short of four feet, maybe forty-two inches. But the wind and movement undermined my confidence and added too many variables to the physical momentum calculation in my head. I couldn't risk the jump. Plus, I was scared and shaking.

I climbed half-way down the ladder, then reached over and grabbed the ladder on what I thought was car twenty-one. Its roof hatch was locked, too. I moved on to car twenty. Another locked hatch. I was starting to think I'd have to cling to a roof until I could get off. Maybe several hours. My hands were already numb from the cold wind, but I didn't dare try to dig out my gloves for fear they might get blown away.

I climbed over the lip of twenty and was just about to duck my head below the roof.

"Hey! You the one they're looking for?" said a voice on the wind.

I whipped my head back and forth. I couldn't see anyone, so I waited, motionless, hanging on the ladder, my head just above the roof.

"Did you hear me?"

I looked around again. "Yes," I said into the wind.

"Then you better get your ass in here."

The hatch on twenty opened. I could see the whites of two eyes peering at me in the darkness.

My mouth voiced my hesitation. "How do I know you're not one of them?"

"'Cause I could have shoved you off from behind."

He was right. With the wind noise, I wouldn't have heard him until it was too late. I climbed back up the ladder. The hatch remained open, but the head disappeared. I felt around inside the hatch with my foot, found the ladder, and climbed down, closing the hatch above me.

"No need for light. Nothing in here but you and me."

I found the wall and slid to a corner. "Thanks."

"Welcome." After a few minutes of silence, he said, "Why are they chasing you?"

"From what I overheard, they wanted me to pay them to pass through their train switch."

"Their switch," he snorted. "More like their camp. Quite a few camps around the big switches."

I had questions but I was exhausted from the last few hours. If he was going to harm me, he'd already had ample chances. I tucked my hands in my armpits, leaned my head back, and fell asleep.

#####

I awoke with a jolt as the train crossed a series of switches. It had slowed to a crawl.

The voice in the dark said, "You best get ready to run. Soon as we stop, they're gonna open these doors."

I knew that but wondered how experienced my traveling companion was. "Why not go out the hatch and climb down a ladder?"

"'Cause you're too easy to spot on top of the train. They'll send cops to catch us. This way, it'll be some low-paid guy who doesn't care about us, and we'll just slip away."

I had already learned that in Peebles hobo school, but I wanted to know how much this guy knew. Apparently, a lot. "Why are you helping me?"

He was silent for a moment. "I did my time for the Man. Pisses me off when some asshole hobo tries to grab power and tell free birds what to do."

"You skirted them. That was you in the plowed field."

"Yeah. Watched 'em beat the bushes looking for you. Saw you take out one of them, too."

The train stopped. I was hungry and thirsty but didn't know how much time I had before the door opened. I gulped down some water anyhow and moved to the wall next to the door.

We could hear them coming. Two of them chattered in indistinct voices. A loud clank cued us that they'd opened the latch on our door. The door began to slide open and early morning light bloomed inside like a spotlight. I hugged the wall, trying to let my eyes adjust.

"…wish they'd git the National Guard out to those camps and clean out those hobos. Get the boys from Kent State. They'd do it."

"Ain't no need to kill anybody, Roy. They deserve to live, too. You need to be cool."

"Bunch of lazy bastards. Get a job. Stop livin' off everybody else."

"Maybe they giving you a job, Roy. They didn't close up these boxes all the time, you and me might need to look for real work."

"Shit, I ain't afraid of work…" The two turned away as they moved on to the next car.

On the other side of the door my traveling companion sat on his haunches, smiling. He had the palest blue eyes I'd ever seen, almost like a wolf. His reddish Fu Manchu mustache drooped past his chin. He looked like a hippy army guy. Olive drab pants and coat, but a ponytail tied behind his Army ranger-style hat.

He pointed at my backpack. "You gonna be an astronaut?"

I'd sewn a NASA patch on my grubby-colored pack just so I could recognize it if needed. "Maybe. Have to be a pilot first."

"Where are you headed?"

"Missoula. Meeting up with some people there."

He nodded. "I'm Sam. Best of luck to you. Ready?"

"I'm Tink. Thanks for the help." I rose and moved closer to the door. We shook hands.

"See ya." Sam leaped through the door and to the ground, landing almost silently. I poked my head out to see if the guys opening the doors even noticed. They were two cars down now and didn't even turn. Sam disappeared under a tanker car two tracks over.

I checked for approaching trains and slid down to the ground, rolling under the car I had been in. From my low perch I could see Sam making his way under cars towards what looked like a fence about six or seven tracks over. When he disappeared, I took off and followed his route to the fence. I climbed over and dropped into the weeds.

I wanted to find a northbound train and hop it immediately, but I still had six weeks before I needed to be in Missoula. Food, restroom, and other traveler amenities were surely nearby, so I convinced myself to take advantage of them. Plus, no one was chasing me. At least not right now.

CHAPTER 17

The second spring with the Gleaner marked the beginning of my teenage years. I'd plowed through most of the Newtonian physics books in the library, having set aside Dr. Einstein's relativity for now. Chuck found a loaner program at Wright Patterson Air Force Base that allowed him to borrow published papers related to aircraft. We reviewed the list together.

"None of these about maintenance or logistics is of interest," I said, pointing at a section in the table of contents.

"If you prioritize the sections, I can order them sequentially. Will one section a month work?"

"Order the first section on 'Structures and Materials,' and then I'll know how fast I'll be able to read through them."

Chuck nodded. "Okay. Should take about a week."

I flipped through the six-page list. "There's a lot of things missing. I expected a bunch of papers on the F-4 aircraft. Or at least the B-52."

"Security. We don't want the Russians or Chinese to know what we know. Anything very new is probably considered secret."

"Let's see what's in the materials papers. I'm not sure they'll be very interesting unless they go into some depth."

Chuck stared at me for a moment. "I have a friend who works at NASA. Let me call him and see if there's any way to get information from them."

The bell rang, signaling I was tardy for math class. "I have to go. Thanks, Chuck. See you tomorrow."

As it turned out, most of the WPAFB papers were a regurgitation of well-understood physics with a few sentences of what-if ideas and plans to explore. The follow-up paper that explained what they discovered, proving or disproving their hypothesis, wasn't in the shared lot.

On the other hand, Chuck landed some exceptional information from his NASA connection. I had to read those in the library on Saturdays, so Chuck always had "physical control of the documents." Some were stamped with "Confidential." Others had blacked-out borders redacting the classification markings when the paper was copied. Even whole paragraphs were sometimes black.

Chuck explained that he had a secret clearance because of his previous government job. I figured he was violating security rules by letting me read these, but I didn't ask. It wasn't like I was going to tell anyone, Russian or not.

He explained that a whole document might be classified "secret" because of one sentence or paragraph. As a result, each page of the document would have a secret stamp. But individual pages might be unclassified and that's why the borders were blacked out sometimes.

The gem in the NASA trove was a package that included drawings and materials testing data sheets. It included detailed structural specifications of the Apollo command module and the Lunar Excursion Module (LEM) that had landed on the moon. They were bookends of spaceflight structures, one dealing with the Earth's forces and the other with the moon's. Both dealing with the emptiness of space.

On my way home that Saturday, I realized that although laws of physics seemed to be universal regardless of where you were in the universe, variations in astronomical bodies shifted base forces like gravity and temperature. What worked in one environment might be a catastrophe in another. Like the aluminum alloy used in the LEM—the engineers worried that the constant low temperatures in space and on the moon would cause the alloy to become brittle. On the other hand, the moon's twenty percent gravity allowed much lighter and simpler structures. The laws of physics were the same, but the environmental application of those laws changed everything. It wasn't enough to know the laws, or even the theories and mathematical underpinnings. You had to know how to use those laws to your advantage. And not get killed. Or kill someone else.

A chill ran up my spine. I was glimpsing a world most humans never thought about and barely knew existed. It put perspective on my existence against the universe backdrop. My lifelong mission had always been flight and space, helping the human endeavor to reach beyond our earthly bounds. I dreamed of flying. But as I thought about the hobos in Peebles and the hungry kids in my school, I squirmed. Maybe I should be more worried about helping those in need. Working to improve the plight of humankind instead of trying to thrust the chosen few into orbit.

This conundrum put me into a funk for several weeks. But an unbent cotter pin would soon change that.

CHAPTER 18

The streets in this town were numbered and lettered, arranged like a checkerboard. Easy to navigate and find my way back to the trainyard, even if the train whistles hadn't provided an audible homing signal.

A few blocks into the town, the late 50's houses gave way to three- and four-story business buildings. A tired main street—oddly named Main Street and the only deviation I found from the letter/number combo—had few cars and even fewer people drifting along. Two blocks down I found an old Texico station with a single pump. It had the globe on top and the port that contained spinning balls when you pumped the gas.

Along the back, I found a locked restroom. The sign on the door said to see attendant for key. After some debate, my bladder overruled my fear, and I trudged inside. I snagged a Milky Way from the candy rack and fished a nickel out of my pocket. The acne-faced boy behind the counter eyed me, looked at my pack swung over one shoulder, at the candy bar in my hand, then at the nickel as I laid it on the wooden counter.

I nodded. "Thanks."

The boy flicked a greeting with his index finger.

"May I use your restroom?"

He stared at me for a moment. I thought he might be deaf. Or mute. But he finally said, "It's busy."

I wasn't sure what that meant. Was it an excuse instead of no, or was someone else in the restroom? "I can wait."

He nodded once. I drifted around the corner of the counter to a magazine rack. Most of the magazines were years old with dirty, worn corners. Car and car repair seemed popular. *Life, Time,* or *Newsweek* were nowhere to be found.

I heard the front door open and turned to find Sam walking in. He aimed for the counter, and then seemed to catch sight of me.

"Hey, Tink." He held up a twelve-inch ruler with a key wired to the end. "You looking for this?"

I nodded, took the key, and headed around back. The door had a lock on the inside, and the sink had hot water. I stripped, did a stand-up bath, and changed into my other set of clothes. After washing out the dirty ones, I wrung them out as much as I could, and then stuffed them in an outside pack pocket.

When I returned the key to the counter, the boy didn't even glance at me. I walked a little lighter towards the door, now clean and in fresh clothes. But it was mostly because I was invisible. At least to the boy behind the counter.

Retracing my way back towards the railyard, I turned right on E, then left on Twelfth. As I stepped off the curb to cross the street, a police car turned the corner a block down the street. It headed my way. My heart raced, but I maintained my pace, trying to appear confident in where I was headed. The urge to run thrummed in my chest.

I reached the other side of the street and continued down the broken sidewalk. My eyes kept trying to turn my head so I could see where the police car was. My ears figured it out, though. It was idling at the intersection. The hair on my neck rose. The cop was staring at me, probably trying to decide if I belonged. Or maybe not. My imagination could be playing tricks.

Deciding to cross the street mid-block, I turned and looked both ways. No police car in sight. My damp pits heaved a sigh of relief. I hitched my pack on my shoulders and picked up my pace. It would feel good to hunker in some weeds by the fence where no one could see me.

As I passed the corner of a one-story brick building, an arm shot out of the alley and grabbed me by a pack strap, pulling me into the alley. I grabbed the wrist of the attacker and whirled away, twisting him to the ground with an arm wringer, hyperextending his elbow and shoulder.

"Jesus, Tink!" hissed Sam. "Trying to help you."

I released his wrist. "Help me how? Dragging me into an alley?"

He scrambled up. "Come on. Unless you want a seat in that cop car." He started running into the dim alley.

A car motor revved in the street behind me. Sam darted behind a dumpster. I sprinted after him and shrunk behind the dumpster, too. A bright light played on the wall and down the alley. Several rats scurried behind some trash and through a hole at the base of the far wall. The light played around for a minute, then went out. The sound of the police car motor receded.

I could hear Sam breathing next to me. I stood and peaked over the dumpster. No sign of the cops. "I think we're clear."

Sam stood, rubbing his shoulder.

"Sorry about that."

"No, I deserved it. Didn't think you were a fighter, though."

"I'm not. Just self-defense."

"You're too young for 'Nam. Where'd you learn that?"

"Brother and his wrestling team. They practiced at our place sometimes."

Sam laughed. "Bet your house was a mess."

I smiled. "They used the barn."

He stared at me for a while. I finally said, "Thanks for the help," and started walking towards the street.

He fell in step. "Heading back to the yard?"

I nodded. We walked in silence for a few blocks until we came to the yard fence.

He pointed to the right. "There's a little knoll about a half mile down that way. You can see the whole end of the yard from there."

We turned to the right, Sam leading the way down the path in the weeds next to the yard fence.

"You've been here before?"

"Yeah. Used to have an army buddy who lived here. Visited him a lot."

"He moved?"

"You could say that."

"What's that mean?"

He stopped walking and stared into me with those wolf eyes. "You ask a lot of questions."

"Sorry." I tried to change the subject. "So that's how you know the police tactics, how you knew they were circling me."

"I've been running from police most of my life." He rotated his shoulder a couple of times and flexed his elbow.

"How come?"

He just kept staring at me.

"I'm only asking because you invited me into the alley."

His mouth dropped open. "Invited?" He turned and continued walking. "Had a boy in my sister's class like you. Victor. Got kicked in the head by a cow when he was little. Seemed perfectly normal until he talked. Then it seemed like he wasn't completely connected to the world around him."

"Aphasia."

"Yeah, that sounds like what they used to call it."

"You think I'm brain damaged?"

"Probably."

"And the use of 'invited' is your single data point for drawing this conclusion?"

He stopped again, this time putting his hands on his hips before spitting into the weeds. "You're an odd one, alright. Clearly not a train kid, but you got a real brain if you figure out how to use it right." He walked on.

"Let me see if I got all of this. I'm brain damaged, inexperienced, and subject to malapropisms. And I can kick your ass. That about it?"

We walked on in silence for ten minutes until we reached the knoll. Sam veered off the path, parted some bushes, and stepped into a small clearing that afforded a view of the yard. The bushes shielded us from the town while sandwiching us with the yard fence.

I took in the scene with the movement of train cars on a dozen tracks. The assembly of cargo on cars bound for various destinations via groups we called trains was marvelous to behold. I wondered how many people worked the schedules and cargo manifests to make this work. "Wish I had a camera."

"You got one—in that head of yours."

"Why are you travelling?

"Life is either a daring adventure or nothing at all."

"You make that up?"

"No. My sister. She read it to me from a book written by a blind woman."

"Helen Keller."

Sam glanced at me, and then stared out at the trains. After a while, he said, "Why are you out here?"

I'd rehearsed for this question for years. There were several flip answers I had at the ready, but I felt like Sam deserved an honest answer. I still wasn't sure I had one. "I'm looking for something."

"What are you looking for?"

"Me."

Without turning, he nodded his head. "Yeah. I get that. How you'd lose you?"

I didn't know how to frame an answer to that one. There was a long, tortured answer I didn't want to get into. I opted for the Cliffsnotes version. "My daddy was killed in a farm accident."

He looked at me. "What happened?"

"He got caught up in the Gleaner—a combine."

"I'm sorry. How old were you then?"

"Fourteen."

"And now?"

I laughed. "About forty."

"Ain't that right." He stood. "It's time to go."

I stood next to him, and, for the first time, noticed I was an inch or so taller than him. He caught me off guard when he put his arm around my shoulder and pulled me into a hug. It was only awkward for a moment before I hugged him back. Twilight hid my red face. My pulse raced. I'd had a few "guy-to-guy" embraces before, but this was different. I liked Sam. He'd saved me from harm several times. If he was around long enough, we'd become friends. Or more. I bit my lip for focus.

"Stay safe out there, Tink. Hope you make it to Missoula and meet your friends. You're a good man." He stepped through the weeds and swung over the fence, disappearing in the dusky shadows.

I couldn't tell if he looked back, but I waved. "Woman. I'm a good woman, Sam."

CHAPTER 19

I sat back down on the knoll and waited for it to get darker. I didn't want to run into Sam or seem like I was following him. But I wanted to run after him, ask him to come to Missoula with me. I told myself it would be safer to travel with him. Momma would approve. But I knew myself well enough by now to know hormones were involved. Libido. I'd come of age in the sixties with the "free love" mantra everywhere. Except me. I've been dead to everyone since Daddy died. Momma even pointed this out to me before I left. I didn't feel anything about anyone. Even Momma or Bobby. They were my family, so I accepted that and treated them accordingly. But everyone else was just interchangeable bodies floating through my life like leaves in a stream.

Except Sam. He'd chipped open a crack in my shell. It felt good. Promising. Maybe this trip was already cathartic. But I had to be careful. If I let myself open too fast, I knew I'd drown from the flashflood of emotion.

The stars were coming out. The waning moon had risen with the sliver making a nearly perfect sad face. I felt sad, too. And lonely. I missed Sam.

I slapped my hat against my knee and stood to pick a fence crossing spot. I moved off to my right, towards the yard exit gate, and waded through the weeds for a hundred yards. A locomotive rumbled by pulling seventy cars or so. While it blocked the yard from view, I scrambled over the fence and squatted until it passed. It was completely dark now and I'd only be spotted as an outline or if someone shone a flashlight my way.

A pair of open-door boxcars stood three tracks over, ten cars back from the locomotive. I didn't like to be that close to the front of the train, but I didn't feel like waiting around. I crouch-ran across the tracks, threw my pack inside the second boxcar, and pulled myself inside. My little flashlight ensured I was alone. The car smelled like rubber tires, probably from its recent cargo.

I crammed myself into a corner, looped the pack strap through my arm, and put my head down. Every few minutes I felt the car bump as more cars were added to the train. A half hour later, we began to move out of the yard, and I soon fell asleep.

Unlike my usual nightmares of severed heads and endless struggles to save Daddy, I dreamed of Sam. We were at the willow next to the creek pool where the snake bit me. Sam wanted to go for a swim. I warned him about the snakes. He waved me off and stripped to his underwear. I hadn't realized how muscular he was. There was an ugly scar on his lower back. He was also missing a chunk of his calf behind his right knee. Before I could ask about those, he dove into the water. I waited for him to surface. And waited. I jumped up and ran to the water's edge, shouting his name.

He finally surfaced on the other side of the pool. I yelled at him, chastising him for scaring me. He couldn't hear me over the stream noise, even though he cupped a hand behind his ear. As he began to swim towards me, I recalled the lesson Paul Hines taught me when we were eleven.

Paul lived on the farm next door. It was a mile-long bike ride to his house, mostly on a gravel lane. Maybe because he was the only kid my age who lived nearby, or maybe we just hit it off—we were friends and spent a lot of our pre-teen free time on joint adventures. I knew his family was poorer than us, but the only evidence was that he was always assembling and re-assembling his bike to keep it running. He had three or four discarded ones from which he borrowed parts. His four older brothers had moved out and abandoned theirs, all Western Flyers, like mine, so everything was interchangeable.

In the spring before we acquired the Gleaner, Paul and I discovered a treasure trove of weekend intrigue. Not far from our houses—a fifteen-minute bike ride—they were constructing "the new highway." It was mostly a four-lane divided highway of two-foot-thick concrete. Paul and I explored their equipment extensively, pretending to operate most of it. I spent my time figuring out how it all worked. He was more intent on snagging some of the girly magazines he found behind a seat or in an unlocked cab.

One day we discovered that the bridge I-beams had been installed across the new Straight Creek bridge they were constructing. The beams were about ten inches wide and now spanned the 280-foot ravine. It seemed obvious to me that we should walk across the ravine on the beams. I took off practically skipping. About a hundred feet out I heard Paul yell behind me. "God damnit!" I turned to look, and there was Paul lying belly down on the beam with his arms and legs wrapped around it. He was only about ten feet from the abutment.

"What are you doing?" I shouted.

His eyes were closed. "I can't do this. Jesus Christ. Son of a bitch!" A tear trickled down his cheek.

I scampered back to him and sat down on the beam, legs dangling on either side. I grabbed his arm. "Come on. I'll help you scootch back."

With my coaxing and a lot of grunting and cussing, he inched his way back to the abutment. Once his feet felt the concrete, he was able to work his way back until he was off the beam. He stood up and pointed at me. "I ain't gonna follow you across there. But if you fall, it ain't my fault."

I nodded and practically ran across the beam to the other side. He stared at me. I walked back more carefully and stepped onto the abutment next to him.

He had tears in his eyes and wiped his nose with his shirt. He turned away.

I was confused. "Why are you crying?"

"I wudn't cryin'. I was just scared. Fer you."

A chill went up my back and I shivered. He'd been scared for me. My actions had caused him to be afraid—for me. It was the first time I realized this cause and effect was possible between two people. Despite my big brain, I felt blind to people and emotions sometimes.

I slung my arm around him. "Next time tell me, and I won't do it."

"Shit, Tink, you do it all the time!"

I laughed, trying to cover my alarm. Was I so self-absorbed I hadn't noticed before? Now I was embarrassed.

I stopped and grabbed his other arm, turning him to face me. "Look, Paul, we're buds. You gotta tell me when I scare you. That's part of the bud contract. Okay?"

He smiled and wiped his nose on the back of his sleeve. "I ain't seen no damn contract."

I tapped his head with my index finger. "It's in there. Maybe you got drunk and lost it."

He laughed. "I ain't been drunk. But you wanna give it a try?"

"Try what?"

"Gettin' drunk."

"No. We're both too young to drink alcohol. You know that."

"My brother Phil stayed at our house last night. I'll bet he's got part of a Bud six-pack in his car. Wanna try to snag it?"

I shook my head. "No. And you don't try it either."

"Might be fun."

"Now you're scaring me."

He shrugged. "First time, I 'spect."

I kicked off and biked home, leaving Paul standing there with his chubby hands on his hips. Along the way, I replayed what had happened and how my fearless adventures frightened Paul. I'd never seen him so upset. My heart was sad because I'd caused such a terrible situation for him. I was also shocked to realize how oblivious I was. I shed a few tears on that ride home. Tears of guilt.

I was in my room reading that night, just before lights out, when the phone rang. I heard Momma answer it in muffled tones, and then Daddy started talking. I opened my door and crept to the top of the steps to listen. All I heard was the click as Daddy hung up the phone.

"Come on down here, Tink," said Momma.

I poked my head around the corner. "How'd you know I was listening?"

"I'm your mother," said Momma. "Now git down here."

Her tone alarmed me. Were they mad that I had tried to listen? She was certainly upset. I scampered to the bottom step and stared from Momma to Daddy.

Daddy sat down beside me. He put his hand on my knee. This was bad. Worse than I'd ever seen. I hugged my knees to my chest. Daddy pulled me into a hug.

"Tink, there's been an accident."

"Who got hurt?"

"Paul. Paul Hines."

"Is it bad?"

"He's dead, Tink. He rolled a tractor, and it pinned him to the ground."

"It crushed him?"

"No, just pinned him. Under the rear tire. On his chest. Didn't crush him, but he couldn't breathe. He suffocated."

I put my forehead on my knees to hide my face. He'd found his brother's beer and gotten drunk. But I wasn't going to tell Daddy or anyone about that. "I'm sorry."

"Me, too, Tink."

I wouldn't have to worry about scaring him anymore. And then I felt guilty for thinking that. It must have been an awful death. He didn't deserve that. He was kind and gentle. He made me laugh. We had good times. Things would change now. I'd have to go to the funeral.

"When's the funeral?"

"Don't know yet. In a few days."

"I'd like to go."

"Sure." Daddy gave me another hug. "You run on to bed now. School tomorrow. I'll check in on you when I come up."

I hiked upstairs with leaden feet and stood looking out the window towards the train track. After a while, I crawled into bed. My friend was dead. I'd never see him or talk with him again. A little piece of me seemed to die with him. I hoped I'd keep a piece of him in my head forever. I wondered how his parents felt. And his brother—if he knew about the beer.

CHAPTER 20

Even though I slept incredibly well on the trains, my nightmares about Daddy continued. Sometimes I'd wake up sweaty, scared, or screaming. Sometimes, all three. But tonight was different. Sam was swimming towards me in that stream where I was snake bit. As he reached the near side he stood and began wading towards me. "Are you okay."

"No. You scared the hell out of me. You were under water a long time."

Sam shrugged. "Sorry. Didn't know there was a time limit."

"And now you're flippant, like you don't care how badly you scared me."

"I said I'm sorry. But how did I know that was going to scare you?"

"When you do dangerous things, people who care about you get concerned. Frightened. Scared. That's basic rules of friendship."

Sam put his hands on his hips and stared at me. His pale eyes twinkled. "So, you care about me or we're friends? Which is it?"

A dark shadow swirled through the pool behind him. "It's both. Now get out of the water. *Hurry!*"

"Am I scaring you by standing here?" He shook his head. "I think you're mental."

The shadow reared from the water—a snake twice as big as me. It struck from above, taking Sam's whole head in its mouth and snapping it off. The snake splashed back into the pool. Sam's headless body stood there spewing blood in great streams from his neck. The blue water turned crimson as the thrashing snake flailed behind him. His body fell over backwards, and the snake snagged him, diving deep into the pool. A putrid wave of horror wafted ashore.

I tried to scream. No sound escaped. I took a step towards the pool. The snake's tail splashed the surface. I turned and ran towards the willow, thinking it would provide safety from the snake. But when I got to the tree, it's branches turned into tendrils and cocooned my body, immobilizing my legs and arms. I struggled, trying to break free. The snake reared from the water, its face now Sam's. My mouth finally began working and I screamed. A tendril snapped across my mouth.

I woke in a battle with my backpack, its straps entwined with my arms, my hat plastered across my face. It was a nightmare far worse than those familiar ones with Daddy. Maybe even worse than that day itself.

I pulled the backpack loose and shoved it back into the corner. Sitting there panting and sweaty, I watched the sun come up outside the open boxcar door. We were stopped. And that putrid smell was still with me. It seemed familiar and then I realized it was manure— a mixture of pig and cow manure.

Peeking outside toward the rear of the train, I confirmed that we'd stopped at a stockyard. There were hundreds of pens and several large arenas where they auctioned the stock. Things were just waking up with the sunrise. Lights winked off here and there. Pigs and cows voiced their displeasure in a cacophony of protest. I picked out some bleats of sheep in there, too.

This wasn't a place to get off the train. There were too many people, and they were moving around too much. The boxcar jolted several times as empty livestock cars were swapped for loaded ones. They were behind me so the smell and occasional manure splatter wouldn't be something else I had to deal with.

I slunk back into my corner and thought about my new nightmare. Dreaming of anyone other than Daddy was new. It was a triad of relief, nightmare, and tectonic shift. I hoped it would prove to be a positive step and a toehold in dealing with my grief. Momma was right about not living. I wasn't sure there was ever going to be a chance. If this trip didn't rip open my cocoon, then I'd decided I'd never make it back from Missoula. There were mountains with cliffs aplenty where I could join the bleached bones of other lost souls.

#####

By late afternoon, the train approached St. Louis. The downtown outline was visible for miles, but the Gateway Arch stood 630 feet, towering above the other buildings. It was distinctively St. Louis. I wondered if other cities considered landmarks that gave them identity. Did the elected officials, mayors, councilmembers—even the police—think about the image and reputation of their city? Did the people who lived there care? It was, after all, their taxpayer's money that built it.

I knew that country folk, at least farmers, didn't have time for such concerns. They were more worried about their crops. Would it rain at the right time, or would it storm too severely and destroy their crops? Mother nature ruled their purse. The only identity for them was whether or not they put food on the table. Survivor or loser, the only two options. There were no winners because there was always next year. What mother nature gave, she could take away.

Financially, I'd had four great years on the farm after Daddy died. In the months that followed that wheatfield ordeal, I struck deals with several nearby farmers to lease their land, and using the no-till technique, I double-cropped wheat and soybeans. Altogether, we farmed nearly six-hundred acres within a five-mile radius of our home.

Bobby had his driver's license and carted me back and forth to the extension office in Georgetown at least twenty times that summer. The extension office was a department of The Ohio State University staffed by farming experts with an eye towards tomorrow's farming future. At first, they urged us to join FFA or 4-H, but we didn't have time for that. I had no time for social involvement or dealing with other people. We finally met Jim Wells who ran the Brown County farming experiment station under the extension office auspices. In short, he tried to put into practice the new ideas, methods, seeds, and technology on his farm. It was owned by the university, and they hired him to run it for them. His "experiment station" was aptly tagged.

Mr. Wells first came to our house to meet Momma. She had to sign a stack of forms to allow us to work with him and make sure none of us sued him or the university. She signed contracts with him and the farmers where we rented land.

With the wheat cut, we should have been planting beans. But Daddy hadn't made plans for that. We had no seed beans. Mr. Wells had no ideas about where to get seed this late in the season.

Three days after Daddy's death, I had Bobby drive me to Jake Cluxton's house. We arrived just before dark. As we pulled up, a half-dozen hound dogs began barking and running around the car.

As I opened the truck door, Mr. Cluxton pushed open the screen door. "You best be careful. Those dogs ain't so friendly."

Bobby said, "Tink, they'll take your leg off."

"Can't talk to Mr. Cluxton from here. Besides, I'm not afraid of dogs."

"Maybe you should be."

I squatted for a moment and eyed the pack. Two or three came over and I gave them a quick pat on their head. They wandered away. The alpha seemed to be standing his ground and growling at me. I looked him in the eye and snapped, "Come here."

He stared at me, then shook his head. He looked away and I knew I had him. "Come on." I reached my hand toward him. He sauntered over, head down, seemingly ashamed of himself. When he got within arm's length, he laid down and rolled over, exposing his belly. I scratched it for a minute, and then stood.

A growl came from behind me. I wheeled to find a small mutt charging me from behind the car. Sneaky and sly. Ugly combination for a dog. A whack to his head with my boot would make him think about trying to bite me next time. But I was too slow. The alpha, though, had jumped up and lunged at the mutt, snarling and trapping him on the ground. In a moment, the mutt squirmed away, looking back over his shoulder as he sought safety by the corn crib.

Jake cackled and shook his head. "Don't reckon you need my help."

I walked toward the open door. "Actually, Mr. Cluxton, I need your help in a big way."

The smile slid from his face. "Missy, you done made yourself look like a boy. That mean you running the Truesdale place?"

I nodded. "And a lot more. We're leasing several hundred acres."

"Ha! Gonna run the shit out of that Gleaner. Make it pay for what it did to your daddy." He scratched his head. It would have been called a comb-over, but he only had a half-dozen strands of hair to flop across his head. "How can I help?"

By the time we left, Jake had made several calls and located sixty bags of soybean seed which he delivered the next day. We'd also agreed to a deal for him to truck our wheat and soybeans to the grain elevator in Mowrystown starting with our soybeans in the fall.

Mrs. Cluxton had forced a slice of warm peach pie on me while Jake was on the phone. When I left, she handed me a wrinkled paper bag of cookies. "Don't be too hard on your brother, Tink. Ain't many gets to our door without a dog bite or two. Can't blame him for staying in the car."

Jake squeezed my shoulder and handed me a dollar.

"What's this for?"

Jake's face turned red. " no girls. Wish you was mine." Tears filled his eyes. "Will'd be damn proud of you." He turned and walked out of the kitchen.

Mrs. Cluxton stood there smiling. I think she was as stunned as I was.

"Thanks for the pie and these cookies." I pushed the door open and stepped outside. The mutt was waiting for me. He jumped at my leg and tried to bite me but got my boot in his gut. When he landed, the alpha and two others jumped him, snarling and biting. The mutt raced away towards the corn crib.

CHAPTER 21

Voices drifted in through the boxcar door. I shrunk into my corner hoping the dimness would conceal me. I couldn't make out what the two men were saying, but one grabbed the door and rolled it shut. Pitch black bloomed.

Ten minutes passed before the train started moving. I ate a peanut butter sandwich and drank some water. After digesting for twenty minutes, I stripped off my shirt and pants. I did some exercises to keep strong. Push-ups, sit-ups, etc. Three sets each. Using my shirt, I wiped my sweat away. It was getting warm in the closed-up boxcar.

I put my clothes back on and felt my way to the front corner ladder. As I climbed up, a niggling voice in my head told me it was going to be locked. But that wasn't normal. The hatches latched from inside. Rarely were they locked from the outside. The odds of getting snake-bit were low, too, but here I was.

Relief and cool air washed over me as I threw the hatch open. I stuck out my head cautiously, only high enough to see over the hatch lip. We were skirting south of St. Louis in a westerly direction. That was good enough for me. If we went to Kansas City, then I'd have to find some way to start heading north. I didn't want to get too far south because there were few north/south trains once you hit the Rockies. I needed to get north of Denver before heading farther west. But if we were headed to Oklahoma City, I'd need to get off. That was too far south for the path I had in mind. With livestock onboard, it was unlikely the train would go that far though. Oklahoma City was at least 500 miles, a good twelve-hour run.

It turned out to be a high-speed run, maybe because of the livestock. The train never stopped and kept up its sixty-plus speed until we got to the Okie stockyard a little after midnight. The smell permeated everything. Between my exercises and the livestock odor, I was a walking stench bomb. But there was nothing I could do. With no reason to get off the train at the stockyard, I settled down in my corner until the train got to a railyard and I could find another one headed in my direction. I guessed it wouldn't be more than an hour and thought the noise of the yard switches would wake me. I was wondering what I would dream about this time, whether it would be a re-run or something altogether different my brain concocted. It was something different. But it was real this time.

#####

I awoke with a start. No recollection of dreams. I had slept hard. Soundly. And the train was crossing some big switches. There was weak daylight streaming through the open hatch.

I darted up the ladder to look around, see if I could tell where I was. A huge sign on the yard control building was a dead giveaway: Amarillo.

I was in God-damned Texas. I'd slept at least six hours, probably on another non-stop run. Why were they balling the jack on this train? Maybe it was a livestock express.

Texas. I was too far west. There were no trains north now, except the little pissant ones that had a dozen cars and trundled through the foothills of the Rockies. They rolled sometimes for days with no place to get supplies. Even if I could stock up, it could take me a month to reach Montana that way. And then I'd have to roll west all the way across the state. I'd never make it by May 31st.

I had to go back, at least to Oklahoma City, then north through Wichita.

I packed up in the dim boxcar and remembered to use my precious flashlight battery life to make sure I hadn't missed anything. My Beagle hat, as I now thought of it, lay on the floor. I grabbed it, pulled it down to my ears, and scooted up the ladder. By the time I rolled off the train, we were well within the yard. This was Texas. There were no weeds or shrubs to hide me. It was dirt, dirt, and more dirt. Low buildings and grain silos abutted the yard. The fence, such that it was, lay mostly on the ground with an occasional rusty post poking stubbornly from the near-desert soil. It was 7:30 am and already the temperature was pushing eighty. I smiled. Hobos said there was no such thing as dry heat. Heat was heat. It's what fried you in a boxcar when you weren't paying attention.

I moved off the tracks into the shadow of a grain elevator. I needed to get my bearings, resupply for several days in case I got stuck on another long run where I couldn't get off.

Judging from the shadows, the main tracks ran east/west. I had to go east but had to make sure I didn't pick a train that turned south—I sure didn't want to end up in San Antonio or Houston. I didn't want one that went north, either—there was just too much open country that way to test my stamina and hobo ability. East. I needed to go east. Due east.

There was an outside ladder on each grain elevator. If I climbed up one of the ladders on the yard side, I could get a view of where the tracks went. But there were switches. Trains that looked like they were going east could pass through multiple switches and change their direction entirely.

I might get spotted on the ladder, too. I hadn't seen anyone around except a couple of train brakemen busting up the train I'd just been on.

The only sure answer was to move east out of the yard beyond the switches where I could be sure the train was truly headed east. I decided walking through the yard wasn't a good idea. Remain invisible.

I slid by the grain silos and looked eastward. It was near the edge of town. No business signs dotted the buildings I could see along the tracks. All industrial stuff.

Sighing, I dropped my pack and grabbed the bottom rung of the grain elevator ladder. Eight rungs up and I was above the one-story buildings that dominated this city. Eastward was a desert. Nothing. Westward was almost as bad. More railyard. Three more trains. And one sign. Some kind of bar. I could get food and water there.

I started to climb down and glanced south. I stopped, staring. This wasn't Amarillo's railyard. It was just a baby feeder yard. The real yard was a north/south one about a mile away. It was at least twenty tracks wide.

I climbed down and shouldered my pack. The bar was nearly a mile in the wrong direction, but I couldn't chance running low. I treaded westward in the dirt alongside the tracks.

The Red Rock Bar was a tiny place. I was surprised to find it open. To be fair, I wasn't sure it was open, but the door wasn't locked. Inside was deep darkness. I stood there for several minutes adjusting to the gloom.

Kitchen noise came from a door next to the bar that spanned the room. Four small tables with four chairs each filled the rest of the place. I ambled up to the bar, but it was clear they weren't open. From the noise and voices, workers were in the kitchen cleaning, stocking, or getting ready for when they did open.

A loud crash caused me to jump. A short burst of angry male voices was replaced with continued crashing and grunts. It sounded like a fight. I wanted no part of this. But my curiosity overrode sensibility.

I snuck up to the kitchen door, one of those two-way swinging doors you often saw in restaurant kitchens. It had a ten-inch circular window at eye height. When I looked through it, two men were wrestling on the floor. Next to them, a wall phone handset dangled from its base. The one face I could see was bleeding from the nose. Four hands were grappling with each other, clawing, and pushing. A gun. They were struggling over a gun.

I ran. Nothing to be gained here. As I hit the front door, a shot rang out from the kitchen. Then two more quick shots. Outside, I heard a siren in the distance. It was coming from the north.

I turned left, past the corner of the building and raced across the vacant lot next door. Angling back towards the trainyard, I reached the first track and rolled under a tanker car to the other side. At least I was shielded from view now. The siren was much louder. I glanced back between two cars. A man was running towards me. He had a gun in his left hand. The shooter was coming my way.

He couldn't have seen me. It was just the logical place to run, given the surroundings. The siren stopped. It would be the logical place for the cops to look, too. I needed a better plan. Fast.

A voice rang out. "Stop! Police."

I needed to disappear. Fast. Two tracks over an open boxcar beckoned me. I ran to it and rolled inside as a series of shots rang out. Peeking around the door, I saw the man with the gun from the bar limping towards me. He still had a gun in his left hand.

Movement on the first track. A cop jumped up from a roll under a train car. "Stop," he yelled.

The man from the bar reached my boxcar, but before he could pull himself inside, two more shots rang out. The man twitched with the second shot, and then slid to the ground.

I was trapped. There was nowhere to go that I wouldn't be seen. If they found me, I'd be associated with the man from the bar just because we were in the same place. They'd never believe my story. I'd end up in jail. Never make it to Missoula. Never make it to the stars.

I gritted my teeth and tried to calm down. Deep slow breaths. Relax my shoulders. Ouch. Pain jolted my left shoulder. I tried to rotate my shoulder again and the pain shot up my neck. Poking around with my right hand, I found a hole in my jacket. Under the jacket my hand found the source of the pain and a lot of slickness. I smelled rusty fence posts again. When I looked, my hand was covered in blood.

At first, I thought I'd been shot. But there was a sliver of wood sticking out of the backside of my jacket. It had gone between my arm and my ribcage, grazing the inside of my upper arm. As the cowboys said in the old movies, it was just a flesh wound.

I shrank into the corner, making myself as small and invisible as possible, tucking my right hand against the wound for pressure.

Outside, there were a dozen voices yammering about the guy on the ground. Apparently, he wasn't dead because I heard one man say something about "hospital." One head poked into the boxcar for a quick look, but he passed right over me. I thanked the sun for blinding the human eye in this dimness.

When they left fifteen minutes later, I dug out a T-shirt and tied it around my arm. I washed down a couple of aspirin and my antibiotic pill. At least the snake bite antibiotics would help prevent infection in my arm, too. I needed a day or two for it to heal up and I'd be fine.

The boxcar jolted. We were moving. I sighed. I really couldn't choose my train right now. Unlike the cowboys who ignored flesh wounds, this hurt a lot. I knew it would be okay, but I had to get it to stop bleeding. Moving around wasn't an option right now.

I smiled to myself. I was a farmer at the mercy of mother nature. Or fate, if you preferred. I'd walked in on a robbery or disagreement of some nature. Violent nature. All by chance. I could have been shot by the man with the gun or by the cops. I felt lucky to have just this flesh wound. Next time I'd make sure to assess my surroundings and make sure I wasn't stepping into someone else's shit.

Regardless of my timeline or destination, right now mother nature was taking me wherever this train went.

CHAPTER 22

Christmas 1967 was a somber affair, but it was a financial repeat of the previous year. We sat around the dining room table where I shared the financial success. We'd maintained the financial arrangement Daddy and Momma had used during their married life. Daddy gave Momma a monthly check which she used to manage the house. Food, family clothing, maintenance, etc. It was her house to manage. The other buildings, equipment, fences—the farm operation—was Daddy's. I wasn't yet old enough to sign checks, but I managed the finances and brought Momma the checks to sign as needed.

Net of all of this, we had $1823 left over. Momma suggested we do another trip to Cincinnati like we did the previous year. I couldn't stomach the thought of retracing our steps without Daddy. In the end, Bobby and Momma drove to Cincinnati for a shopping trip. Momma divided the money 50:25:25. She got fifty percent. I didn't care.

On Christmas morning, we exchanged gifts. I gave Momma an apron. It was the best I could do to acknowledge her as my mother. But since Daddy died, we hardly ever spoke. I knew she blamed me, and I did my best to stay out of her way. She did her best to apologize for blaming me. It was an awful way to live, but I wasn't ready for the alternative yet.

I gave Bobby an 8-track player for his car, a sky-blue 1959 Chevy Impala he cherished only slightly less than he did his girlfriend, Janet.

He seemed happy with it when he opened it. "Thanks, Tink. I really appreciate." He stared at the box.

"Don't worry, Bobby. I'll install it for you."

He nodded. "Thanks. Um, I'm gonna wait 'til Janet gets here 'fore I give you your gift. That okay?"

"Sure."

Momma handed me a box. It had a red bow on top, but wasn't gift wrapped. "Didn't figure you cared much about wrapping."

"Thank you, Momma."

She looked away. The box was plain but had an 'Edmund Scientific' label on the side. When I saw what was inside, I looked at Momma. "How'd you come to pick this for me?"

"Figured it was somethin' you'd like." She waved her hand in the air. "You always looking at the stars. Figured you'd like to see 'em better."

I stared into the box. It was a kit for grinding your own glass blank into a 4.25-inch mirror for a reflector telescope. I was baffled at how Momma even knew this existed let alone how she figured out where to get it. "It's a really nice gift, Momma. Thank you."

"Rest of it's in the trunk of the car. You get it when you want."

"What do you mean, rest of it?"

"The tube and tripod thing. Eye thing you look through."

It was a whole telescope kit. I wanted to hug Momma but still hated her, too. I grabbed the box and ran upstairs to my room. I flopped on my bed and cried for a while. There was a tornado of emotions in my head. Missing Daddy. Hating Momma because she blamed me and missing her at the same time. Hating my solitude, my loneliness. Doing my duty. By myself. What friends I'd had, even Susie, gave me a wide berth anymore. I fell asleep.

A tapping on my door woke me. I sat up and looked at the clock. I'd been rolling in my nightmares for nearly two hours.

"Come in."

Janet pushed through the door and shut it behind her. "Merry Christmas, Tink." She came and sat on the bed next to me.

"Merry Christmas, Janet. But it's not very merry in this house."

She stroked my short hair. "I know, sweetie. Everyone is sad because they miss your dad."

I pursed my lips, trying to hold it together.

Janet laid a magazine on the bed next to me. She flipped through some pages to a fashion ad. She pointed to a woman in the pictures. "You know who this is?"

"No. Pixie comes to mind."

"She goes by the name 'Twiggy.' She's a model in Europe."

"She's cute."

"Reminds me of you."

"Me? Why?"

"You've got the build and the haircut."

"Maybe the haircut. Sort of. But not the build. I'm probably a foot taller than her. Like I said, pixie comes to mind. Maybe Peter Pan."

Janet laughed and stood up. "How are our bodies different, Tink?"

I rolled over and sat up. "You're bigger than me."

"How? What are the differences?"

"You have broad shoulders, bigger hips."

"What else?"

"Bigger breasts."

"But we're the same height."

I stood and nodded. "I guess so."

She pointed at the magazine. "I'd look ridiculous in that outfit, right? You, on the other hand, are perfect for it. You'd be stunning." She walked over to my closet and started rummaging through the clothes. "Work pants, work pants, work pants. Don't you have any dresses or skirts?"

"No. I burned them all."

"Why?"

"I have to be taken seriously if I'm going to run the farm, deal with men. Farm men. If they see me as a boy, they'll work with me. If they see me as a girl, they'll just laugh."

"You know I couldn't do that—pretend to be a boy."

"You have…curves."

"I have big boobs. They're impossible to hide. And they attract men's attention. When I talk to men, or even boys, their eyes drift to my boobs. It's annoying, but it's not my problem and I refuse to take the blame for it." She sighed and walked to the door. She retrieved a box wrapped in white with a huge Christmas bow. "Merry Christmas."

I set the box on the bed. Inside I found a Twiggy-type mini-dress. It was clingy jersey fabric in a paisley design of primarily green, red, and yellow. Just like the one in the magazine.

"It's beautiful. Where did you get it?"

"I made it."

I stared at her as I held it up to me and looked at myself in the mirror. The hemline wasn't more than a few inches below my butt. "It's beautiful, Janet. But I could never wear this. It's too short."

She reached into the box and handed me a small plastic bag. "You wear this underneath. It's called a body stocking. Go on, try it on. I'll wait downstairs." She closed the door behind her.

I changed into the bright yellow body stocking and the paisley dress, and then stood before the dresser mirror. I did look like Twiggy. Like a girl. Funny how clothes can change you so much.

A knock on my door. "You coming down?"

I opened the door and stood there in front of Janet. She grinned from ear to ear. "Holy shit. I had no idea it would be this dramatic." She led me to the bed. "Sit." She pulled open her purse and spent the next ten minutes doing my makeup, something I never wore even before I cut off my hair. When she was done, she got some water from the bathroom and wet my hair. She parted it on the side and combed it straight across. She pulled me up in front of the mirror and held up the Twiggy picture next to me.

"See. You could be walking right into those exclusive dance clubs in New York. They'd think you were a famous model."

I saw someone else in the mirror. It wasn't me. The eyes were the same dead blue, but the makeup, hair, and clothes made me someone else. I did look like the Twiggy pictures. Serious, no smile, all business. But I was bigger. Less pixie. Formidable came to mind. I felt powerful, in a weird kind of way.

Janet called down the stairway, "Bobby, come up here, please.".

I turned toward the door just as Bobby came lumbering in. His mouth dropped open.

Janet began to giggle. "See, Tink. I told you what you'd do to boys." She reached over and closed Bobby's mouth.

"I would swear it wud'n you, Tink, if I didn't know better."

I looked in the mirror again. It really was someone else looking back. Someone scary. Even more scary than the regular me.

I hugged Janet. "Thank you so much. I really do appreciate you going to this trouble. But it's not me. Not today. I have enough trouble just being the regular me and keeping things together.

"I get it, Tink. Just trying to show you there are options." She shooed Bobby out the door and closed it behind her.

I took off the dress and hung it on a hanger in my closet. I folded up the body stocking and tucked it into my underwear drawer. As I re-dressed in my farmer outfit, I decided there were innumerable me's I *could* become. But how did one choose and decide who you *would* become?

CHAPTER 23

Apparently, my boxcar was being shuffled onto a sidetrack. After three starts and stops with several switches in between, it was left on an isolated sidetrack about halfway between the switches and the much larger trainyard.

I stayed in the boxcar all day, nursing my arm, sipping water, and eating a few small meals. After dark, I climbed out and explored the area, walking north along the sidetrack. There was a liquor warehouse right next to me. Adjacent to that was a restaurant equipment supply store. Warehouses of various kinds lined the track. Some had signs but none seemed to contain anything I could use, even if I could figure out how to break in. I stopped walking and crouched down next to a track switch box. I checked my forehead to see if I had a fever. I wasn't delirious, but I had just nonchalantly considered breaking into a warehouse if the contents suited me. Where and how had I evolved from a high school student to a female hobo, known as a *boyette* on the rails? I'd dodged a gunfight, been wounded, and had now become a thief. Even if I hadn't yet stolen anything, it was clear to me that I would do so if presented with the opportunity. Maybe it was the grit I'd grown in the last few years on the farm. Maybe it was that I kept proving I could do whatever I set out to do. But breaking the law? That wasn't who I wanted to be. It wasn't who I needed to be, either. At least not yet.

I thought of Hoss and his brothers. The laws they followed, and the ones they didn't—were they the same as mine? This was America. They should be the same. But there were thousands and thousands of people in the streets demonstrating because they felt discrimination and racism were predominant. The rules and laws applied differently, depending on your skin color or your hair length. Or if you fought in Vietnam. I shivered. Laws weren't absolute. Enforcement wasn't consistent. Fairness, honesty, and respect were relevant.

My brain felt flooded, like someone had pulled back the curtain in that Dorothy movie. The real world was out here on these tracks. The world wasn't like a Sardinia farm. The laws were still the same, but the way they worked varied a lot. It wasn't just the laws of physics that were affected by the environment. It was the man-made laws, too.

Herb, my chief hobo teacher, tried to tell me about this, but at the time I didn't know enough to understand. Now it made sense. "Jumpin' off a train ain't like jumpin' off your hay wagon. Never know where you landin' with a train. Who's waitin' for you. What trouble is brewin.' Bein' invisible is your only chance to dodge what you don't know is comin'."

Wise man. Invisible. I looked around. Across the tracks was a train station. Something Herb avoided. Probably good advice. But it looked closed, and I needed a bathroom, water, and maybe some supplies.

I remained hunkered behind the switch box while a train went by. As soon as it was clear, I scampered across seven tracks. The station was surrounded by a ten-foot fence with razor wire on top. Each of two gates were padlocked. I followed the fence a hundred yards south to where it stopped, then turned right with the fence. It continued for a half-block to Grant Street where I turned right again and continued until I was opposite the station. Here, the fence was only three feet tall, and I easily hopped over it. The station was permanently closed and at least semi-abandoned.

I stood in the parking lot looking around and listening. To the southwest, the loom of bright lights above the buildings caught my attention. I hopped back over the fence and zigzagged through a few blocks to find the lights were from a local park and baseball diamond. There was no game going on, but a few kids ran about while some adults sat on old wooden bleachers. In a few minutes I'd found a one-person restroom with sink and toilet and I locked myself inside.

Twenty minutes later, I felt like a new person. I'd had a stand-up bath, filled my canteens, and brushed my teeth. With salve on my arm wound, I headed out northward on Buchanan Street. A block later I spotted a pizza store across the street. Just as I got there, an acne-faced boy pulled the blind on a window next to the door. When I opened the door, he said, "We're closed. Sorry."

I nodded. "Got anything left? I'll take what you have."

He called over the counter towards the back. "Jose, any no shows?"

"Si. Dos queso, grande."

"How much?"

The boy looked at me. "We just throw 'em out. You can have them." He walked around the counter and disappeared. When he came back a moment later, he set two large pizzas and a liter of Pepsi on the counter.

"Are you sure I can't pay?"

"Nope. Me and Jose are fat from eating these leftovers anyhow. Take 'em off our hands."

"Thanks. I appreciate it." I grabbed the boxes and Pepsi and turned for the door.

"Be careful out there. Heard there was a gunfight this morning near the tracks."

I smiled and waved as I closed the door. Invisible. Stay invisible. Would the boy remember me if he was asked? I wished I could quiz Herb again on his invisible tricks.

By the time I got back to my boxcar, the pizza was cold. But I didn't care. They were both cheese, Bobby's favorite. I usually ate so little pizza that the toppings didn't matter to me. Tonight, I ate all the first one and downed it with warm Pepsi. I had two full canteens and a pizza for tomorrow. I hunkered down in the boxcar and was asleep in a few minutes. It was a relatively peaceful night without nightmares, but the Pepsi worked on my kidneys. I had to get up twice to pee.

#####

When I woke at sunrise, I was dreaming about the bar gunfight yesterday. Walking into it really wasn't my fault. It was just chance. The hobos had warned me about the fringes around the tracks. The folk who frequented them might be just as likely to shoot you as to give you water.

When I got off that train yesterday, I could have walked away from the tracks and found a diner that might have been a lot safer. Lesson learned. Don't stop at the first place you see. Assess the situation and potential for risk.

After I ate half my leftover pizza, I walked north to where the tracks turned east/west and then eastward between the outer track and the occasional building. I soon left the switches behind and passed the Grand Street overpass. A little further on the two eastward tracks passed over another track headed north in one direction, and southeast in the other. Towards Dallas maybe. Another place I didn't want to go.

I stopped and looked at the northward track. There were other tracks around me so that the one I was on and the one to the north all connected in both directions. It was like one of those Interstate highway cloverleaf things, but I'd never heard of or seen one with train tracks. It was a big, and likely busy, intersection for some reason. It had been quiet for the last couple of hours, though. Not even any gunshots.

I turned north and walked across dirt and sand for a few hundred yards until the north track came back up to ground level. It was wide open space, a small field adjacent to the track. Up ahead, there were more buildings on both sides.

Looking back at the overpass, I wondered if I could use that to my advantage to hop a boxcar. Strength-wise, my arm was fine, but I didn't want it to start bleeding again. Maybe I could somehow jump from the downslope into the boxcar instead of pulling myself in with my arms. It wasn't much farther to jump than my boarding ramp back in Ohio. And I'd have a downhill running start. The train would be going slow because the track curved under the overpass, too. I couldn't sit around here to wait, though. I was completely exposed and would attract attention.

I made my way onto the lower track and walked back under the overpass. I was out of sight here, in the shade, and I'd feel the vibration of any train headed my way. As if on cue, two trains rumbled across the overpass above me.

The breeze was coming from the north and smelled foul. I guess I had tuned it out, but when I stopped to listen, I could hear cows bawling not far away. Probably a slaughterhouse since it was so close to the tracks.

The ground under me began to vibrate, but I couldn't tell if it was an overhead train or one on the track I was sitting next to. I got up and moved through the underpass to the south so I could see trains coming my way. The curve made the line of sight fairly short, but it was enough to give some warning. A lone pine grew halfway up the embankment and I moved into its shadow.

It was a busy intersection. I counted eleven trains going in one direction or another in the half-hour I sat there. There were three on my track going south, all with empty hoppers. Two northbound trains were coal-filled hoppers. A coal-fired power plant must be to the north not too far away.

Just after another train passed on my track going south, I saw the headlight of a locomotive headed north. I stayed behind the pine until the locomotive passed by, then moved down the slope hoping for an open boxcar. Most of the cars were empty hopper cars again, but if they were hauling coal to a power plant to the north, I didn't understand why these were empty. An occasional tanker was interspersed. No boxcars. None. I watched the last car as it went around the curve and under the overpass.

A train whistle sounded right behind me. I turned to see another locomotive nearly in my face on the same track. The noise of the first train had masked this one sneaking up on me. As the locomotive passed me, the engineer leaned out a window eyeing me. I waved. He waved back. I hoped that would be the end of his curiosity. Just a kid watching the trains. Nothing to report.

This train was loaded. It had several center beams of lumber and some covered hoppers and flatcars. I could see some boxcars coming, but everything seemed to be loaded. No empties.

After seventy cars or so, three empty flatcars came by. They were followed by five empty center beams. Some boxcars followed. Three of them. The first and third were closed, but the second had an open door.

I hitched my pack on my shoulder and clamped my wounded arm to my side. I'd already calculated my estimates of when to start running, where I'd jump, and how I planned to land. When the door of the first boxcar got to me, I took off. When I jumped, I knew I was late. The train was going faster than I had estimated. Sailing through the air toward the blackness of the open door, I turned my head away as I realized I was going to clip the edge of the door in my flight. I was also higher than I anticipated and would fall a couple of feet onto the boxcar floor once inside. Newton was going to make a mess of this boarding attempt. Folding myself into a ball, I didn't have time to analyze how I had got this so wrong. My right side clipped the door, spinning me clockwise like a top. I crashed onto the floor. But Newton had other laws to deal with now. I pulled my hands and legs tighter, trying not to have an appendage ripped or broken by the combination of centripetal force and the train's momentum. When I hit the far wall of the boxcar, it knocked the wind out of me. I lay there gasping while I checked for anything broken. Eventually, I inhaled a sip of air and kickstarted my breathing again. When I sat up, my head was spinning, and my pants were wet. At first, I thought I'd peed myself, but a short investigation revealed my Pepsi bottle lashed to my pack had split open when I landed on it.

My scan around the inside of the boxcar revealed what I'd hoped—nothing. It was empty except for me and my gear. It was still early morning, maybe eight o'clock, so there was plenty of daylight left for a long ride today. Although we were headed north, I had little idea what the next town might be. The map I had memorized didn't start until Colorado. We had a long way to go before I could get my bearings.

#####

I spent the time fueling up, drinking most of one canteen and eating a decent meal of Pop-Tarts, dried beef, and a bruised apple. Around noon we pulled into another, smaller trainyard. We'd been moving painfully slow, and we weren't even in the Rockies or going up hills. Maybe there was a schedule to keep with all the trains in the area and they had to run at a particular speed.

In any case, I could see the signs in the adjacent city. We were in Dumas, Texas. The train stopped and I could feel cars being cut loose and rearranged. My boxcar was cut out and shuffled off to a sidetrack by itself. Out the door, the other two boxcars were joined to the train behind the last of the loaded flatcars. It began to rain, lightly at first, and then it became a downpour. Shortly thereafter, the train disappeared as it moved out of sight northward.

I sat there trying to decide what to do. We weren't that far from Amarillo. I guessed about fifty miles. Somewhere to the north was the Kansas/Colorado border. Between me and that border was more of the Texas panhandle and a sliver of Oklahoma panhandle. Not more than a hundred miles total.

My boxcar jolted and I could feel it moving forward. We crossed several switches, moving to the right side of the yard. It felt like they were maneuvering the car into position for loading. I could hear voices shouting outside over the din of the rain on the roof.

I packed up everything and moved over to the opposite hatch ladder. If they were going to load, it would be from the closed-door side. With people right outside, I couldn't afford to jump out the door. I'd be fully exposed and subject to a chase from multiple rail employees. The hatch on the side away from the load was my only option.

I raced up the ladder and jammed the collapsed Pepsi bottle under the latch. I couldn't afford the hatch to lock and not be able to get back inside.

The closed door banged and began to open. I scampered through the hatch and onto the roof, staying away from the loading side. Swirling rain blasted me in the face. I set the hatch back down gently, hoping the Pepsi bottle wouldn't be noticed. I flattened myself on the roof, trying not to be seen and not to slide off the slippery wet roof.

The boxcar shifted and its springs squeaked as they loaded something heavy inside with a forklift. After five trips, I heard both doors slam shut, one after another. The boxcar jolted as the tractor pushed it up the track. There was nowhere to hold on except the roof seams and they were only an inch or so high. Fortunately, it was a flat yard and only a short push through a couple of switches until I felt us latch onto a train.

The rain slowed to a drizzle. I raised my head and looked around, trying to figure out if anyone could see me. There were cars in front and at least two cars behind. To the left one train moved slowly past us. Beyond that was mostly open country. To the right was the city and the yard operations center. I certainly didn't want to be up here when the train started moving out.

I crawled back to the hatch, seam-by-seam, so I didn't slide off. At first, the hatch seemed to be locked, but a panicked heave got it loose. I stepped down the ladder, pulling the hatch closed, but leaving the Pepsi bottle in place.

Five crates filled the bulk of the boxcar space. As the train began to move, I trained my flashlight on a crate label. *Milling machine parts.* Big chunks of metal. The crates weren't strapped down. They didn't think they were going anywhere, but I didn't want to get crushed from someone's bad assumption. Besides, it had been raining and that was a good reason for them to skip safety concerns. I'd have to ride this segment on top of a crate.

I stripped and laid my clothes out to dry. Cracking open the boxcar front hatch allowed some airflow and kept the temperature inside reasonable. I didn't like being shut inside, but at least I was on the move and in no imminent danger.

Around midnight, I popped my head out the hatch. The rain had stopped. We were cruising through open, arid fields of what I thought was southwest Kansas. Dark clouds swathed the eastern sky in blackness, but the nearly full moon overhead gave the flat nothingness land around us an eerie mystic feel like wolves were going to give chase at any moment. I shivered and decided to get dressed even if the clothes weren't dry.

A few hours later, I woke because the train had stopped. I poked my head out the hatch. Several clusters of grain silos flanked the triple tracks on the left. The lights of a small town twinkled on the right. Small was good. People were usually more friendly. Police were scarce. Bigger city conflicts like bar gunfights were a lot less frequent.

I packed, checked all around with my flashlight, and climbed out the hatch. I felt it latch shut behind me. The train began to move, picking up speed quickly. I wasn't sure how long we had been stopped, but surely not long. Maybe they had dropped or added a few cars and the jostling woke me. Hobos are supposed to be light sleepers. It's a lot safer that way, but apparently I hadn't yet learned to sleep that way when I wasn't having nightmares. Since I'd had the one about Sam, my nightmares had stopped. Or at least I didn't remember them when I woke. And I was getting real sleep for the first time in years. The rocking train motion probably helped, too.

I had no way to know how long the train had been stopped, but as I hurried down the outside ladder, the train was really starting to move. There was no frame at the bottom of the ladder. I had to jump from the bottom rung, swinging out between the cars as the same time. Herb would say this was a foolish exit, but there wasn't time to waste.

I leaped off, landing in railbed gravel, and rolling as best I could with my pack strapped on. I stopped against the adjacent track, a dangerous place to be at any time, day or night. I scrambled a couple of feet away and lay there taking inventory.

The right knee in my jeans was ripped, but my kneecap didn't seem to be scraped much. I had a rock scrape on my hand near where the snake had bit me. I was still taking antibiotics so I didn't think that would compound anything. All in all, I was in pretty good shape for leaping from a moving train in the middle of the night.

The red light on the last train car grew smaller in the distance. Quiet washed over me like heavy fog. You get used to the noise of the train, but when it's gone and every other noise seems to be asleep, it's eerie.

A dozen grain silos flanked the left side of the track just behind me. A few lights shone on them and illuminated the outline of four covered hopper cars. Grain transport.

In the dim light, two men walked out from behind the first car. The lead one shone a flashlight in my face. My instinct was to run, but the flashlight man spoke before I could decide. "You fall off that train, boy?"

I wondered which way this conversation would go. It could turn into a chase, or it could become a helping hand kind of thing. I crossed my fingers. A small town equals friendly.

"Jumped."

"Jumped? What the hell for? You lost?"

"No. Just passing through. Needed to refill my canteen."

"Passing through. You must be lost 'cause ain't nobody in their right mind passes through Sublette."

"Why?"

The two men laughed. The one without the flashlight said, "We ain't nowhere. And we ain't on the way to nowhere, neither."

Flashlight man said, "There's a hose over at the shed by the last silo. Help yourself." He pointed up the track. "Diner down that way probably give you a free breakfast."

The two walked on to a pickup truck, got in, and drove across the tracks into the town. Sublette. I looked up and down the tracks. The whole town wasn't a half-mile long and it was all on the right side of the tracks. Except for the grain silos on the left.

I found the hose and filled my canteen. The eastern sky was starting to hint at the coming sunrise. I walked along the track defining the town's border. There was a bar I skirted even though there were no lights showing through the windows. Even after I walked by, I kept checking the bar over my shoulder.

I passed Dennis Street. The town looked about two blocks wide from there, but there were no visible business signs along that street. I moved on. A small Mexican-looking hole-in-the wall restaurant peeked between two warehouse buildings. Too close to the tracks.

At Inman Street, there was a Sunoco gas station on the corner. As I looked down the street into the town, business signs dotted the buildings. I made a right turn, eyeing the not-yet-open gas station. Through the plate-glass window there wasn't much to see. No soda machines. No food.

I passed a supermarket on my right. The sign said it opened at 7:30. Further down the street I could see a flag where I'd probably find a post office. Another block down I passed a restaurant. It opened at 6:30. There were lights on in the back. I envisioned a cook breaking out the eggs and bacon and toasting a whole loaf of bread, getting ready for the morning rush. Could a town this size have a diner rush? Hard to tell.

Another block down was the post office. I sat on the step and pulled a pen and a pre-addressed/stamped postcard from my pack. Dear Momma, Just wanted you to know I'm safe and making my way to Missoula. Trains don't always go the direction I want, but I'm making a zigzag path westward. Love, Tink. I dropped it into the blue box.

Diagonally across the street was a building that looked like the heart of town. Maybe a courthouse and administration building combined. A school stood on the opposite side of the street. Given the town size, I guessed it was the only school for all grades. Like us, they probably weren't large enough to field a football team. Basketball was the likely leading sport here, too.

A ray of sunlight sparked over a tree. I stood in the middle of the street surveying this little town. Sublette. It was about the size of Sardinia. Had the same problems. Same attitudes. No hippies here. No demonstrations. Probably some Vietnam vets with stories they wanted to forget. A farm town and those who supported them.

A couple of trucks turned onto the street by the tracks three blocks away. I watched them pull up in front of the café. Two men got out of each truck and went inside. I waited. I wasn't wading into another conflict among the locals. My flesh wound was still tender. It had only been twenty-four hours.

A Corvair drove by me and pulled up at the cafe, too. A man and a woman got out and went inside. Six people. That should be enough to make sure no guns were drawn. As I strolled back toward the restaurant, another pickup pulled up and a single woman went inside.

By the time I pushed open the door, another car had arrived. Altogether, there were nine people there when I walked in. I took a seat in a back booth. A waitress came by shortly and dropped a plastic menu on the table in front of me.

"What can I get you, honey?"

"I'll have a Coke, please."

"You ain't old enough to drink coffee yet." She smiled and walked away. I didn't know if that was a statement or a question.

When she returned with the Coke, I ordered the morning special—bacon and eggs with toast. I laid a twenty-dollar traveler's check on the table. "Want to make sure you take these."

She picked it up and looked at it. Turned it over. "I don't know. Ain't never seen one. I'll ask Agnus." She walked off and I sipped my Coke. I looked around at the other customers. They were all speaking in quiet voices and sneaking glances my way. Except the single elderly woman with her hair in a gray bun. She was wearing a blueish uniform which I eventually recognized as a postal worker uniform. Given the town size, I thought she might be the only postal employee in this tiny town. She was reading a newspaper and seemed to be minding her own business.

The waitress brought my breakfast. "Agnus said this traveler's check is fine." She laid it on the table. "You that boy fell off the train this morning?"

News travels fast in small towns. That's why everyone was looking at me. "Jumped," I said. "I didn't fall off."

She pointed at my knee. "Either way, looks like you landed a bit rough."

I glanced at my knee. A two-inch flap of my pants was torn open and there was a baseball-sized red stain around it. I held up my skinned left wrist. "Perfect landings from a moving train are tricky, particularly in the dark."

She grunted and headed back towards the kitchen.

I ate in silence, trying not to make eye contact with the various stares. A few customers left and others drifted in. The waitress came by, refilled my Coke, and dropped the breakfast bill on my table. "Pay up front."

I had nearly finished my refill and was about to leave when a slim elderly woman marched in and headed my way. She had a John Deere cap tilted back on her head and wore a blue work shirt and denim work pants. All talking ceased as her boots echoed on the wooden floor. Everyone's eyes followed her as she marched up to my table and stopped. She pulled her sunglasses off and stared at me.

"Who are you?"

"I'm Tink."

"Well, Tink, why are you sitting at my table?"

"Your table? I didn't know this was your table." I grabbed the check and my pack and started to stand up.

"Sit down. You're here now and you'll have to explain yourself."

I sank back into my seat.

She thrust her hand at me. "I'm Fanny Chouteau."

I shook her hand. "Tink Truesdale."

Fanny sat down across from me. The waitress appeared. "Your usual Mrs. Chouteau?"

Fanny gave a faint head twitch and the waitress retreated.

"What is your business here, Mr. Truesdale?"

Under other conditions I might have given more consideration as to what to say or been reluctant to share my hobo line about passing through. But this woman seemed to be well known, and in charge. I didn't want to get on her wrong side. Sliding by her with as little notice as possible seemed to be the best strategy. "I'm just passing through."

She squinted at me. "If that was meant in jest, Mr. Truesdale, you failed to convey any accompanying facial cues or body language. Therefore, I must presume you are serious. And lost. No one chooses to 'pass through' Sublette."

I felt my face redden. I hadn't heard anyone speak this formally since my freshman Latin teacher, Mrs. Perilli. She had a way of making you feel stupid without coming close to making direct accusations. She was a master at innuendo and pomposity. This woman could have been her verbal twin. And, as I'd learned with Mrs. Perilli, the best approach was to match her formality and fortitude as best I could. Return in kind, so to speak.

"No. Not lost. I'm traveling and my transportation happened this way. I intend to resume that transport with the next train that stops in town."

Fanny let out a little bark. It was likely intended as a sharp laugh, but it sounded more like the yap of some tiny dog, like a chihuahua. She smiled at me. "What are your plans until then? Until next Monday when the same train stops again?" She bark-laughed twice more.

"I'll catch some other train, maybe this afternoon."

"Is English your first language, Mr. Truesdale? Perhaps not. I just told you that the next train to stop in this quaint little paradise will be early next Monday morning, shortly before sunrise."

I swallowed. Stuck here for a week? Surely there would be other trains. She must be joking, trying to upset me. Maybe I could hitchhike. Or get a bus. "Perhaps. Perhaps another will stop sooner than you expect."

She raised an eyebrow and looked at me for a while. "Why would the train schedule change when it's been working perfectly well for thirty-four years?" She pulled off her cap and set it on the seat next to her. "You seem to give meaning to the phrase 'falling off the turnip truck,' Mr. Truesdale."

The waitress brought her a steaming bowl of oatmeal, a small pitcher of cream, a cup of coffee, and a glass of orange juice. She placed a tray with three tiny bowls in front of the woman. The bowls contained walnuts, raisins, and brown sugar. The woman began to spoon them onto the oatmeal, and then stirred the mixture as she added cream from the pitcher.

"If that's the case, I suppose I'll catch a bus or hitchhike if needed."

"Young man, we're two hundred miles to anything that smells like a city. For some, that's uncomfortable, even frightening. For others, like those of us who choose to live in our little town away from the craziness of this world today, it is, indeed, paradise. You won't find demonstrations on our streets. No one burns flags here. Should your chosen hair style lean towards those filthy hippies, then you would soon find yourself availed of our town barber and subject to our hospitality as our guest for…a few cycles of your train, shall we say.

"You, though, Mr. Truesdale, appear to be of clean and proper character. A conservative haircut, not the flattop style of my late husband nor the crewcut style of the military. Yet a cut that reflects moderation and respect for societal norms."

I was wrong to compare this woman with Mrs. Perilli. Fanny, as I now thought of her, was intentionally offensive. Innuendo was not her intent. I'd never met anyone quite this pompous. She probably thought I was easily intimidated because I was young. Or maybe disdain was her normal demeanor with everyone. I looked around the restaurant. There seemed to be a sense of unease in the air. These people were afraid of her.

I smiled. "Thank you, Mrs. Chouteau. Did I pronounce that correctly? Those of us with an English native tongue often butcher words of other languages with which we are not familiar. *N'est-ce pas vrai?*"

She looked at me with a blank look, a spoonful of oatmeal paused midway to her mouth. I realized she didn't speak French. She was just aloof and full of herself, even though she had a French name. But she parried well.

"Not being from Kansas, you obviously don't recognize my family name. Francois Chouteau founded Kansas City. His great uncle, Auguste Chouteau, founded St. Louis. You see, I'm from a lineage of important people. Yes, French ancestry, but we chose to come here to America where the language is English. Proper English, I might add. And we chose not to teach our children French so that they would never be mistaken for half-American."

"I'm sure your family ancestry is fascinating and filled with incorrigible scoundrels," I said. "But I must confess that you misjudge me. Misjudge me so badly that it is incomprehensible how to explain your multitude of errors. It seems your assessment of hair style, and your implied character thereof is woefully misguided. Take, for example, Sir Isaac Newton, certainly someone you recognize and admire, as do I. His foundational works underpin the entire space program of this country. And yet his carefully quaffed hair extended to mid-shoulder.

"And surely someone as educated as you have seen pictures of Albert Einstein. I'm sure I don't need to remind you of his brilliance. Or his hair style."

Mrs. Chouteau stared at me, her mouth slightly agape. I don't know if others in the restaurant heard the conversation, but it was deathly quiet. I glanced around. No one was looking our way. It seemed everyone was holding their breath.

She set her spoon down beside the oatmeal. The wrinkles in her face shifted a few times like she was trying to stifle a smile. Or she was having a stroke. She finally pursed her lips and looked at me. "Mr. Truesdale, please allow me to finish my breakfast and then we will resume our conversation."

I sat there silently while Fanny spooned oatmeal into her mouth at a rapid clip. She chugged her coffee, wiped her mouth and stood up. With her back to the restaurant, she whispered to me, "Please accompany me to my office."

She turned and strode out of the restaurant. I grabbed my pack and followed. Fanny turned left and started walking down the sidewalk at a good pace.

I grabbed my bill and my traveler's check. "Wait. I forgot to pay my bill."

She never turned, just waved a hand, and shouted. "We're good for it. Come on."

She might be good for it, but I certainly wasn't. I glanced at the restaurant door. Inside, everyone seemed to be looking our way, but no one was running to the door to call me back. I tucked the bill and my travelers' check into my pocket, intending to come back shortly and settle up.

I jogged down the street after Fanny, wondering if I should be going the other way to escape this woman. But I'd never met anyone quite like her. I wanted to see what happened next, as long as it wasn't a jail cell.

Catching up just as she crossed the street, she headed towards the courthouse-like building I had seen before. She marched through the front door and turned left into an office suite. The sign on the office door said *Mayor*. That explained a lot. She might be chief of police, dog catcher, and postmaster rolled into one in a small town like this.

Fanny strode into an inner office and pointed to a chair in front of a giant oak desk. "Please have a seat, Mr. Truesdale."

She dumped her purse on the desk and sat down behind it. She watched as I put my pack on the floor next to the chair and sat.

She said, "Who are you?"

I'd already told her my name. Maybe she was also senile and had forgotten. "Like I said before, Tink Truesdale."

She waved her hand. "Not that. Who are you really? We have the occasional lost hobo or drifter wander into town. I usually scare them off quickly without a fuss. We have a reputation for not tolerating outsiders who try to prey on our good fortune.

"You seem so young, but you weren't intimidated and aren't going to run. In fact, you rose to my challenge and, I dare say, beat me at my own game. So, who are you?"

Her demeanor and tone were completely different. More normal. Not the pompous woman from the restaurant.

"That was all an act in the restaurant? Your attempt to urge a drifter out of your town?"

She nodded.

"But you dragged me to your office. Why?"

"To figure out who you are. Out of earshot of the town and the gossip mongers."

"Why do you care?"

"You're a unicorn. An enigma. I've never met someone like you, particularly so young. You're fascinating. Piqued my curiosity." She stood, staring at me, arms crossed over her chest.

I was always an enigma. Odd was the word most people used. Other than Chuck, the librarian, no one ever much cared to know my story. I wasn't sure I wanted to share it with this stranger, though. Her personality reversal felt contrived. Well, she'd already admitted it was.

"I'm a hobo riding trains to get to Montana. Ran into some trouble in Amarillo and hopped a train in the wrong direction, I guess."

"What kind of trouble?"

"I walked into a bar that, I think, was being robbed. Police showed up and there was a gunfight. I managed to dodge most of the bullets and get away before they lumped me in with the robbers."

"Most of the bullets—did you get hurt?"

I raised my left arm and pointed at the inner side of my upper arm. "I took a wood splinter through here from a bullet hitting next to me. Mostly just grazed and burned. I think they called it a "flesh wound" in the Westerns."

"There's a doctor in town. Do you want to see him? I can arrange it."

"No, I'll be fine. I'll heal up just like the cowboys did."

"If it's money, I'll be glad to pay for the doctor's services."

Her whiplash change was disturbing. Fanny was being nice and caring now. I was starting to worry about who she really was and why she was now treating me this way.

"No. It'll be fine" I stood. "I guess I'll be moving on now."

"Please. Sit down, Tink, or whatever your name really is. I wasn't kidding about weekly train service. And there's no bus. No locals are going to pick you up, either. It's a philosophy well entrenched in this area. Trying to preserve what we have and not let the outside world pollute us." She glanced out the window toward the school building.

"We can't stop it, but we can delay it. For as long as we live. We enjoy our lives here and just want to be left alone to raise our families and live our lives peacefully. Sublette is an out-of-the-way place that has attracted folks who like being out-of-the-way. Symbiosis, right?"

"I guess you can see it that way."

"How do you see it?"

I shrugged. "None of my business. I'm just passing through."

"Yes, but I asked for your opinion. I want to hear your thoughts."

"Why? You don't know me. My opinion doesn't matter to you or to this town. I'm just passing through. I might throw rocks at your glass house. Why go down that path?"

"Because you have perspective. You've seen a lot, been to many places. And maybe most importantly, you're highly intelligent and perceptive." She paused and looked out the window again. "It's selfish of me. My husband Johnson passed away four years ago. I've had no one to really talk with since then. The locals are wonderful people, but they offer little mental stimulation. No one in that restaurant has read Chaucer. But you have. And much more."

"I think you misjudge me. I'm an astrophysicist at heart, or at least want to be. I've read Newton, Einstein, and Planck. Studied their writings quite a lot. Learned German and French so I could read their original works. And others like Bohr, Heisenberg, and Schrodinger."

Fanny pursed her lips, stared at me for a while. "And Chaucer?"

I laughed. "Yes, Chaucer. *Canterbury Tales.* English class requirement."

"What tale did you like most?"

"I understand the significance of the work in literary history, but the oppression, religious rule, and class system were disgusting. Chaucer's depiction makes me glad we don't live in that era."

"You don't think we have all of that today?"

"Maybe some but not to the same extent."

"You might change your mind as you get older and experience those things for yourself."

I heard a door close in the outer office behind me. As I stood up, a woman dressed in a white silk blouse and a short tan skirt sauntered through the door.

Fanny introduced her. "Sharita, this is Mr. Truesdale. He'll be staying with us for a few days. Maybe a week. Sharita is my assistant."

"Nice to meet you, Mr. Truesdale," said Sharita. "Let me know if there's anything you need."

I'm sure my face was a bit red from my charade as Mister. But I'd been living it for several years now and it had become second nature. I shook Sharita's hand. To say her hand engulfed mine would be an understatement. She was a tall black woman in her mid-twenties, but she was at least six inches taller than me. When she moved, it was cat-like, almost bouncing on her toes.

"Sharita is our star basketball player," said Fanny. "She's been invited to the World Championship for Women in Sao Paulo, Brazil. She'll be leaving next week to make the trip."

Sharita blushed. "Thanks to Fanny. She pulled some strings and got me on the team."

Many questions came to mind as I recalled my conversations with Hoss. I wanted to ask Sharita about her relationship with the other players and whether they were white or black. In this small burg in the middle of nowhere, I expected racism to be alive and well, if it was anywhere.

As if reading my mind, Fanny said, "Sublette, and the people who live in this area, are progressive in most ways, Mr. Truesdale. For example, we don't let skin color factor into our relationships, be they personal or otherwise."

Thinking back to the diner this morning, I realized there were a few black customers and at least one Asian woman sitting at the breakfast counter.

A man in a police uniform knocked on the doorframe. "Excuse me."

"Oh," said Fanny. "Come on in, Jeb. Sharita, see if you can find something to entertain Mr. Truesdale until dinner time."

Sharita grabbed my hand and pulled me along with her out of the office, shutting the door behind us. She walked over and shut the outer office door, leaving the two of us in the room with her desk and four guest chairs.

She put both hands on her hips. "You fall off the train this morning?"

"Jumped."

"You sure plopped down in a funny kinda place. You know why Fanny didn't run you out of town?"

"I guess she liked our breakfast banter."

"She figure out you're a woman yet?"

My heart wanted to stop. I thought about running and glanced at the outer door.

Sharita waved her hand in the air. "It don't make no never-mind to me. You want people to think you're a man, that's your business. But don't let 'em get up close. Else you need to grow some beard and an Adam's apple."

She was probably right. My disguise was only good from a distance. That's why I mostly tried to skirt people and not get too close. A girl traveling alone would get attention. Unwanted attention.

"Maybe I'm younger than you think."

"That don't 'splain nothing. You still a woman."

I shrugged. "Like you said, it doesn't matter."

"It will to Fanny. I 'spect she already figured it out. That's why she didn't run you off. Only reason I can think of."

"Why does that make a difference?"

"'Cause her daughter run away. And got herself killed."

CHAPTER 24

An hour later, Sharita walked me to Fanny's house. We went through the white picket fence gate and around to the back. Sharita fished a key out of her purse and unlocked the back door. Even so, I felt like we were breaking into Fanny's house.

As we walked into the kitchen, I asked, "How did you get a key?"

"I'm secretary, housecleaner, cook, and all-around Fanny helper."

The kitchen was large, nearly as big as our house near Sardinia. It had a big center island with a sink. Eight stools flanked the island. Sharita motioned to one.

"Have a seat. I'll fix us some lunch."

"What are we having?"

Sharita stood at the open refrigerator door. "How about ham and cheese sandwiches?"

The refrigerator was huge. It had double doors as tall as Sharita. I could see inside. The shelves were stuffed.

"What do you want on it? Ketchup, mustard, mayonnaise…"

"Mustard is fine, thanks."

Sharita busied herself slicing the ham and cheese. In a few moments, she set a plate in front of me with a perfect pair of white bread slices cut diagonally into four triangular sections. She set a plate for herself on the island, retrieved two Cokes from a smaller refrigerator and popped the caps. She sat down next to me and began eating.

"Sharita, do you live here?"

She smiled. "Nah. My momma lives on the edge of town. 'Bout four blocks. I live with her mostly."

"Mostly?"

"Sometimes it gets late and I don't wanna walk home. Fanny fixed up the garage so I can stay there instead. It's a little loft with a bed above the cars."

"This place is huge. Why don't you stay in one of the bedrooms in the house? There must be half-a-dozen empty ones."

Sharita stared at me for a moment, sandwich poised in mid-bite. She waved the sandwich towards me. "You that dumb?"

My face flushed. "What do you mean?"

"What color my skin, Tink?"

My mouth fell open and I shifted my eyes to my sandwich. My face raged red. "I'm sorry. It never occurred to me."

"Why not? You never seen a black person before?"

"Yes. Of course. Several in my class."

"Lemme guess. The boys played basketball. And nobody wanted them in the white boy locker room."

I nodded. "There were often fights and they were blamed."

"'Course."

"Sharita, I met a black man and his brothers during my trip. He pointed out some things about racism I never recognized."

"Such as?"

"He said the civil war might have ended slavery, but racism is still alive and well. And he didn't think you can change people's ideas. He thinks it will take generations of raising more and more kids to not be racist before it really starts to fade out."

"And you? What do you think?"

"The hippie movement preached equality. I think some of that rubbed off on young people today. We're making progress but there's a lot to be done yet. And the older folks haven't changed the way they feel. They just tolerate it better and don't comment as much as they used to."

"I asked about you."

I fiddled with my sandwich. "I don't think I'm racist, but I keep finding new symptoms I didn't know were there. It never occurred to me that you couldn't sleep in the house because you're black."

"What about at your house? Your momma?"

I thought about that for a moment. Momma never showed any prejudice for the neighborhood blacks. Two black girls came to my seventh birthday party. They used our bathroom. They played in our house. But that didn't say much. I didn't know how Momma felt.

"It's frustrating and embarrassing because I don't know. Maybe I didn't pay attention."

"Ain't nothin' you can do about it. You can only do you." She took another bite of sandwich and washed it down with her Coke.

She was right. But if I didn't even notice the symptoms, I wouldn't know how to do better. It was like the way the farming community wouldn't really do business with a woman. I saw that growing up. It didn't have to be that way, but that's how it was. I became enough of a boy to dodge most of that bias. Their eyes slid right over me and we did farm business. My approach didn't do anything to change the way they thought. But I only had a few years to make the farm profitable and no time to try to change them. Still, some of them knew who I was—Will Truesdale's daughter—and they went along with my charade. I wondered why.

As we were cleaning up the lunch dishes, the phone rang. Surprisingly, Sharita answered it. "Chouteau residence. How may I help you?"

Sharita listened, her eyes glancing my way.

"Yes, ma'am. I'll see to it." She hung up. "Fanny said to park you in a bedroom and to tell you to take a bath and wash your clothes. I'll show you where, but I have to get back to the office."

CHAPTER 25

Mrs. Martin called a couple of weeks after we bought the Gleaner. It was just at the end of supper, and she talked with Momma a few minutes before Momma handed the phone to me.

"Tink, this is Emma Martin. I was just talking with your mother about a good time to come over and teach you a few of my baking tricks. I thought we could start with my Chinese Chews."

"Sounds great to me."

"Alright. I guess I'll see you the day after tomorrow. Around four o'clock."

"Mrs. Martin, how are you doing?"

"Well, I'm getting along. Thank you for asking." She was silent for a moment, and I thought she might be crying. But then she said, "We'll talk more when I see you. Goodbye."

"Bye."

#####

Two days later, when I got home from school and opened the door, I could hear Mrs. Martin's voice in the kitchen. She and Momma were chatting away. The house also smelled of cinnamon. I rushed upstairs to change clothes.

When I walked into the kitchen, they clammed right up. "Did I interrupt?"

"No, no," said Momma. "We were just yammerin' about our school days." She pulled off her apron and hung it behind the door.

"You two go on about your business. I have to run to the bank before it closes."

Mrs. Martin, who insisted I call her Emma henceforth, dove right in. We mixed up her Chinese Chews, and while they were baking, she taught me how to make an apple pie. While the pie was baking, we munched on the warm chews.

"How did you learn to bake, Emma?"

"My momma taught me some. Swapped recipes with others at the fair. You know I won a blue ribbon at the county fair for my angel food cake. Thirteen years in a row. Lotta them women there wanted my recipe, but I kept it my secret. Traded my apple pie recipe, though. Got a buckeye cookie recipe and a 7-up poundcake." She winked at me as she said, "I've tinkered with those and made 'em a might smart better."

We talked for a good while about baking. She didn't seem to know why some things worked and others didn't, but she was a natural baker with a head of experience. I think she realized right away that I was never going to be much of a baker. I followed the rules and the recipes. If it said one-quarter teaspoon of vanilla, then that is what I was going to use. No trying it a little differently for me.

As we were cleaning up the dishes and pans she had brought over, I said, "Next time, I could come over to your place so you don't have to bring all this over here."

Her face fell and she patted my hand. "Tink, I won't have any place to bake after next week. I sold the farm and got a little house behind the Pepsi plant in Ripley."

"Does it have a kitchen?"

"Yes, but it's tiny. Not much of my stuff will fit."

"What are you going to do with the rest?"

"I've given some away. The rest I'm going to sell to that feller that runs the flea market in Aberdeen."

I felt so bad for her. Her whole world was crumbling. And yet, here she was trying to teach me to bake. I wanted to help her, but I wasn't sure how.

"When are you moving?"

"Next Saturday."

"Do you have help?"

"It's not so much. Just my clothes and the kitchen stuff. My brother is moving the furniture I'm keeping."

"I'd be glad to come help you. Saturday? What time?"

"That's so sweet of you, Tink. But you aren't old enough to drive and I don't want to burden your mother."

"That's okay. My brother Bobby drives. I can get him to bring me over. And maybe I can get his wrestling buddies to join us."

She wrapped her arms around me and hugged until we heard the door open. "Smells good in here," called Momma. She snagged a chew from the plate and tasted it. "Tastes as good as it smells, too."

"Momma, Emma is moving to town next Saturday. Would it be okey if Bobby and I go over and help her out?"

"Of course. If your Daddy's not got me tied up in some of his unannounced plans already, I'll join you."

Emma had tears in her eyes. "You are the kindest people. I wish I could repay you somehow."

"You already did. Look, you've taught me to make apple pie and chews."

She patted my cheek. "You're a special one, Tink."

#####

Two of Bobby's wrestling buddies joined us, and we helped Emma move the next weekend. She was right about her new house, though. The kitchen was tiny. Of course, her farm kitchen was huge, and she had been collecting cooking stuff for fifty years. That didn't even include the "summer" kitchen in the outbuilding she had for canning.

Bobby or Momma took me to Emma's every month or so for nearly a year. But being alone affected poor Emma. Conversations began to take abrupt twists and turns, even though she was still a marvelous baker. By the end of the year, she only seemed to know who I was about half of the time. Six months later, her brother moved her to a nursing home on the hill. I went to visit once, but she didn't know me and didn't even acknowledge that I was there.

The nurse said, "She just stares out the window all day."

I cried on the way home with Momma. There was nothing I could do for Emma. She was drifting away, waiting for death to take her out of her misery. She'd lost the centerpiece of her life and didn't know how to go on living. She'd lost her farm and her kitchen, too.

On that ride home, I realized Emma wasn't alone. Farmers died every day, leaving widows on farms. But most had family to keep them going. Still, I wondered if the nursing homes were full of old women who'd suffered like Emma.

I reached across the seat and squeezed Momma's hand. "I love you."

Momma pursed her lips. "Life's a real bitch sometimes, Tink."

I nodded, knowingly. But I was young and had no idea how bad it could be.

CHAPTER 26

I heard the front door close and the clack of Fanny's steps on the hardwood floor. Maybe I am getting better at sleeping light. I rolled off the bed and padded downstairs. Fanny was standing at the kitchen island sorting through her mail.

She looked up as I walked into the kitchen. "You certainly look like a new person. Did you get some sleep, too?"

"Yes, thank you. The bath was relaxing, and I fell asleep for a while."

"Good." She looked around the kitchen. "I don't cook anymore. Just me. Doesn't seem worth it. We'll go to the diner for dinner."

"I'd be glad to cook. I'm sure you have plenty to work with."

She stared at me for a moment. "Maybe tomorrow. I want to hear your story tonight. Over dinner." She glanced at my feet. "Fetch your shoes and we'll go."

We sat at Fanny's table. The waitress immediately brought a glass of red wine to Fanny and set a Coke in front of me.

"We'll have the special, Carolyn," said Fanny. She raised her glass in a toast. "To a safe journey."

I clinked my Coke glass with hers and took a sip.

"Do you have a driver's license, Tink?"

"Yes."

"May I see it?"

"Why?"

"I want proof of your age."

"What for?"

"So I can be assured that you are not an underage runaway."

"You don't believe me?"

"I've learned to verify everything. That's how I've survived in this position for so long."

"Why does it matter? I'm moving on. And what is your position, anyhow?"

"First, you spent the afternoon at my house. If you're a runaway, I'm abetting you and that's a crime. Second, have you heard any trains pass through? No, of course, you haven't. Because there aren't any. Until Monday. So, you may as well enjoy my hospitality until then. But I need to know who's in my house. And I need to verify it."

She was right about no trains so far. I hadn't heard anything but a few pickups on the streets. No semi's, either. Just local traffic "When does the gas station get resupplied? I could hitch a ride with him."

"Monthly. Was here last week."

I had the time, and this seemed like an okay place to be. But I felt a little trapped and that bothered me. It felt a little *Twilight Zone-*like. If I started hearing creepy music or met someone named Norman Bates, I'd have to make an abrupt course change. For now, I decided to trust Fanny and see where this went.

I unbuttoned the flap on my jacket pocket and pulled out my driver's license. I slid it across the table.

Fanny barely glanced at it. "You can put it away."

"You didn't look at it."

"I don't need to. You showing it to me demonstrates trust. Now let's start over. Who are you?"

I returned the license back to my pocket. Fanny had a way of winning you over. The license thing, not checking my age…that was something Chuck would have done. With my license, I had offered to reveal who I really was. She didn't rub it in my nose. Instead, she used the moment to show she trusted me now. And left me feeling less vulnerable. In some odd way, it lessened her authority position in my head and instead made her seem more genuine. Trustworthy. I couldn't explain it more because it was all emotional, and emotions are so complicated and unreliable.

I told her my story. Almost all of it. Chuck, the library, my reading. Momma. The farm. Missoula. Mrs. Morgan's letter. Even Daddy's accident, except the part about me causing it.

By the time I was done, we had finished dinner and some coconut cream pie. Fanny asked a few questions along the way, but mostly let me reel out my story at my own pace.

"You're a brave young woman, Tink." She seemed to study her coffee for a few minutes. "I had a daughter about your age. Ella. We didn't get along. Maybe because we were too much alike. She had your spirit. My mouth. Never lost an argument." She went silent, staring at the cup.

"What happened, Fanny?"

"She decided to leave. With her friend. Sharita's sister, Tiara." She shook her head. "Truck they were in had an accident on the freeway. Twenty-car pileup. Nine died. Both went through the windshield. No seatbelts. Tiara's in a wheelchair." She shrugged. "But the truck burned up. Driver died, too."

"I'm sorry."

"It killed my husband, too. He committed suicide a week later. Shot himself in the head."

"And you blame yourself?"

"Wouldn't you?"

Of course I would. I still blamed myself for Daddy's death. I'd known this was supposed to be some kind of cleansing journey. There were others like me. I knew that. But Fanny was the first one I'd met.

Fanny waved a hand at me. "That's why you're running away. Think you can leave your past behind?"

"I'm not running away."

"You think your pain and nightmares won't follow you. I get it. But it won't work."

I glared at her, furious that she would so flippantly dismiss my journey. She didn't know me. She didn't know where I was going. Or what I'd been through.

The waitress came and refilled Fanny's empty wine glass. I'd lost count of how much she'd drunk. At least six or eight glasses. Probably well into her second bottle. But I guessed that stuff came from a jug in the kitchen refrigerator.

Before I could say anything, Fanny cut back in. "No matter, Tink. I don't have a better solution. The wine just dims my whole brain for a while. The nightmares still come."

She drained her glass in a few gulps. "Let's go before I'm too drunk to walk home."

Once outside, she took my arm. I steered us down the sidewalk to her house. She wobbled a few times but otherwise seemed relatively steady on her feet.

When we got to her front porch, she fumbled in her purse for her key but finally found it. She handed it to me instead of trying it herself.

Inside, she shed her coat on the floor and kicked off her shoes. She then staggered towards the stairs. "Tink, help yourself to whatever. We'll talk more tomorrow." She made her way up the stairs and disappeared around the hallway corner.

I picked up her coat and hung it in the hall closet. I set her shoes on the bottom step. Having had a brief nap today, I wasn't really tired. Plus, I'd had three Cokes filled with sugar and caffeine. It was only 9:30 so I wandered around the first floor, turning lights on and off as I went.

In what Momma would call the parlor, there were pictures sitting on the mantel where a toddler grew to a young woman about my age. Ella. There were several of Fanny with Ella and a man. Her husband, Johnson. In what appeared to be the most recent, he had thinning black hair slicked back. My head played the Brylcreem TV jingle. He was handsome and resembled William Shatner, Captain Kirk on *Star Trek*.

I sat down on the sofa and pulled out a picture from my wallet, the only picture I carried. It was of my family and me on Easter Sunday the year Daddy died. We looked happy then. Smiles on our faces and twinkles in our eyes. I didn't keep any pictures of us after Daddy died. Momma and I had dead eyes in all of them, so I threw them out. And stopped taking pictures. Since Janet had come into Bobby's life, his eyes had awakened. She brought him back to life and I loved her for it. She was making my brother happy again.

Thinking back about the evening, I tried to refute Fanny's comments about my journey. But I couldn't find a valid defense. *When you have eliminated all which is possible, then whatever remains, however improbable, must be the truth.* I suspected Newton and Einstein had their own versions of Sherlock Holmes' famous quote.

I retrieved the latest volume of my journal from my backpack and returned to the sofa. I recorded today's events and the conversations with Sharita and Fanny. The journey hadn't been as cathartic as I had hoped. But the journal writing did seem productive. Once on paper, events and emotions alike seemed to calm, if not disappear. My nightmares about Daddy had all but disappeared. I was getting some real sleep. And I'd only had one Sam nightmare. I worried that I'd jinxed that now, thinking about Sam. Maybe he'd be back in my nightmares tonight. I considered rummaging in the kitchen for some of Fanny's wine. But I knew I'd feel horrible tomorrow. Susie once convinced me to share her Boone's Farm bottle under the grandstand at the county fair. I'm sure she drank twice as much as me, but I remembered the feeling the next day. My brain was muddy, and my head pounded most of the day. And then there was the bottle of Ripple the week after Daddy died. Susie found me in the barn where we talked for hours. I drank the whole bottle while she smoked a couple of joints. The next day's hangover was much like the first. I didn't have time for that anymore, so afterwards I avoided alcohol completely. Now didn't seem like a good time to suspend that rule.

CHAPTER 27

When I woke, it was just getting daylight. From my sprawled position on the sofa, I could hear Fanny moving around upstairs.

In thirty minutes, I'd showered and changed into some clean clothes I'd washed yesterday. When I walked into the kitchen, the smell of bacon frying greeted me, along with the sizzling sound as it danced in the pan.

"Good morning, Tink."

"Morning, Fanny. Sleep well?"

"Like a bat…awake most of the night. You?"

"Fine. No nightmares."

I heard the front door open and close. Fanny called, "Good morning, Sharita."

Sharita walked into the kitchen. "What's going on, Fanny?"

"I'm cooking breakfast. Eggs, bacon, toast. Same as the diner. But cheaper, easier, and quicker."

"They gonna come lookin' for you, you don't show up there this mornin'."

"I called. They're fine."

Sharita looked at me. "You put her up to this?"

Before I could answer, Fanny said, "Sit down, Sharita. And leave Tink alone. It's not her fault."

"Figure out Tink's a girl yet?"

"I figured that out in the diner when we first met, Sharita. It's Miss Trudy Truesdale, but she goes by Tink."

Maybe she had looked at my license closer than I thought. But I felt like a third wheel in this conversation even though I was the topic.

"Trudy, huh? Yeah, that ain't a good name for you. I like Tink better."

I said, "Me, too."

"She doesn't care what you think, Sharita. She has a mind of her own." She turned and slid a plate across the island to me. It had two eggs over easy, several strips of crispy bacon, and buttered toast cut into triangles. "And now I'm feeding that mind." She waved a spatula towards Sharita. "Sit."

Sharita slid onto a stool and looked at me. "You got her drunk last night. She's punishing herself 'cause she's hung over."

I shrugged.

"What about you? You get drunk, too?"

"No," said Fanny. "Straight Coke all night. Don't know how she did it, but didn't pee all night, either.

"You was drunk. How would you know?"

Fanny slammed the spatula on the countertop. "Sharita! Give it a rest."

Sharita laughed. "Yes, ma'am."

It was quiet for a few moments. Fanny slid a plate towards Sharita, and then sat down at the island with one of her own. We ate in silence for a while until I said, "You two always banter like this in the morning?"

"Like cats and dogs," said Fanny.

Sharita grinned.

"Sharita isn't sure if she's my mother, teacher, or something else."

"Well, I sure hope my children don't behave like you," said Sharita. "I'd whup them all the way to Sunday."

"I'm most grateful that you refrain from that form of punishment with me."

After breakfast, Sharita washed, and I dried. Fanny had disappeared for a few minutes but returned as I hung up the dish towel.

"Tink, I have a task for you. Would you please follow me?"

Sharita growled, "I don't like that tone. Watch your back."

I followed Fanny through a few doorways in the back of the house until we stepped down into the garage. It was the largest garage I'd ever seen with eight parking spaces, all empty. She led me to the far side, through another side doorway, into another double garage. The overhead lights were already on. A large tarp-covered vehicle sat in the middle of the space.

"This was my husband's favorite car. But it hasn't run for several decades. He bought the parts and everything." She swept her arm around indicating multiple stacks of boxes. "He just never got the time. And then Ella became an endless need, requiring constant attention." She turned and handed me a pair of keys. "You're a mechanical genius. Do you think you can get it running in six days?"

"I don't know. I was planning to leave today."

"Oh, Tink, don't be so vapid! There's no transport until Monday." She smiled and turned towards the car. "At least, none that runs right now."

I peeled the tarp back from the car. Sharita, whose eyes were bugging out of her head, helped roll the tarp completely off the car. We stood staring.

"It's a 1949 Packard convertible coupe. A little rusty. Needs a new top. All cosmetic. But Johnson said it 'threw a rod,' whatever that means. All I know is the engine broke. Can you fix it?"

"Probably. If the parts are here." I had never seen a car quite this beautiful. It was dusty and old, but it had such beautiful lines. Chrome everywhere, which needed serious polishing. It was a car made in a time when style was important.

"Girl," said Sharita, "you ain't never showed that smile in Sublette before. You gonna kiss this thing, or what?"

I felt my face turn red. "It's a magnificent piece of mechanical genius. It's so pretty and…and elegant."

"Indeed," said Fanny. "Perfect description. Well, I'll leave you to your work. Sharita, let's get to the office. See you at dinner, Tink." Fanny turned on her heel and disappeared through the door. Sharita shook her head and followed Fanny.

CHAPTER 28

In the year after Daddy died, Bobby and I convinced Momma to borrow money to build three grain bins. I pointed out that we could make twenty percent more profit if we held our grain until winter or spring when prices naturally went back up after harvest time.

After the bins were built, we shuffled the grain elevator from bin to bin, as needed. But keeping our one tractor to run the elevator meant we had no way to pull the grain wagons from the fields to the bins. So we unhooked the tractor from the elevator, got a loaded wagon from the field, pulled that into position, unhooked it, and then hooked the tractor back up to the elevator. This was repeated for every wagonload. I often waited a half-hour with a full Gleaner bin before Bobby got back. This hooking and unhooking took too much time.

Momma resisted buying another tractor. Financially, it was risky at this point in our budding grain operation. I raised this issue with Jake Cluxton.

He said, "You could get a little Farmall Cub or Model A. They're cheap. Won't pull a loaded wagon, but it'll run your elevator."

"Where could I find one of those, Mr. Cluxton?"

"Try that Holton fella in Russellville. If he don't have one, he'll know where you can get it."

Bobby drove us to Russellville, and we found Holton's Case Dealership on Main Street. Mr. Holton was a big man with glasses that constantly slid down his veined nose. If he'd been green, I would have sworn he was the giant Hulk's brother. When I told him what we wanted, he mopped his sweaty brow with a blue handkerchief and pushed his glasses up his nose.

"I got two used I can sell you." He stood there looking at us for a moment, and then flicked a finger my way. "You Will Truesdale's daughter, ain't you?"

I nodded. "This is my brother Bobby."

He nodded towards Bobby, and then said to me, "Heard you was real handy with engines and such. Natural ability to see how they work and how to fix 'em."

I shrugged.

Bobby said, "She's a wizard. Ain't nobody ever seen anything like her at this age."

"Where'd you hear about me?" I asked Mr. Holton.

He rubbed his chin and glanced around like he didn't want to tell me. "Emma Martin. She's my sister."

"She's a lovely lady. Been teaching me to bake."

"That's what she told me. Said you been damn nice to her."

We stood there awkwardly for a few moments, Mr. Holton eyeing us and pushing his glasses back up, us shifting on our feet. I finally said, "How much for one of those little tractors?"

"Nine hundred. Maybe eight-fifty. But I got one that was in a fire. Burned the tires and wires right off. I bought it just for the motor. I'll sell it to you for fifty dollars. You go over to Schadle's junkyard. They got a couple of these tractors with no motor at all. Another hundred bucks, you can put the two together."

That's what we did. It took me three days to shuffle the engine and transmission from one chassis to the other. When I started it up, the engine blew a lot of smoke from burning oil. I pulled the head and changed the rings to cure that.

It was a great little engine. Four cylinders, about ten horsepower, and relatively light so I could easily sling the engine in and out of the chassis.

As far as I knew, Junior (Bobby named each piece of equipment) was still sitting next to the grain bins running the grain elevator to this day.

Looking at Fanny's Packard, I didn't think it would be more complicated than Junior. Both were originally made in the late 1940s so there weren't any complicated aspects I couldn't figure out. The

Packard was just bigger. Johnson had a chain hoist in the garage so I could easily pull the engine if needed.

I peeled the convertible top off first. It was ripped in several places, and several snaps had popped off or rusted out.. Poking around in the workbench and cabinets, I found a full set of nearly new tools that also carried the Packard brand name. In those days, the owner of a car did most of his or her own maintenance to keep the car in good condition. I wondered if Johnson had purchased the tools separately or if they came with the car when he bought it.

There was a pair of repair kits for the top. I wondered if they came with the car, or Johnson had added them to his repair supplies. In any case, there were patches for the rips and replacement snaps that came with canvas reinforcement around their attachment points.

I found the hood latches under the dash. The hood could open from either side, depending on which under-dash lever you pushed. After getting the lay of the engine, I figured I'd have to pull the whole engine if a rod was thrown. By pushing both hood latches, the hood tilted forward, but it was too heavy to lift off by myself. I rigged some straps to the overhead chain hoist and wrestled the hood aside. .

In a couple of hours, I had the engine head off and found the rods were broken on two of the eight cylinders. There didn't appear to be any damage to the block or head, which made the repair a lot easier. I did find plenty of spare rings, so I replaced all of them and the two rods. The other six rods seemed to be in decent shape. I hoped the new ones didn't throw the balance off.

By late afternoon, I had the engine back together. The battery was dead, so I decided to wait until tomorrow to get a new one or get this one charged. Oddly, it seemed that the electrical system used a positive ground. The negative ground approach must have won out in the fifties because that's all I'd ever seen before.

Not knowing how long this car had been idle, I figured I should at least change the oil and flush the radiator. The radiator was easy. Although I didn't have any antifreeze, water would be fine for now. Oil was another matter. I found the plug to drain it, but I didn't know what oil or how much to use to fill it. In most cars, there's a manual in the glovebox that details that kind of information. The Packard's glovebox was empty. A thorough search of the workbench and cabinets yielded a complete set of service manuals. Six quarts of oil,

16.9 gallons of gasoline, one quart of transmission oil. The battery was an odd shaped six-volt, 100 Ah, which I probably could never find. Cars were all twelve volts now.

In my search, I also found a case of oil and a gallon of transmission fluid. I drained the engine oil and transmission, replacing both fluids. I even found wiper replacements which I finished putting on just before Sharita walked in.

"Hey, Tink the tinkerer. You 'bout ready for dinner?"

"Sure." I glanced up.

Sharita's mouth fell open. "You got grease and shit all over your face. Go wash up. Fanny will be here shortly, and she don't like to wait."

As I walked by Sharita, I pretended to wipe a greasy hand across her nose. She ducked.

"Don't you be touching me with that paw. And wash it off in that garage sink. I don't wanna be scrubbing another bathroom for the rest of my life."

Over dinner at the diner, I updated Fanny and Sharita on my Packard progress. Fanny seemed pleased. Sharita seemed shocked.

I concluded with a question for Fanny. "Do you know where we can get a new battery?"

She frowned. "Normally, I'd say the Texico station. But I don't know if they'll have this unusual one. I can call Ronald—he owns the station—when we get home."

#####

At 7:30 the next morning, Sharita picked me up at the garage door in her '63 Ford Galaxy.

"Well, look at you bein' a girl today."

I shrugged. "Same as always. T-shirt and jeans."

"You don't have that boy aura around you. Curves showing. You look downright feminine."

"Hope that's not a problem at the station." Gas station guys were a lot like the farm equipment guys. Lots of testosterone that went haywire when a girl walked in.

The inside of Sharita's Galaxy was as clean as it was the day it drove off the showroom floor. She spread several layers of newspaper on the floor of her car's trunk. With her help, we lugged the Packard battery into her trunk, and I added an empty five-gallon gas can

When we pulled into the station, a whopping three-minute ride across Sublette, a young guy came out.

"Fill her up, ladies?"

I got out. "No, just need to fill this can." I got the can out of the trunk and set it near the pump.

"What's a couple of ladies need this much gas for?"

I couldn't help myself. "Airplane. I gotta fly her to Brazil later this afternoon."

He looked at me. "Airplane, huh? You a pilot?"

"Yeah. Amelia Earhart was my grandmother."

I could see him twist up his mouth, probably trying to decide if I was crazy or not. But he might know Sharita. And her basketball plans.

He finished filling the can and hefted it into the trunk. He stood there leaning on the fender with one hand. "Where's your airplane?"

"About a mile east. Fanny Chouteau's farm. It's got a nice flat dirt road."

He nodded and went back to working his mouth.

I pointed at the battery in the trunk. "Do you have one like this?"

"Dunno. Have to ask Willy inside."

Gas man helped me pick it up and carry it inside. We hefted the battery onto the counter. A scruffy guy with a Texaco hat stood behind the counter eyeing a percolating coffee pot, an eager cup in hand. He turned to me. "Can I help you?"

"I'm looking for a six-volt battery like this one."

He eyed it and rubbed a finger across the faded battery label. "Six-volt. Old one. What'd it come out of?"

"Forty-nine Packard."

"Humph. Johnson's old car?"

"Yes."

He pulled his cap back and scratched his head. "I don't have anything that size. Lots of six-volts for tractors and older cars. But they're a lot different shape. Might not fit."

The Packard battery was about twenty inches long, but only four inches wide. "Can be taller, but the base fits in a pretty tight spot."

I could smell the coffee now and saw gas man pouring a cup. He walked over and set it in front of me. "Battery truck's due here anytime. He might have one." He flicked a finger towards the coffee. "Cream or sugar?"

"No, thanks." I picked up the cup and took a sip. I never liked coffee much, but being around farm equipment dealers, granary operators, and farm supply stores, everyone seemed to have a cup in hand most of the time. Long ago, I decided I needed to be sociable. I sipped again.

"Okay if I wait for the battery guy?"

The Texico guy dipped his cup my way. "Help yourself."

The two guys wandered into the back, their muffled voices indistinguishable.

I went out and updated Sharita.

"I can't wait around, Tink. I gotta get to work at Fanny's. Bein' tardy is a mortal sin with her."

"How should I get back? Can't lug a battery that far."

Before Sharita could reply, the big battery truck pulled in. It had a company named painted on the door: Volt Battery. Under the name in plain letters it said *Dodge City, Kansas*. I could hitch a ride with this guy if he was going back home by the end of the day.

I looked at Sharita. She was looking at the battery truck door, too. She turned away. "You got your ride."

"Probably."

"Sorry to see you go. I liked you. 'Spose Fanny'll blame me."

"For what?"

"Lettin' you get off."

I put a hand on Sharita's shoulder. "I've got the time, Sharita. Fixing the Packard is kinda fun, too. Don't worry. I'm not leaving." At least not yet. But I'd sure find out how often the battery truck passed through Sublette. "This won't take but a minute, then we can go."

The battery truck driver held the station door for me. I looked at his embroidered name on his shirt. *Gus.*

"Thanks, Gus." I pointed at the battery on the counter. "You got anything like that?"

He barely glanced at it. He was eyeing me up and down. "Maybe."

"Sorry, Gus, but I'm in a hurry today. How often do you come through here? Maybe we could get a bite at the diner next time you come through."

A huge smile washed over his face. "I make my rounds once a week. Be here next Wednesday."

"Okay. Sounds like a date. About this time? We'll have breakfast."

"Sure."

I pointed at the battery. "Got anything?"

He nodded. "Think so. Lemme go look."

I followed him to the truck. He opened a couple of doors on the side and soon pulled out a near-model match. "It's a 2E battery. Use these in older combines. Tractors. Still being used out here in the boonies."

He fixed a plastic handle to it and carried it around to the Galaxy's trunk. I climbed into the passenger seat and said, "See you next week, Gus." Under my breath, I whispered to Sharita, "Let's get out of here now."

Gus grinned and waved. As Sharita backed out, he called, "Hey, who's paying for the battery?"

"See the man who wears the star. Inside." I figured Fanny was good for it. But I didn't want to be anywhere near Gus any longer than necessary. The hair on the back of my neck had been dancing since he opened the station door. He was exactly the kind Janet warned me about. I could feel his eyes boring into me from behind. But he didn't try to hide his eyeball assessment of me, even when we were face-to-face. I recalled an article I'd read about Singapore laws. "Lascivious Looking." Had we been in Singapore, I could have had him arrested. I think twenty lashes was the common punishment. I wondered if they'd let me give him the lashes.

Sharita glanced at me. "Did you just make a date with that creep?"

"He thinks so, but I'll be long gone."

"Ha! That type makes you want to disguise yourself as a boy!"

I looked at her. We both laughed until we had tears running down our cheeks.

CHAPTER 29

Johnson had laid in Packard spares of every kind, including a kit for a new canvas top. After I drained the old gas and dumped the five gallons of new gas into the tank, I installed the battery. When I turned the key, the ammeter didn't move. But the battery tested good, so I replaced the ammeter. As soon as I hooked up the battery and turned the key again, the meter jumped to life.

I tinkered for a while, checking and double checking to make sure everything was in place and ready before I tried to start the car. By late morning, I'd run out of things to recheck. I rolled up the garage door—I didn't want to die of carbon monoxide poisoning—and stood looking at that Packard beast. Without its top, it reminded me of the old flat-top haircuts some of boys used to wear. Maybe that's why Johnson liked this car. It reminded him of his own haircut.

I climbed in, made sure it was in neutral, pushed in the clutch, turned the key, and then pushed the starter switch. The engine rolled over, a little sluggish at first, but picked up speed after a few revolutions. But it didn't catch and keep running.

Four hours later, I'd disassembled the carburetor. It was filled with gunk from the old gasoline, and it took quite a while to soak it off with carburetor cleaner.

On the start retry, it took right off. It wasn't running very smoothly, so a tune-up was in order. But I had several days to get to that. I couldn't resist a test. I put the old behemoth into reverse and backed out of the garage. Just as the front bumper cleared the door, I heard a pop and the left rear side of the car seemed to drop lower. I knew before I looked—flat tire.

I pulled back into the garage and shut the engine down. By the time Sharita stopped in, I'd finished changing all four tires and the spare. Johnson knew what he was doing. But even those spare tires were old—at least twenty years. I wouldn't want to go far on these things.

I didn't think wrestling the new convertible canvas by myself made any sense. Fanny agreed to let Sharita off for the afternoon to help. I busied myself with cleaning and polishing as much as I could. Some of the rust on the body needed the skill of a body shop, but the chrome was thick and old-school, so I could sand that a little and then polish it back up to a luster.

I found time to make some brownies and had lunch ready when Sharita arrived.

"Well, look at you. Miss Betty Crocker after all."

"Soup and sandwiches. Nothing much."

"Brownies? Do I have to scrub the oven?"

"Nope. Not a crumb in there from me."

She walked over and opened the oven door. "No offense, but my name's on the cleanliness of this kitchen. And my paycheck."

"I get it. I'll clean up after we eat and you can inspect all you want."

By 3:30 p.m. we had the repaired top on. I was anxious to show Fanny what we'd done. "Let's drive by and pick up Fanny."

"Can't. License plates are expired. Fanny'd have to call up Jeb to give her a ticket."

"Who's Jeb?"

"Town cop. He came in Fanny's office Tuesday while you were there. And you met his brother, Ronald. Texaco hat."

Everyone was intertwined with everyone else in Sublette. Small towns were like that. In Sardinia, my hometown, the town cop also owned the Dairy Queen and was married to the mayor's daughter. Her brother ran the drugstore. It was endless.

"Is there an office in Sublette that could issue temporary tags for the Packard?"

"I think so. Second floor in Fanny's building."

"How do you mean, 'Fanny's building?'"

"It's her building. She owns it. Leases it to the town and a bunch of other businesses."

"How much other property does she own?"

"I don't really know. A lot. I think she owns most of both sides of this street. Had to sell a few parts, though. Post office. Police station."

"She owns the diner?"

"Just the building. Alem owns the diner business. Course, Fanny loaned him the money."

"Is she the bank, too?"

Sharita nodded. "She owns that. And most every business in town. Or she holds a loan on it."

"It really is her town."

"For a smart woman, it sure takes you a long time to figure out the lay of the land. Her ancestors founded this town. At one time, they owned all of it and most of the surrounding ranch and farmland. They've sold some things here and there, but Fanny is the queen bee in these parts. And the last Chouteau."

#####

At the license office, we discovered we needed the vehicle number and the title to get tags. Sharita went back to Fanny's office to find the title while I went back to the house to try to find the vehicle number.

A couple of years ago they passed a law requiring all vehicles to have a Vehicle Identification Number (VIN) in a standard format and in standard locations. Prior to that, manufacturers had their own number system. On the Packard there were two plates on the engine side of the firewall. One was clearly the Packard plate with a vehicle model number of 2232 and a body number of 2279-0671. The other plate was a body number plate stamped with 2292-9978. But no VIN number.

By the time I'd retrieved these numbers and taken off the rear license plate (the license bureau wanted to see the old license plate, too), Sharita and Fanny arrived home. Fanny rummaged in her office for ten minutes or so while Sharita and I had a Coke at the kitchen island. She returned triumphantly with a thick worn envelop in her hand, shouting, "Let's go get those tags."

It took less than twenty minutes. Sharita had to head home to help her mother with something. Fanny and I carefully taped the temporary tag to the plastic window in the convertible top. I started to hand her the key.

"No, you drive, Tink."

"It's your car, Fanny. You should drive it."

"I already spoke to Jake at the insurance agency. You're covered under my policy."

"Never thought about insurance." I climbed in and backed us out of the garage. "Why don't you have a car, Fanny?"

"I never drove. Johnson had quite a collection. After he was gone, they were useless to me. I sold them all. Except for this one. He always said it was the most valuable."

My hands fidgeted on the wheel. I wondered how valuable this thing was. I sure didn't want to wreck it or I'd be in Sublette forever paying Fanny back.

We reached the end of the alley at Maple Street. "Which way?"

"Turn right. Let's make our way to the highway. We'll run out of town, then turn right on route 160."

When we turned onto route 160, Fanny said, "Pull over there at that gate in the fence."

I stopped and Fanny got out. She proceeded to fold down the convertible top, something she had apparently done many times before.

She hopped back in and shut her door. "Let her rip, Tink. Let's get some wind in our hair."

The car was a three-speed on the steering column. The speedometer went to 110, but I wasn't about to push the crate that hard. It was made with quality workmanship and materials for the time it was made. But I didn't want to test any of the twenty-plus-years-old components. The tires particularly seemed narrow and fragile compared to truck tires on our farm.

It was a straight shot down the highway and Fanny grinned and let out an occasional whoop. I didn't know if I was giggling at her or at the ride.

After about five miles, Fanny said, "Turn left up here. Haskell County Cemetery."

My glee immediately dampened. I didn't like cemeteries. Dead people were buried there, each with a death story to tell.

I pulled in through the overhead iron sign. Fanny directed me down the gravel road to a side path that looked more like a pair of cow paths wandering between the tombstones. It dead-ended at a small white building. *Chouteau* was carved into the white stone above the single door.

"Johnson's resting place. Haven't been here for a while. Thought I owed it to him since you got his favorite car running."

Fanny opened the door and stepped out. She started towards the building but turned and looked at me. "Coming?"

"I'll just wait here. Give you some privacy."

"Nonsense. You fixed his car. He'll want to meet you."

I did not want to meet Johnson. He was dead. I felt cold but sweat rolled down my spine under my top.

"He won't bite, Tink. He's dead. But I still talk to him."

I opened the door and got out. This didn't feel right. I glanced around at the other tombstones staring back at me. Each one had a story, a story I didn't want to hear.

Fanny came and took my arm. "Tink, why are you so nervous? These people are all dead. They can't hurt you."

"But their stories can haunt you."

Fanny stopped and turned to me. "What's haunting you, Tink?"

I looked beyond the cemetery out over the open farmland. The sun was dipping low in the sky. It would be dark in twenty minutes. I'd gotten good at finding other things to occupy my mind whenever Daddy came up. When others stumbled across the topic, I found a way to shift the topic. But I was at a loss for words here among the departed.

Fanny took my hand and led me to the building. "This is called a Mausoleum. My grandparents and parents are here. And Johnson." She opened the door and led me inside. It smelled sweet like someone had been burning incense. A stone bench stood between a pair of shelves on each side wall. The shelves held caskets, four on each side. There was one missing. The one where Fanny would be…what was the right word? Not buried. Laid to rest? Interred?

Fanny pulled me to the bench, and we sat. "My grandparents are behind us. We don't talk much anymore. I've said everything I can think of. All the things I never thought to say when they were alive.

"My parents are here." She pointed to the right. "And there's Johnson. We argued a lot about whether he wanted to be in here or not. He claimed he wasn't a Chouteau; he was a Taft. But he married into the Chouteau family." Fanny shrugged. "That was part of the deal. He wanted to be on top, too." She giggled. "I usually get my way."

The open slot for Fanny's casket was above Johnson's.

Fanny reached over and tapped on Johnson's casket. "Johnson, I brought this young lady to meet you. She's refurbished the Packard. We drove it here. Her name is Tink Truesdale." She turned to me. "Say hello."

I didn't know what to do but stare at Johnson's casket. It was like I expected him to say something. But this was stupid. These people were dead. They weren't going to talk.

Fanny elbowed me in the ribs and gestured towards Johnson.

"Hello, Johnson. Nice to meet you."

"Tell him about the Packard."

"Um. You have a nice car. Very elegant lines and artful design."

"Tell him what you did."

"Well, I fixed the thrown rod. There were actually two. Replaced the ammeter. Polished some rust off the chrome."

"Go on."

"I found your spare parts. You had quite an extensive maintenance store. Nice tools, too. Did they come with the Packard? The service manual really helped. I've never seen a positive ground wiring system before."

I went on talking to Johnson for a while. Fanny finally put her arm around me. I stopped talking. Outside, the sun had set. It had become nearly pitch-black inside.

Fanny said, "What really happened to your father, Tink."

I shook my head and scrunched up my mouth. But she couldn't see me in the darkness. "I told you. Farm accident."

"Why's that seem like the elephant in the room?"

It was always the elephant in the room. For the last six years. Always, every day, all the time.

"You think it was your fault?"

My heart skipped a beat. Why would she ask that? "No. Of course not."

"Then what are you running away from?"

"I'm not running away. I'm going to Missoula to a two-week training seminar."

"Okay." Silence permeated the darkness. I couldn't see the door outline anymore. "Were you close with your father."

"Yes. Very. He was my mentor, coach, and parent all in one. He taught me to read when I was three. And he bought books. Lots of books. Drove me to the library to get more. And he taught me what he called *common sense*."

"As you look back at it, Tink, is there anything that you did that led to his death?"

I didn't even think. It just came out. "The Gleaner." And then it came streaming out of me. It was like a dam had sprung a leak. I poured out the story beginning with buying the Gleaner all the way through to jumping on the train—including my mistake with the cotter pin. When I was done, I felt empty. Tears streamed down my cheeks. Fanny had her arm around my shoulders. I turned toward her and she wrapped both arms around me while I sobbed.

We sat there for a while in silence until Fanny let out a long sigh. "I guess we should go."

We stood and felt our way to the door. I turned back. "Johnson, I had fun working on your Packard. Thank you."

It was equally dark outside. We stood there for a moment, trying to figure out how to make our way to the Packard.

"Fanny."

"Yes, Tink."

"I never tested the headlights."

#####

On Saturday afternoon, Fanny hosted a farewell party for Sharita. A cadre of service people arrived at 8:00 am and strung lights in the front yard and streamers in the entry and living rooms. They brought in a sea of food and set up a buffet on the kitchen island. I stayed out of the way in my bedroom, updating my notebook on my time in Sublette.

Around 10:00 am, there was a knock on my door. When I opened it, Fanny handed me a large flat box.

"What's this?"

"For you. To be you at Sharita's party." She also handed me a shoebox. "I hope you know how to walk in heels." She turned and disappeared down the hall before I had time to reply. It wouldn't have mattered anyway. Fanny ran the show, and she ran it her way.

I opened the boxes and found a Pierre Cardin shift dress. It was sleeveless in green with broad red trim around the neck and arms, and it had a narrow, red patent leather belt. In the shoebox were matching green pumps with medium heels and a pair of green tights. Janet would be thrilled—it was another Twiggy ensemble.

When I took a shower, I considered shaving my armpits and legs, but that seemed like a lot of trouble. Besides, I hadn't shaved either since Daddy died. Some things were easier being a boy. In the end, though, I decided to shave my pits after I discovered Fanny had left a new razor and shaving cream in the shower.

I slicked my hair back like Janet had done for me at Christmas. I had to admit that I did kinda resemble Twiggy in this outfit.

Just as I finished dressing, Sharita banged on my door once and burst in without waiting for me to respond.

"Hi, Tink. Oh." She set a black bag on the bed and stared at me. "That's scary. You look like you walked out of some high fashion magazine. Where'd the grease monkey go?"

"Do I look okay for your party?"

"Okay? You look stunning. You gonna be the star at the top of the Christmas tree today."

"No, this is your day. It's a sendoff for you, the big-time international basketball player."

"Where'd you get that idea?"

"From Fanny."

"She told you that, huh? It's true I'm leavin', but I think today's more about you leavin'."

"No, it's not." I pointed at a box wrapped in red on the dresser. "I even got you a farewell gift."

"We see about that. Anyways, come over here by the light. I need to do your makeup."

"I don't wear makeup."

"I wasn't askin'. I'm doin' what Fanny said. You know the deal by now."

I did. I sat down by the window.

#####

By noon, the setup was complete and the guests started arriving. The afternoon was a blur, partly because they served champagne and I drank two glasses. Given the number of guests, at least half the

Sublette population stopped by. Many brought gifts for Sharita and well-wishes for me on my journey. It seemed like the whole town knew my travel plans and the nature of my journey. It was very strange to realize so many people were, in their own way, cheering me on just as they were cheering for Sharita. I wondered if that was Fanny's influence or did these Sublette citizens really have a genuine caring for their own…even an adopted one like me.

After the cleaning crew left around 9:00 pm, Fanny handed me another glass of champagne, and dragged me into the sitting room. She kicked her shoes off and sat down.

"Have a seat, Tink. I want to ask you something."

I slipped off my shoes—my feet ached from the heels—and curled my legs under me on the sofa.

"How did you feel today?"

"I'm not sure what you mean, Fanny."

"You were a woman today. A beautiful woman. Was that different than your man-masquerade?"

"Of course."

"In what way? How did you feel different?"

I sipped my champagne. "I didn't feel like I was hiding, trying to be invisible."

"Invisible you were not."

"Thanks to you."

Fanny shrugged. "Just trying to open doors. Let you peek at other opportunities."

We were quiet for a minute. "Tink, when's the last time you wore a dress?"

"Long time ago."

"Why?"

I sipped more champagne. "'Cause I burned all my girl clothes the night Daddy died. Cut my hair. Started my 'man-masquerade,' as you call it. Started running the farm. Trying to make money."

"Why?"

"Why not?" I gulped some more champagne. "Without Daddy, there was no one to run the farm. If we didn't run the farm, there would be no money. We'd have to sell the farm. Move to town. Shrivel up and die like the other farm widows."

Fanny stared at her champagne glass for a while, and then took a sip. "I get it, Tink. Makes sense. Safer on the train, too, looking like a man, at least at first glance."

I drank the rest of my champagne, maybe because I was already a little giddy.

"Your Daddy would be proud of you, how you've carried on. I'm sure I'll see your picture on the cover of *Time* someday, too. Come back and visit if you get the chance. You'll always be welcome here."

"Thank you, Fanny. You've been so nice to me. I hope I wasn't too much trouble."

Tears welled in Fanny's eyes. "It was my pleasure, Tink. You're such a lovely young woman. I wish my daughter could have met you. Maybe…maybe things would be different."

"I'm sorry about your daughter, Fanny. Sharita told me."

"People die all the time. All ages. All reasons. But when someone you love dies, you must learn new ways to behave without them. A whole new set of behaviors. Until you get comfortable with the new way, it feels terrible and unfamiliar." She looked at me. "It doesn't stop hurting, Tink. But eventually you recognize it, and you know you'll get through it. You learn to cope."

"It's going on four years, Fanny."

"Are you a slow learner, or just stubborn?" She held up a hand. "Before you answer that, think about what I said. Examine it. Does it apply? Or am I just being a bitch?"

Her comment made me angry. I was neither a slow learner nor stubborn. But I grasped control and considered it. I had tucked my grief away so I could focus on running the farm, so it only came out at night in my dreams when my brain couldn't really process it or learn to deal with it. Maybe Momma was right—I'd stopped living, so I didn't have to feel it, didn't have to deal with it. But the pressure just kept building inside me, like Momma's pressure cooker she forgot to turn off. If I couldn't find a way to relieve it, I'd probably end up like Fanny's daughter—another source of grief for our mother.

#####

For Sharita's first leg in her journey to Brazil, Fanny had arranged for someone to drive her to Dodge City on Monday. They wanted me to ride along, but I'd already lost a week of my journey to Sublette. I wasn't going to chance any more time to a flat tire, breakdown, or other highway mishap. I had to be in Missoula by the thirty-first. Four weeks from today.

The early Monday morning train from Sublette to Dodge City turned out to be only about a fifty-mile ride. Fanny had exaggerated, if not outright lied, about how remote Sublette was. But at this point, it didn't really matter to me. Fanny had befriended me, maybe because she thought of me as a temporary substitute for her daughter. She did a lot for me while I was there. This morning, she even secretly slipped a hundred dollars in my pocket somehow.

Our chat in Johnson's mausoleum seemed to drain a lot of my anxiety. I felt calmer and had a clearer vision of where I was going and why: Missoula was my gateway to NASA. I hoped.

My train was going in the wrong direction when we got to Dodge City. The Sublette track wasn't much more than a spur and entered the yard headed eastward. I waited until the train stopped before sliding off. The sun was up here on the open plains, but there were still long shadows where I could hide.

I moved to the side of the yard among some bushes and tried to get the lay of the land. They were already breaking up my train and moving cars to other tracks. It looked like the west-bound trains were on the far side from where I crouched.

As I rose to dart across the tracks, two shadows fifty yards away ran across the tracks. The men crouched near a car, and then disappeared around it towards the westward trains. I had company.

It was easier to move in the dark and remain undetected, but footing could be challenging. And when it was dark outside, you couldn't see inside an open boxcar to find out if it was empty or filled with trouble. I decided to wait a bit for full daylight and see how things played out. Scooting back into the bushes even more, I pulled out an early morning snack. A Payday candy bar and water.

One of the far trains pulled out. It had a few boxcars, but I didn't spot any open doors on this side. Two eastern trains pulled out, too. Both had open boxcars.

It was getting light fast, and I wasn't very well concealed in these bushes in daylight. I made a break for a lone livestock car. It had been sitting at the west edge of the yard since I had been here. It was loaded with pigs. Noisy, stinky pigs. I presumed some clever trainyard employee wanted to keep them downwind as long as possible.

I slid in behind the pig car, keeping it between me and the rest of yard. I was in relative darkness in the shadow of the car. I watched for ten minutes. No other hobo company revealed themselves.

There were three open boxcars on a train five or six tracks over. They were hitched between tankers and two livestock cars loaded with cows. Not as noisy as pigs, but similarly stinky.

I made my way to the open boxcar just in front of the cows, figuring a rational hobo would want to be as far from them as possible. Company wasn't part of my plan today. Shining my flashlight around the car, I confirmed it was empty and climbed inside. Twenty minutes later, we began to move.

CHAPTER 30

The ride was uneventful. We crawled westward for two days, stopping at every burg and cow-town on the map. Midday on Wednesday, we pulled into Pueblo, Colorado. I knew I had to go north now. The Rocky Mountains lay westward, blocking our path. I needed to follow the mountains up through Colorado and Wyoming and into Montana before turning westward again.

Pueblo's railyard was small, maybe six tracks in all. I spotted a gas station not far from the tracks and headed in that direction. Refilling my canteen was always a priority, but I wanted to replenish the supplies I'd used in the last two days.

As I approached the gas station, I saw two men enter. They were dressed in dark clothes and looked like the ones I'd seen in Dodge City running across the tracks. I hung back and found a dim alley where I could see the station but not be out in the open myself.

A few minutes later the two men came running out of the gas station. They headed my way, back towards the tracks. A large man with a ponytail burst out of the station door. He had a shotgun in his hands. I ducked down behind some trash cans. I didn't want another injury from being in the line of fire. The shotgun boomed.

I waited a beat, then peeked out. The men were running in different directions, one darting behind a building across the street. The other headed right for my alley. I shrunk behind the cans as much as possible and ducked my head. Between the cans I could see his feet. He was just inside the alley against the wall, shielding himself from view from the gas station. I heard crackling and paper tearing. He dropped something on the ground near his feet. It looked like a candy bar wrapper.

A short whistle came from across the street. My alley buddy whistled back and took off. I crept from my hiding place and poked my head around the corner. The two men were half-a-block down the street just walking along towards the tracks. I'd need to make sure to avoid them when I came back.

There were three wrappers at my feet, all from hostess twinkies. I presumed the ponytail guy saw them steal these from the station and he gave chase. I didn't want to confront an angry owner with a shotgun, but I did need supplies. I fished a five-dollar bill out of my pack and carried it in my hand as I approached the station. When I walked in, I caught the eye of the ponytail guy and waved with the bill. "Good morning."

The shotgun was laying on the counter next to him. He just stared at me.

I wandered the aisles collecting what I needed. When I dumped it on the counter, the guy said, "More than five dollars there."

"Okay." I laid the bill on the counter and dug out a couple of ones from my pocket.

He rang up the items for a total of $8.42. I dug some change out of my pocket and counted it out in front of him.

"Those two friends of yours?"

"No. Never saw them before. Did they steal stuff from you?"

"Twinkies. Took six of 'em."

"You didn't shoot at them."

"Twinkies ain't worth killin' for. But maybe they won't come back."

"You get a lot of theft here?"

"Yeah. Being close to the tracks, we get a lot of hobos." He eyed me. "You one of 'em?"

"I'm riding the trains. Does that make me a hobo?"

"Guess so. But you ain't got the look."

"What look is that?"

"Snake-like. Dangerous. Don't turn your back on 'em."

"There are bad people everywhere. Good ones, too. Maybe hobos are no different."

"I'll put a sign out. Good hobos only."

"Hope they can read."

Ponytail laughed. "You take care, kid. Steer clear of trouble."

I loaded my purchases into my pack and left. As I walked back towards the tracks, Ponytail's words rang in my head. "Steer clear of trouble." It gave me cold chills. I wondered if karma was trying to tell me something.

I scanned the street ahead, looking for the two men or any other sign of trouble. When I got to the yard fence, I stood in the weeds for ten minutes watching movements and trying to figure out where the men had gone.

There was a train right in front of me with an open boxcar just two back from the locomotive. Not a good location for a hobo because the engineer or other rail employees are more likely to spot you. But it was also more likely not to have any other hobos in that car.

I waited until the engineer was looking out the other side of the locomotive and no one else was around. Then I vaulted over the fence and scampered across the tracks into the boxcar. I lay on the floor for a minute scanning the interior. Nothing moved and I couldn't see anyone. I'd already decided to roll right back off the car if anyone was in there. But I was alone.

I scooted into a dark corner and tried to get comfortable. A half-hour later, we began to move. The noises of the locomotive were a lot louder this far forward in the train. The smell of diesel was also more prominent. But I felt safer here hoping the locomotive presence would deter trouble from coming my way.

CHAPTER 31

We crawled through the Rocky Mountain foothills to Colorado Springs. It was mid-evening by the time we got there. I packed up and was ready to bolt if someone boarded my boxcar or they pulled it from the train. But twenty minutes later, we were on the move again and I was still alone.

The train rolled along at a slow pace for ten minutes. Then it stopped outside the trainyard. I poked my head out the door and looked around. We were on a sidetrack, maybe to let another train pass. But this close to the yard, there were plenty of tracks to switch to so another train could pass. This felt more like a layup—a temporary stop until a predetermined time. Probably overnight. Likely for several hours. I curled up in the corner and went to sleep. I knew my brain would wake me when the train started moving again.

When I woke, the sun was just rising. Dim light drifted through the open door. I yawned and ripped open a Pop-Tart. It was nice to have a full night's sleep.

Most towns and cities have one trainyard. Sometimes it's just a couple of extra tracks with some switches so railcars can be pulled aside and loaded or unloaded. In others, like the one in Cincinnati where I started, there are a dozen or more tracks with complex switches where railcars are moved among various trains according to their destinations. The large cities, or sometimes just where many tracks intersect, there are roundhouses and turntables where they can service and easily switch a locomotive from one track to another.

Denver, maybe because it was a western city where rail travel developed later than the eastern states, had multiple yards aligned with the various rail companies. I hoped the train I was on would end up at one of the yards I had memorized so I could find my way to Union Station. Denver was a big place, and I didn't want to waste my money on paid transportation.

Union Station, the central passenger terminal, was supposed to be a marvelous old building of unique architecture. Although the hobo scuttle was that the hippies hung out there and frequently clashed with their Latino neighbors to the south, I figured I could pass through safely in daylight hours and check it out.

More importantly, though, I wanted to visit the Margaret "Molly" Brown house that was less than a mile from Union Station. It, too, wasn't in a great neighborhood, but I couldn't pass up the home of the Titanic survivor and first woman to run for Congress. She was also the subject of my ninth-grade essay on historical figures. On the day we got our papers back, Mrs. Swartz pulled me aside.

"Tink, how did you come to choose Molly Brown for your essay?"

"I was looking for a woman pioneer who stood up for women. Someone important, but not a history book-obvious person."

"Well, I wanted to thank you. It was refreshing to have a new character. And it was very well written. I just wanted you to know that I noticed and appreciated it."

So the Molly Brown house became a 'must-visit' stop on this journey.

The open door on my boxcar was on the left, which was good. I kept watching for landmarks I had memorized and was starting to think maybe I was completely lost when we crawled by the Overland Park Golf Course. I knew where we were. There was a big train yard ahead with a dozen tracks. Whether I stayed on the train or not depended on which track we took. Union Station was to the northeast. If we stayed on one of the rightmost tracks, we would go under Interstate 70 and curve to the right.

In a few minutes we entered the yard. As far as I could tell, we were staying well to the right. I considered popping my head out of a hatch, but I didn't want to take the time to get it open, get up and down, and all of that when I might have to make a quick exit decision. Fortunately, luck was with me today. We crossed 13th Street, and I could see other tracks to the west splitting off. We were going right. In a moment we passed under I-70 and curved sharply right.

Shouldering my pack, I took a quick look out the door ahead of us. There were some track turns before we got to Union Station. I wanted to get off before we got there, but not too soon. I waited for the locomotive to navigate the first turn, and then the second.

As I was about to slide out the door, I caught motion to my left behind the train. Two men in dark clothes slipped out of a boxcar two behind me. They rolled to a landing and stood up, and then loped across the other two tracks before disappearing into the weeds.

They looked like the guys from the store in Pueblo. I pulled back from the door, not wanting them to see me. But I had to get off before we got too close to the station, or I'd be spotted for sure. Maybe chased. Or worse.

I slid out the door, running as my feet touched the ground. And I kept running, angling back away from the station, hopping over the other two tracks rail-by-rail, until I slid under a flatcar sitting on the spur next to the fence. For the next twenty minutes I lay motionless, watching all around me for anyone approaching. I kept a hand on the rail so I could feel the vibration if they hooked this hideout flatcar to another train. Although it was the last car on the spur and it would just pass over me if I laid flat, I didn't want to take any unnecessary chances.

Down the track, I could see the station and a passenger train idling next to it. A whistle blew and a deep rumble of the locomotive's accelerating diesel carried down the track. Nine passenger cars swept by with what looked like a dining car caboose. I wondered where those silhouetted people in the windows were going. They'd chosen train over airplane or car. I ticked off a long list of possible reasons like cost, comfort, and time. Maybe there were ten variables they evaluated. But each variable wasn't binary, yes or no. They were all weighted, and weighted differently by each person. And there were personal thresholds for some variables, like it can't cost more than fifty dollars. Those threw off all the combinatoric calculations. Nevertheless, each person, whether they consciously knew it or not, had somehow whittled more than 3.6

million variable combinations into their decision to buy a train ticket.

Those were simple decisions. In space, things got more difficult. The number of variables increased. The timeliness of the decision could mean life or death. The human mind, or at least one trained for it, could make those decisions and make them correctly. As Neil Armstrong began the landing on the moon, he had to take over from the computer and personally fly their spaceship to safety. He processed hundreds of variables instantly and piloted the craft away from the sure disaster the computer had chosen. And after a 250,000-mile journey, he landed with fifteen seconds of descent fuel left.

I wanted to do that.

I rolled out from under the flatcar on the fence side. After climbing the fence, I made my way along a building until I came to an alley. It led out to a street that I followed eastward. In a few minutes I navigated my way to Union Station. I felt like I was visiting an old friend because I'd spent quite a bit of time researching this building. I wasn't sure why I was so fascinated by it, but I'd done my homework. It was a beautiful building on Wynkoop Street, built in 1914 from carved granite in the Beaux-Arts style. I wandered inside and marveled at the architecture and ornate details of the construction.

Thirty minutes later, I found myself sitting on a bench studying the walls and ceiling of the central rotunda. My backpack lay at my feet with one strap looped around my leg. I wasn't about to let my fascination distract me so much that my backpack got snagged.

People wandered through, mostly in a rush to get from one train to another. But it wasn't particularly crowded. The news said rail travel had plummeted as more and more people chose to travel by their own car on the Interstate highways or, increasingly, by airplane.

I sensed someone sit down on my bench. I'd watched several people come and go on the various benches. A few had shared my bench for a while. One was an elderly woman who seemed to be catching her breath before she picked up her petite plaid suitcase and shuffled away.

The person who'd just sat down sucked on a straw in their now-empty drink, making that awful screech that drove me crazy. I glanced toward them, noticing it was a young guy with a silly grin on his face. I shifted my gaze to my pack, thinking I'd better move on before this guy started trying to talk to me. I unhitched the backpack strap from my leg.

"Leaving so soon?" said the guy.

Something about the voice sounded familiar but I wasn't about to engage with a stranger when I didn't have to. I slung my pack over my shoulder and turned away.

"Tink. It's me."

I twisted around and looked at the grinning guy sitting on the bench. He pulled his hat off and then I recognized him. Sam. "Hello, Sam."

"Wow. I thought you'd be happy to see me."

"I am. But sneaking up on me is kind of creepy." Sam had seemed like a normal kind of guy and I'd enjoyed my short time with him. But the hair on the back of my neck was standing up. Part of me wanted to run.

The grin disappeared. He stood. "I'm sorry, Tink. Maybe it was kinda creepy. Probably childish and immature. I'm not very good at talking to women."

My heart raced. Was my man-masquerade that bad? My run instinct kicked in again. But I was curious about what gave me away.

"My man-masquerade isn't working?"

"Mostly it does. I thought you were a guy when we were on the train before. Later, when I was thinking about you, I realized you were a woman."

"Why?"

"Nothing specific. But talking to you doesn't seem guy-like. It's more angry woman."

"I meant why were you thinking about me?"

"I don't know." His face flushed.

"That's a juvenile answer. Very teenager."

He fumbled with his hat in his hands. "I guess I liked you. Felt like we had a connection. After I realized you were a woman, I was glad I hugged you before we went our separate ways."

"Do you hug a lot of random strangers?"

"I don't hug much of anybody."

I had a swirl of thoughts going on in my head, a combination of warnings, curiosity, and unfamiliar attraction to this guy. My subconscious brain seemed to sort it all out before I did because I stepped towards Sam and wrapped my arms around him. He was stiff for a moment, then I felt him relax and put his arms around me.

He whispered into my ear. "You're full of surprises." I stood there for a moment examining the sensations caused by his breath in my ear. Susie came to mind, and I immediately shut those thoughts down. I'd never had a boyfriend, or even a date. Or a kiss. At least not from a guy. At fourteen, just before Daddy died, Susie instructed me on kissing techniques. It had been…wait, why was I thinking about this. I wasn't going to kiss Sam.

I stepped back and looked at him. "I'm not the only one with surprises."

He grinned again. "There's a sit-down restaurant across the street. How about I buy you lunch."

It was my turn to grin.

CHAPTER 32

We slept in an empty boxcar that night. It was probably midnight before we stopped talking and went to sleep. I think it was because neither of us had friends and we found talking to each other about our lives was an elixir for our wounds. Sam had his hell in Vietnam. I had mine in an Ohio cornfield. I had stumbled into someone else plagued by self-imposed penitence.

The next day, Sam showed me his rented locker in the train station. We stashed our packs there for the day. Instead of looking like the vagrants we were, we now passed for a couple of college students. I'd stopped wearing my hat pulled down over my ears and didn't try to maintain my man-masquerade.

After a real sit-down breakfast, we visited the Molly Brown house. I knew a group of concerned citizens had recently formed Historic Denver and were attempting to restore the house and turn it into a museum. When we found it on Pennsylvania Street there was a knot of people chatting on the sidewalk in front. We hung back trying to figure out what was going on. After a few minutes, a young lady in the group climbed up a couple of steps towards the house and turned to face the group of ten or so people. She clapped her hands. "Okay, everyone, I'm Pam Mahonchak. Thank you for coming. I'm so appreciative of you members taking the time for this inaugural tour of the Molly Brown House Museum. Let's get started and please ask questions as we go along." She waved a pad of paper in the air. "I'm taking notes so we can improve for our first paying tours this weekend."

Sam grinned at me. Even though I'd been with him for the last twenty-four hours, those wolf-like eyes were continually a little unsettling.

"Guess you couldn't have picked a better time to visit."

"Why? She said they're not open for tours until the weekend."

He took my arm and started walking towards the group. "This way, madam. The tour is just starting now."

I would never have even thought about crashing this tour group. Sam, I was learning, didn't always follow the rules. I could see why, as he'd told me he'd been in lots of trouble during his teen years.

We fell in behind the group of mostly older adults. No one seemed surprised that we were tagging along. Sam even asked Pam several questions along the way.

A couple of hours later, as the tour ended and the group was dispersing on the sidewalk, an older lady approached us.

"I don't believe I've met you two." She stuck her hand out towards Sam. "I'm Pam's mother."

He shook it. "I'm Sam Forbes. This is my friend, Tink."

"Pleased to meet you, Mrs. Mahonchak," I said.

"Are you two members of Historic Denver?"

"No, ma'am. We just came by because I wrote a paper on Molly Brown and her work for women's rights. Since I was in Denver, I couldn't pass up an opportunity to see where she once lived."

"Oh, I'm so glad you joined us. What did you think?"

"There's still a lot of work to do, but I can see where it's going. And Pam had so many fascinating stories. I'll bet this will be enormously popular. And I'm so glad your group honors such an important lady."

Mrs. Mahonchak grabbed my hand and squeezed it. "Aren't you the kindest, dear." She looked towards the house for a moment, and then back at me. "You're from out of town, then."

Sam said, "Yes, ma'am."

She glanced at him, and then back at me. "Have you seen much of Denver?"

I said, "No, we just got here yesterday."

"Have you plans for this evening?"

I glanced at Sam. "No. Nothing in particular."

She opened her purse and fished around in there for a moment. When she pulled her hand out, she had a small envelope. She handed it to me. "Maybe you can use these. They're tickets to *The Unsinkable Molly Brown* at the Aladdin, downtown. It's on Colfax. The story's not accurate, but it's a fun show."

Pam rushed down the steps. "Mother. We need to go or we'll be late."

Mrs. Mahonchak said, "It was so nice meeting you two young people. I hope you'll enjoy the show and see the sights of our wonderful city."

Sam and I stood there for a moment while Pam and Mrs. Mahonchak climbed into a yellow Cadillac parked curbside and drove off.

Sam said, "Tink, would you like to go to the theater with me tonight?"

I put the envelope in my pocket. "I'll pay for the tickets if you'll buy dinner."

"My pleasure."

#####

We slept in an empty boxcar again that night. At first, we chatted about the play, its music, and the story.

"She reminded me of you," he said.

"Who did?"

"Molly Brown."

"You think I'm looking for a rich husband?"

"No, not that. But you're on a mission. You have a goal and you're going after it."

"I can't sing."

"You've got something better. You're resilient."

"Now you're comparing me to a tardigrade?"

"A what?"

"Tardigrade."

"Never heard of it."

"It's the most resilient animal in the world. Microscopic, eight-legged, been around for 600 million years. They're nicknamed 'water bears.'"

"I thought mountain goats were the most resilient."

"So I'm a mountain goat? Nice."

"Better than a parasite like that water bear."

"They aren't parasites."

"We had a lot of parasites in 'Nam. Mostly intestinal. From the local food."

"Did you bring any home?"

"Only the kind that eat the brains of wannabe astronauts."

Although I elbowed him, I couldn't help but giggle. He made me laugh. And that made me forget the awful part of my life for a moment.

We seemed to chat forever before falling asleep around midnight. Sam being there with me made me feel secure and safe. My sleep was deep, and I had no nightmares, or at least I had no recollection of having them when I awoke.

That afternoon, Sam said, "Let's walk up to the bus station and take a ride."

"To where?"

"Boulder."

"Is there something special there."

"I think so. I think you might like it. But I want to surprise you."

I didn't generally like surprises. Most of them in my life had been awful. But I liked Sam and trusted him. Besides, Boulder was a college town, so I knew there had to be a lot there to entertain the students.

After a late afternoon bus ride, we arrived in Boulder. As we walked through drizzling rain down 13th Street, Sam took my hand. It was warm and calloused, like mine. I felt flushed holding his hand. It was almost like holding on to a live electric wire. I glanced at him. With those eyes, I felt like I was holding hands with a wolf. But he was a kind, gentle wolf, or at least he had been with me.

The building we approached had a flat roof extending over the sidewalk and some outdoor seating. It was a bar named Tulagi. Sam pulled me under the roof, out of the rain. We stood in a short line to get in. Since they served 3.2% beer, at eighteen I was allowed in and got a red stamp on my hand. Sam got a green stamp.

I asked, "How old are you?"

"Twenty-two. You?"

"Eighteen. Going on forty."

He nodded. "Different parts of us age at different rates. My body is twenty-two, but I think I'm a lot older in some ways. I guess war does that to you. If you survive."

"I know what you mean. I've been running our farm since I was fourteen. I know way more than I should in a lot of ways. It was a war of a different sort."

"Maybe not so different in the important ways. Seems like they both do things to your head. Makes you see the world differently."

"I used to know who I was and where I was going. Now…I spend a lot of time thinking about who I am, who I could be, and who I should be."

He squeezed my hand. "Never heard it put like that, but tonight, at least, let's just relax and enjoy some live music."

We found a small table near the side wall in the front. It wasn't a great view of the stage but people on the parquet dance floor wouldn't block our view. An emergency door in the side wall behind us seemed to be a kind of stage door, with guys carrying in lots of equipment and disappearing backstage. The stage was concealed by a drooping gray curtain.

Sam ordered drinks and then leaned in next to my ear. "I know it's kind of loud in here now, but once the band starts playing, it will be too loud to talk."

I leaned into his ear. He smelled of Irish Spring soap, the kind everyone in my family used. A twinge of homesickness plucked at my heart. "Do you come here often?"

"I try to when I pass through Denver. Several army buddies go to school here and in Colorado Springs. Tulagi has very cool bands. Some big names you'd recognize."

"Why would they come to this little bar in Boulder?"

"Caribou Ranch recording studio. Up in Nederland. It's got some new high tech recording equipment that other studios don't have. At least not yet."

"Who's the band tonight?"

"I'm not sure, but I heard a rumor. I want to see if you recognize them. Kind of a surprise."

"I do well on tests."

He looked at me for a minute. "I bet you do."

Our heads were only inches apart. I thought he might kiss me. It was suddenly hot in here and my mouth was dry. I licked my lips and Sam's gaze flicked to them.

The drinks arrived and Sam paid the waitress. I took a sip of beer. The best thing I could say about it was it was cold. But it tasted like beer, as close to a vomit taste as I could imagine.

Sam took a swig from his frothy glass. A little bit of foam stuck to his moustache. He smiled at me, and my stomach muscles seemed to tingle.

He took another drink. I stared at the foam on his moustache. Goosebumps popped up on my arms. I grabbed his elbow and pulled him toward me, putting my mouth next to his ear. "That foam in your moustache is giving me goosebumps."

"Why?"

I glanced at it again. "I, um, don't know. But it makes me, want to, kinda, um, wipe it off."

He wiped a napkin across his mouth, clearing the foam. "Sorry if it grosses you out."

"No, it's not that. I like it." It was definitely getting hot in here. And I was flirting with a guy, something I never did. But I felt safe with Sam. Maybe because he was older than the high school boys who spent most of their time drooling over one girl or another. I thought of Susie and all she'd ever told me about boys and sex. My brain seemed sluggish. I couldn't focus on what Susie had told me. I just kept staring at Sam's moustache.

He took another sip. This time there was even more foam on his moustache. He grinned at me.

I pulled him toward me, but this time he turned his head to face me. I leaned in and wiped the foam with my finger, and then licked the foam off my finger. It was salty and caramel flavored at the same time.

"What is that beer?"

"Schlitz Malt Liquor."

"I can taste caramel. And it's sweet."

"Like me?"

I eyed him for a moment. He really was kinda sweet. And those were the kind Susie said were the most dangerous. At least you could count on a bad boy to be bad. They were consistent. But sweet boys broke your heart because you fell in love with them.

"I don't know. Do you think you're sweet?"

"Sometimes. How about you?"

"Me? I'm…" What was I? Probably not sweet. Focused. Driven. Screwed up. Some combination. "…on a mission."

"But tonight, the mission is on hold. Okay?"

I looked at him not knowing quite what to say. My mission was never on hold. It was always there. The path, though, could wander a bit.

"Just relax and have fun." He smiled and sipped again, this time I was sure he purposely got even more foam on his moustache. I couldn't resist. I leaned in and tasted the foam with the tip of my tongue. His moustache hair tickled. I licked it again, getting a full taste. Jeez, it was hot in here. I needed some air. But Sam's lips found mine and we kissed.

He tasted of caramel and beer, like the foam on his moustache. Less salty, but it was delightful. His lips were warm and soft, too. Pleasant twinges rippled through my lower belly.

Someone opened the door behind us, and cool air washed in. I leaned away from Sam, trying to take full advantage of the breeze. My armpits were moist, if not downright wet. My already-awake nipples jumped to attention. My confused brain finally worked out that I was turned on by Sam and my body was responding. I wanted to kiss him again, but I tucked my hands under my legs and smiled. I was in quicksand and had no idea how to navigate. Maybe he thought I was a naïve young girl, unlike the many women he'd surely been with. I pursed my lips. He'd be right. It was the first time I'd ever kissed a boy. Or a man. Sam was definitely a man.

Someone began testing the drum set backstage, thumping the bass, rapping on the snare, and banging on others. A couple of guitars tuned up. Someone said "Test" several times into a microphone. And then the drum and a couple of guitars started playing. It was a familiar tune I'd heard on the radio, but I didn't know its name. Nor the name of the band.

The curtains pulled back revealing five guys. Drummer, guitarist, bassist, and keyboard player. The fifth guy in the center without an instrument was their singer. The music started and everyone jammed the dance floor. Sam and I rose to our feet and started dancing at our table where we had a great view of the group. I noticed immediately that the singer had particularly big lips. He strutted around the stage during the intro, and then began singing. The song was familiar. I couldn't name it until he got to the fifth or sixth line: "Jumpin' Jack Flash."

Oh my God! The Rolling Stones. And I was less than fifty feet from Mick Jagger. It was like being lifted onto a magic carpet and taken for a two-hour ride. I had never seen a real, live legend before. I knew, then and there, that I'd remember this night for the rest of my life.

They played for two hours. I'd never heard most of the songs. After the second or third song, Mick Jagger explained that they were in town to record at a nearby studio. This performance was a warm-up for recording their new material. Often, they had conversations between songs, and a couple of times they started playing and then stopped. After a little discussion, they started up again and finished the song. Most of the songs were their traditional rock and roll sounds. We danced to all of them.

The next to last song was named "Angie." It started out with an acoustic guitar, then Mick started singing. Sam took my hand, and we began slow-dancing. Other than Bobby and Susie, I'd never slow-danced with anyone before. But Sam seemed to know what he was doing. After the first verse, he pulled me close. It really was hot in here and we had danced a lot. Our clothes were wet from sweat. His wet hair stuck to his neck and shirt. When he put his hand on my back, I could feel that my top was wet clear through.

It wasn't the kind of romantic scene I had ever imagined. Mick Jagger was right there singing to us—in person. We were both soaked. But we were swaying in an embrace that allowed me to feel every curve in Sam's body. I'm sure he felt mine too. In a few moments I could feel his erect penis pushing against my hip every time we swayed to the left. I pulled him closer and closed my eyes, wondering if this was really happening or if I was dreaming.

The song ended. "We've got one more song I think you'll know. Thank you for being here tonight."

The band launched into "Satisfaction." The lyrics rang in my head, made me think about what I couldn't get. It wasn't satisfaction. Maybe it was redemption. Did the Stones have a song about that?

Sam and I just stood there, hand-in-hand, swaying to the tune. I was exhausted. Soaked. Amazed. And then the thought exploded in my brain—I was happy. I hadn't been happy in a long time. Since before Daddy died. But here it was, and I greeted it like a long-lost friend.

I snuck a sidelong glance at Sam. He was smiling from ear to ear. He looked happy, too. He was a special man who'd given me a gift, part of him, part of his happiness. Another moment I'd remember for the rest of my life.

CHAPTER 33

The rain had stopped, but it was still cloudy and looking like more rain might be on the way. The temperature had dropped, too. It was downright cold now, particularly in these damp clothes.

We walked back down 13th Street towards the bus stop, chatting endlessly about what we'd just witnessed. Sam agreed that it was a memorable night.

"But the memories weren't just the Rolling Stones," he said.

"Yeah, I almost fainted when they walked right by us on their way out."

Sam laughed. "Yeah, that was pretty cool, too."

"Too?"

"I was talking about you. Being with you, Tink. That made it even more special."

I hated compliments. They made me uncomfortable, like now I was indebted to this person. "Thanks." But I knew he was right. Being there with Sam, sharing that experience with him, made it so much more special. "Thank you for taking me."

I'd switched to Coke after Sam figured out that I didn't like beer. We had to walk across campus about a mile to the bus station. And I had to pee. Soon. Before we got to the bus station.

"I have to pee."

"The bus station has restrooms."

We were at a point where Boulder Creek went under Arapahoe Avenue. Some bushes and trees lined the stream.

I let go of Sam's hand. "Be right back." I made my way off the paved path towards the creek and found a small opening between some bushes. In two minutes, I was back. Sam pointed at a water fountain at the corner of a tennis court.

"Useful?"

"Thanks." I washed my hands and took a couple of gulps.

Sam came over and did the same. He took my wet hand in his and glanced at his watch. "We better run. Bus leaves in ten minutes."

Fortunately, Sam had taken this route before and knew which station was ours, so we didn't need to go into the terminal to sort out our bus. We flashed our return stubs to the driver and found open seats halfway back. I curled up in Sam's arms with my head on his chest. I was asleep before the bus pulled out.

Forty minutes later, Sam woke me and we filed off the bus. The train station was across the street from the bus terminal. We went into the station and retrieved our backpacks from the locker.

I shouldered my pack. "You headed out tomorrow?"

"Yeah. Planned to. You?"

"Yeah. I still have three weeks to get to Missoula. Shouldn't be a problem."

We stood there for a minute or so, awkward silence enveloping us. Then it started to rain. Heavy rain. Lightning flashed and thunder boomed nearby. The night sky lit up. We scampered back under the station's platform overhang.

Sam set his pack down. "We need a dry place to sleep."

I jerked a thumb towards the trains. "Boxcar."

"You see any?"

I looked through the rain towards the tracks. There weren't that many cars standing in the yard. The boxcars were all closed. I didn't know what else to say. I didn't have any other ideas.

"I have a tent. Let me go get it."

I pulled my rain poncho out of a pocket on my pack and pulled it on. I stood with the poncho covering his pack, protecting it from rain. It was really coming down now, but it was just splash and mist hitting me under the roof ledge.

In a few minutes he came out carrying another pack.

"Where'd you get that?"

"I have another long-term locker with some supplies and this. For emergencies."

"Convenient. Why Denver?"

"I have them in six cities. Just in case. Figure if I never go back, it's like purchasing insurance. The cost of doing business."

"Clever."

"Thanks. You're welcome to share my tent."

I nodded.

He led me to a grassy area surrounded by small pine trees. The needles from the trees made the ground soft.

Sam handed me a sleeping bag. "Keep this dry while I set up the tent."

I pulled it under my poncho. He set up the tent in less than a minute. It was a large puptent, but it had an external frame I'd never seen.

"Where'd you get that tent?"

"Japan."

"Interesting. External frame. I've never seen one like that."

"It's for mountain climbing. Lightweight. Easy up and down."

He held the flap. "Ladies first."

I tossed the sleeping bag inside and shrugged out of my poncho. I set my pack down outside the tent door next to Sam's and tucked my poncho over both to keep them dry. Then I crawled inside.

It was pitch black, but Sam had a little flashlight he used to find the sleeping bag zipper. He unzipped the bag and started removing his boots. I followed his lead.

"You use your tents often?"

"This the second time."

"Really."

"Yeah. This one's been here for nearly a year. I slept in it once before putting it in the locker. Wanted to make sure it worked."

"With a woman?"

"What?"

"Did you test it out with a woman?"

"No. Why would you think that?"

"I'm just kidding." Or was I? I wasn't sure.

He turned off the light. There was the sound of a zipper and some rustling noises. He was taking his pants off. My chest tightened. Part of me wanted to run out of the tent and find a boxcar. I wrestled that around in my head for minute and decided I needed to start acting like a woman instead of a high school teenager.

"Sam."

He turned on the flashlight, holding it under his chin so the light made his face look like a creepy ghoul. In a raspy deep voice, he said, "Yeeeessss?"

I laughed and slapped his arm. "Stop. I want to be serious."

He gave a ghoulish laugh and turned off the light.

I felt his hand find my shoulder, and then it was up in my hair. His lips found mine and he kissed me. I felt muscles tingle all the way to my vagina.

I reached out a hand and found his bare chest, pushing him back a little. The hair on his chest tickled my hand. Muscles twitched.

"Sam, I've never done this before."

"Done what?"

"Had sex."

"Okay."

"I know it's the era of free love and everybody screws everybody these days, but I've been too busy running a farm, keeping my family together, trying to make a living for all of us."

His hand stroked my hair. "It's okay, Tink."

"I know guys call me a prude, but I've never been attracted to anyone. You're…you're the first guy I've ever kissed and I'm eighteen years old. That's how much experience I've had with guys."

He kept stroking my hair. "It's okay, Tink. Now's not the time. Maybe I'm not the right guy."

"Wait. Are you saying you don't want to have sex with me?"

He laughed. I swatted his hand away from my head. "No. I'm not saying that. I'm saying we're not ready. Maybe we will be ready someday. But not now. We're passing in the night, so to speak."

"It's not that I don't want to have sex, it's just that…"

He clamped his hand over my mouth. "No more talking." He took his hand away. "I'm going to lie down now and get some sleep. You should do the same."

"What are you wearing?"

"What?"

"What clothes do you still have on?"

"My boxers. Why?"

"I just didn't want to run into, you know, any surprises."

He laughed. "Are you done talking?'

"Yes."

"Goodnight, Tink."

"No kiss?"

He sighed.

"Never mind. If it's that much effort, just go to sleep."

"Are you always like this? It's like a pinball bouncing from one thing to another since we got into this tent."

He was right. This was all new to me. Emotions raged. I couldn't focus, and parts of my body were giving me new signals I had no idea how to process. I thought about ripping his boxers off and having sex just to get it over with. Maybe that would be like being thrown into a pool and you sink or swim. But I'd never do that to my kids.

"Sorry." I unzipped my pants and pulled them off.

"You can roll them up to make a pillow."

"I planned to use your arm for that."

He was silent.

"Sam."

"I'm right here."

"I have small breasts. I'm downright flat-chested. My brother's girlfriend Janet said I could be another Twiggy."

"Okay."

"I don't own a bra. Have never worn one."

"Okay."

"Did you see *Love Story*? It's kinda like Ali MacGraw."

"Okay."

"My nipples are…"

"Tink!"

I clamped my hand over my own mouth. Why was I such a motormouth? I knew it was nerves. I knew that. What kind of astronaut would I make if I got nervous. The voice in my head had an answer: the kind that gets people killed.

I lay down and scooted up next to Sam. He pulled the sleeping bag over us and wrapped an arm around me. Susie called this spooning. I thought it was more like sleeping with fire because we had so much skin touching each other. I was tingling in a lot of places, but I was also dead tired. I shifted on the pine needles and tried to get closer to Sam. We were both on our right sides with his left arm draped over me. I found his hand with mine and pulled it to my chest.

As I drifted off to sleep, I wondered if my smile was giving off enough light to illuminate the tent. It had been a wonderful day. And it ended with me curled up half-naked next to a nice guy who was also half-naked. Maybe this was a perfect day. At least it was the best one in a long, long time.

CHAPTER 34

Although the movement of train cars went on all night, the pace picked up as daylight approached. A loud bang of several cars being pushed into a train nearby woke me. Sam still had his arm draped over me. His hand now cupped my left breast. I almost giggled. He probably didn't even know. Or maybe he did know. While I was asleep, he could have been fondling my breasts.

He shifted a little. I could feel his erect penis against my butt. Susie told me most guys woke up like that. But she didn't know if that was from their dreams or what caused it. Good to know Sam was normal.

I raised his hand and arm and started to roll away.

He muttered, "Good morning."

"Good morning. You sleep okay?" It was getting lighter.

"Um-hum. You?"

"Yup." I pulled on my pants.

"Are you as chatty in the morning as you are before you go to sleep?"

"Maybe."

He grabbed me and wrapped his arms around me, tickling my ribs. I wanted to scream, but I knew better here. Someone might hear us and who knows where that might go.

I grabbed his arm and used my wrestling training to pin his arm behind him. Pretty soon I was sitting on top of him, and he was flat on his back with both arms held over his head.

"I give up. You win."

I let go of his arms, and then leaned down and kissed him. "Did you let me win?"

"Maybe."

I slugged him in the chest. Then I noticed the dark curly hair that covered it. I ran my hand through it. Now-familiar tingles twitched. I rolled off. "We better get going."

"I would argue, but I have to pee." He began pulling on his pants.

That was another thing Susie told me. They always have to pee when they wake up. "If you want morning sex, you better get it while their pecker is ready. If you wait for them to pee, it'll be noon before they get it up again." She was such a tramp. And such a storehouse of information about the mysterious world of men and sex.

###

Sam slung his backpack over one shoulder. "Your pack is an interesting color."

"It only came in orange, but I needed it to be more of a neutral color. I used my friend Susie's hair dye. Came out a mottled brown, I think."

"We called it camouflage in 'Nam."

I flipped the top open and loaded my stuff.

"What are those numbers under the top flap?"

"I wrote my mom's phone number on it. Not sure anyone who stole it would ever call, but you never know." I opened the main part of the pack. "And we didn't dye the inside. I didn't think that was necessary."

"Yeah, I can see that."

"Yours looks pretty sturdy with the leather straps."

"It's seen a lot of miles. I think most see it as beat up. No use stealing this old thing." He pulled the pack onto both shoulders. "You heading north?"

I nodded.

"Let me see if I can find the track numbers for you." He walked toward the terminal, and I followed along behind. While he was waiting in line, I pulled out a postcard, scribbled a hello to Momma, and told her I met a nice guy named Sam on my journey. Then I dropped it in a blue mailbox.

Sam walked up to a ticket agent window and chatted for a minute. Shortly, he came back with some scribbles on a piece of paper.

"Track seventy-two goes north. Sixty-eight, too, but not for a couple of hours."

"How does that lady know that?"

"They get a daily printout of the yard schedule. Sometimes it changes, but it's mostly right. You have to sweet-talk the agent, though. Sometimes they won't tell you."

"Where are you headed?"

"Going to Chicago to visit my sister. I heard she had a baby a few months ago. My nephew."

We stood there awkwardly for a few moments.

"Tink, I hope I'll see you again."

"Me, too."

"You remember Momma's phone number?"

"Yeah. You better get going before you miss your ride. It's supposed to pull out in a couple of minutes."

We hugged and I kissed him on the cheek. "Thanks, Sam. I had a great time with you."

He nodded. I turned on my heel and walked out the door.

By now I'd figured out how to navigate track numbers. It was a weird system that was mostly based on the main track or tracks coming into a railyard. Seventy-two and sixty-eight were next to each other. I looked up and down for an open boxcar. There were only forty or so cars in these trains, probably because we were in mountains. Most of the cars were tankers, but the last four or five were boxcars. The next to last one had an open door on the right side. I poked my head in and looked around. It was empty. I tossed my pack inside and climbed up.

The train began to move almost immediately. I wasn't sleepy, so I pulled out my notebook and chronicled the last twenty-four hours with Sam.

CHAPTER 35

The train was slower than most. Maybe thirty miles per hour. There were lots of winding areas and switchbacks. It took us four hours to reach Cheyenne. It was the biggest trainyard I'd been through. The roundhouse was huge and spit out locomotives like playing cards. I was so mesmerized by the size of the place that I was far inside the yard before I thought about getting off. Now I was trapped in the empty boxcar until it moved out on another train, or until I was caught.

I slunk back into the shadows and curled up as small as I could, awaiting my fate. One letdown might end up being my demise. After all I'd endured, I didn't want it to end this way.

But luck was on my side, or so I thought. Some jostling of cars in the train made me think they had added a second and third locomotive, and we were soon on our way northward. My failure hadn't cost me this time.

It was getting dark, just after 7:00 p.m. The train had picked up speed with the additional locomotives. We were doing fifty or more on the straight, flat stretches. And there were a lot of those.

I dozed off for a while and awoke as we were pulling into Casper. It also had a large trainyard, but not as big as Cheyenne. It was just after midnight and I decided to stay in the boxcar this time. Casper was a notoriously rough town and one I didn't want to navigate in the middle of the night. If I continued north, I'd be in Billings by morning and I'd resupply there.

I curled into the back corner in case anyone looked inside. But no one came. And after thirty minutes of jostling cars, we started moving again. I relaxed.

I had just decided to eat a snack and drink some water when I heard footsteps pounding on the roof. I curled back into the corner. There was some banging and scratching at the forward hatch, and then a faint light shone on the boxcar floor. I watched two faint shadows climb down the ladder into the car. The second one shut the hatch.

"Told you we didn't have long," said a raspy male voice.

"We made it, didn't we?" said a higher pitched-voiced man.

One of them turned on a flashlight and shone it around the inside. I pulled my hat lower on my head, knowing they'd find me. I pulled out my flashlight and pointed it their way.

"Who's there?" shouted the raspy voice.

"Nobody you need to worry about. Riding the rails like you."

"What's your name?"

"Don't need a name or any talk. Just want to be left alone." I turned off my flashlight.

They played their flashlight over me for a minute, and then turned it off. I heard them move to the corner by the ladder and begin whispering.

I figured they would leave me alone while it was dark. The map in my head said Sheridan was the next major city on this route. It would be getting light around the time we got there. If the train stopped there, I'd have to get off.

CHAPTER 36

Light flashed in my face. I'd dozed off sitting up, leaning into the corner of the boxcar. The light woke me. One of the men stood a few feet in front of me, shining their flashlight over me and my pack.

I jumped to my feet. "What do you want?"

The man jumped back, apparently startled at my sudden movement. Good. I wanted to intimidate him. There was a light glow from the open door, hinting at the coming sunrise. Buildings and lights slipped by. Either a small town or we were coming into Sheridan. More likely Sheridan, given the sun was coming up.

Raspy voice said, "Thought you might have somethin' for us to eat."

"Why would I share with you? I already let you ride my car."

"That so?" He laughed. "They's two of us and one of you."

In the dim light I saw the outline of the other man against the wall next to me. He wasn't more than six feet away.

In his high, whiney voice, he said, "We ain't lookin' for trouble, boy. But we're hungry. Thought you could help us out."

"Why should I? Looks like you're threatening me right now. Not a good way to make friends."

"Ain't no friends on the rails."

I probably couldn't handle these two together. In the growing light, they looked skinny and…I suddenly realized these were the two from Pueblo. The ones who'd stolen from the store. Maybe they'd been following me. But that made no sense. I certainly wasn't an obvious target. Unless they figured out I wasn't a boy.

I broke out in a cold sweat. This was too much for coincidence. They *had* been following me. And that was the only reason I could think of. My knees were shaking. This was what everyone warned me about. And they had me cornered, isolated, with no chance of anyone hearing or helping.

I tamped down my panic and took a deep breath. I wouldn't go down without a fight. At least one of these guys was going to have some broken bones before this day was done.

The train whistle sounded. Both glanced out the door. We were in a city, but not slowing. I picked up my pack.

Raspy voice said, "Going somewhere?"

"Just digging out some breakfast. Maybe I have some spare."

The guy in front of me licked his lips and stared at my pack.

I fished around and found a couple Pop-Tarts. I tossed one to the man in front of me. He caught it and turned off his flashlight. It was dim inside, but still light enough to make out their movements and faces. They were downright scrawny with scruffy beards, greasy hair, and ragged clothes. Their beady eyes never left me.

I tossed the second Pop-Tart to the other guy. He ripped open the package and began wolfing it down.

I edged a little closer to the door. The one in front of me moved with me. "Don't get no ideas. We gotta get some use out of this here goose 'fore it gets away."

"Shut up, Ray," hissed the other guy. He pointed at me. "Why don't you sit back down, Bo-ette."

Bo-ette. A female hobo. They knew. My heart raced. I had to fight to hold back tears. I thought of Daddy in the Gleaner, his unseeing eyes staring at me. I'd been through worse, no matter how this turned out. But these two weren't going to come out unscathed. My biggest strength was my brain. I could outsmart them. I also had a surprise on my side—I could fight.

I slid to the floor. Best to not betray my surprise until I had a good opportunity.

Raspy voice said, "How 'bout you kick that backpack over here?"

"Come and get it."

"Yeah, you'd like that. We'll get it soon enough."

I pulled the backpack toward me and found the pocket with Daddy's knife. Right now, I was damn glad Momma had given it to me. At the time I thought it wasn't necessary. Even silly. I could take care of myself. But now, my hand was sweating around its handle, and I was counting on it to shift the odds in this little arena.

We rode on like this for twenty minutes, through downtown Sheridan, and then fewer and fewer buildings as we moved out of the city. The sun was up, and we were nearly at full light inside the boxcar. I could see an ugly scar on Raspy voice's neck. He was no stranger to knife fights. That's probably what gave him his voice. His buddy Ray, whom I now thought of as Squeaky voice, would be my target if I got the chance. Besides, he was the one between me and the door. He reminded me of Shaggy from that Scooby-Doo cartoon. He even had a scruffy goatee.

The train whistle sounded again. I popped the knife blade, its click hidden by the whistle. But the whistle must have been some kind of pre-arranged signal for these guys. They rushed me.

I shoved my backpack at Raspy, knocking him over. He grabbed my pack and rolled away. Ray kept coming, aiming to tackle me. I let him get close, and then side-stepped, grabbed his collar, and slammed his head into the wall. He crashed to the floor, and I took off for the door. But Raspy was ahead of me. He'd already dropped the backpack and covered Ray's move, cutting off my exit. Instead of being in a corner, I was now on a flat wall with one guy on each side of me. But I hadn't revealed the knife yet. I could have stuck it in Ray's back, slicing a kidney, but I wasn't ready to kill these guys. Yet.

I'd been thinking about the pack and all that was in it. The only thing of irreplaceable value were my journal notebooks. My cash was in my pants. The bulk of my money in the pack was traveler's checks which they couldn't cash.

I mentally slapped myself. Forget the money. Forget the backpack. These guys might kill me. Forfeit the backpack and get away. Now. "Look, you can have the pack. I'll just walk out the door and be gone. No one will ever know. There's food, water, and several hundred dollars in there."

Ray laughed. "You wanna spoil the party, Bo-ette? We ain't had our fun yet. I got just the thing for you, too."

I held the knife in front of me. "I've got just the right tool to cut it off, too."

Ray's grin vanished.

Raspy said, "Put the knife down, or we'll use it to toss you, piece by piece, out this door. After we have our party."

I took a step towards Raspy, hoping Ray would make his move as I turned my back. Raspy stepped back and, sure enough, Ray came lunging at me. Time seemed to slow as I twisted and squatted to the floor. Ray overshot, and I came up under him driving both legs as hard as I could, tossing him towards Raspy.

I ran for the door and, in mid-leap, felt a vise grip grab my wrist. Raspy whirled me around, right in front of the door. His other fist lashed out and slammed into my forehead. But at the same time, my other arm drove the knife into his gut, slashing as best I could. He let go and I tumbled backwards—out the door.

The physics of jumping out the door of a train moving at fifty miles per hour said you better land smoothly on both feet and roll to a stop on smooth ground. Any variation could cause significant injuries, even death. I'd studied this problem for a couple of years, even doing experiments from the farm wagon with Bobby driving. I didn't have my backpack, so my body weight was all that entered the problem. The loss of my backpack was an issue I'd worry about later, after I landed without killing myself. The second part of the problem was what part of your body landed first and how you might dissipate the momentum from the train. Landing on your feet and rolling was the best option, but that was unlikely, given how I had left the train. I was flying backwards through the air and likely to land on my head. That wouldn't do, so I tucked my head to my chest and folded both arms over my head, making me as much of a ball as possible. The last part of the problem is what kind of terrain you land on. Flat grass is best. The typical sloped gravel of most rail rights-of-way aren't very forgiving, but they're survivable. The worst case is hard objects that damage your body and prevent you from dissipating the momentum. Large boulders, trees, or in this case, a fence post, are particularly troublesome.

My upper body was rolled together with my hands and arms wrapped around my head when I hit the post. My shins took the brunt of the crash, and I ricocheted off the post onto weeds and grass, rolling like a ball. In the moment, I thought it wasn't a bad landing. But my roll carried me over the eroded embankment into a rushing river.

CHAPTER 37

Although the water was running fast, I'd landed in a hairpin curve in the river where dirt eroded into the river during flooding and made this a muddy, shallow area. Only my lower body was under water, the current pulling at my boots. I rolled off my back and used my arms to drag myself onto the narrow strip of land between the water and the embankment. It wasn't more than eighteen inches wide. I lay there and took inventory, checking the condition of various body parts. My wrist, where Raspy voice had grabbed me, was aching, but I could move it and didn't think it was broken. I realized I still had my knife in the other hand. I should have dropped it so I didn't impale or cut myself in the fall. But here I was. I still had a weapon if I needed one. I folded it up and put it in my pants pocket.

I sat up and looked at my legs. My boots didn't seem to be pointing in quite the right direction, but I didn't feel any pain. Maybe shock was holding it at bay, or the frigid water had masked it. I pulled up my right pant leg. There was a giant bruise about halfway down my shin. And the bone was no longer in a straight line. It was clearly broken. My biology class came to mind. We had to get up in front of class and point to and name the major bones of Clyde, a full-sized skeleton. Everyone laughed about it. Some of the girls thought it was gross to touch Clyde. Mrs. Campbell, the biology teacher, pointed out that Clyde was made of plastic. He wasn't a real skeleton. Still, it was creepy moving his bones around.

Fibula and tibia. Those were the lower leg bones. The tibia was the shin bone, the one I'd broken. I moved my ankle a bit and it seemed to work reasonably well. My fibula was probably intact.

I pulled up my other pant leg. Same story. Two broken legs. I wouldn't be able to stand, let alone walk. My clothes were wet, and the east sun cast me in shadow next to the embankment. It wasn't cold enough to worry about hypothermia, but my teeth started to chatter, nonetheless.

Using my arms, I scooted myself six feet along the embankment to a couple of rocks. I took off my shirt and laid it out on the rocks. I knew I'd never get my boots or pants off, so I resigned myself to them staying wet. Maybe the afternoon sun would dry me out. But this strip of land was kept wet by the proximity to the river water.

The embankment was almost straight up. There was no way I could climb it and it was too tall to reach the top, even if I could stand. Which I couldn't.

I looked up and down the river, following the strip of land next to the embankment. Rocks at both ends where the hairpin straightened blocked any option of scooting out to higher ground. But I needed to get somewhere where I could be seen. This little strip next to the embankment was an island in the ocean. No one would ever find me here.

If I could find a decent branch maybe I could float down the river. But how long would that take before I could find some civilization where I could be rescued? The river water's temperature would suck the heat from my body and I'd go into hypothermia in an hour or so. Plus, without my legs, I might end up drowning before I could get from a branch to the shore.

I took inventory of what I had in my pockets. Knife, driver's license, two soggy candy bars, and some change. Plus, there was forty dollars in my shirt pocket. Traveler's checks and Fanny's hundred were in my pack.

I watched a few sticks float by in the river. If I had one long enough, I might be able to put my shirt on it and stick it up above the embankment. As far as I could tell, I was in the middle of nowhere. I listened to see if I could hear anything to indicate people were around.

There was a road not far away because in ten minutes I heard two cars go by. They were faint, but the noise of the river masked almost everything. The road had to be on the other side of the tracks. Even if I got up there, I wasn't sure I could drag myself over the tracks to the road. And there was sure to be another fence on the other side of the tracks. I didn't remember any fencing attached to the post I hit, though. Maybe the wire had rusted away long ago.

Still, how was I going to get up there. A ladder wouldn't work. I couldn't climb. But I could negotiate steps. If I had some.

I pulled out my knife and started digging out an area of the embankment about eighteen inches above me. If I could fashion a step where I could muscle myself up to sit on, maybe I could keep at it until I had enough steps to reach the top. I calculated that four would do it. From there, I'd be able to reach the top and pull myself over the edge. And I had plenty of time to work on it.

After an hour, I had carved out the first step and enough additional dirt above it to squeeze my torso in so I could work on the next step. I hand-walked my body around with my back to the embankment and got both elbows up on the step. Then I shifted around until I got my hands on the step and lifted myself up to sit on it. It worked for a minute, and then the step of dirt collapsed, and I was back where I started. If it had been heavy clay or even lots of rocks, it might have worked and supported my weight.

I rested and ate one of the candy bars. Both legs were starting to throb. If I died here, there'd never be a record of my journey. No one would ever know what happened to me. The next rain would wash my body down the river, just another piece of debris no one would ever recover. Even my journal was lost now. The hobos who attacked me would toss out the notebooks, or maybe burn them for a fire starter at some point. Everything in my pack was lost. Even the wrinkled picture of my family when we were happy.

A shadow drifted across the river water. I looked up to see a bird angling in for a landing on what looked like a sandbar upstream. It had long legs like a heron, but it was too far away to identify the species. I laughed at myself, at my brain trying to identify the bird. What was the point? I should have had more friends in school. I laughed again. More meant more than just Susie. Maybe Susie had it right all along. Her life was about relationships, people, emotions. I should have dated, had a boyfriend, gone to the prom. I should have kissed Sam more. I should have had sex with him when I had the chance.

A tear trickled down my cheek. I tried to flex both legs and pain shot through them. No pity-party for me. I was focused and knew where I was going. I was going to be an astronaut. I was going to the stars. I was going to use this brain to help advance mankind to reach out to the cosmos.

Or I was going to die on a tiny riverbank in Montana. But I was too smart to let that happen.

A noticed a new noise in the background. After straining to hear it over the river, I figured out it was a tractor. And it wasn't too far away. I waited twenty minutes for another car to go by on the highway. When it finally did, the tractor was still going, and it seemed closer than the car. The car noise seemed to be over my right shoulder. The tractor was over my left shoulder. It was on this side of the tracks. Whatever it was doing, it wouldn't last forever. I needed to get its attention.

I needed to get upstream, around the rocks. Without an embankment flanking the riverbank, I might be able to drag myself close enough for the tractor to see me. But there was no way to go upstream. I had no legs to kick.

I wondered about putting my legs back in the river for a while. The cold water might numb them again and even help reduce the inevitable swelling. But I was still in shade and shivering. I'd endure the pain for as long as necessary until the sun warmed me up. Besides, so far, the broken bones were closed. If I moved around and the bone poked through the skin, the risk of infection and the likelihood of losing the leg would skyrocket. Somehow, I needed to stay quiet and still get out of here.

Maybe it was shock or something else, but after sitting still for a few minutes, I dozed off. When I woke, the sun was shining on me. At least a couple of hours had passed. My shirt was nearly dry, so I put it back on. I'd come up with another idea about getting out of here. Since the embankment dirt was soft with few rocks, I might be able to carve a ramp up the dirt. I'd have to make it wider than necessary because of my legs. I would have to go up with my back to the embankment, which meant I couldn't dig behind me. So, I'd have to dig beside me, clear a section, move to that section, then dig on the other side until I was at the top. It would require me to move a lot of dirt.

I moved down to the water's edge and dipped my face in, drinking some water. Once I started up the ramp, I couldn't come back. There would be no more water. I unwrapped the remaining soggy candy bar and ate it. Then I got to work.

An hour later, I had two sections of ramp carved out for a total of about three feet. It was getting harder now as I dug into the embankment. There was dirt overhanging above both me and the ramp. If it fell all at once, it could bury me, or fall on my broken legs and make me immobile. It was delicate, dangerous work.

Somehow, when I stopped an hour later, I was nearly two-thirds of the way up the embankment. But a lot of dirt hung overhead. I'd carved out as much as I could reach, but there was still four or five feet of dirt above me that could cave in at any minute.

Being in this mini cave now, I could no longer hear any noise but the river. The sun was halfway to the horizon. I estimated I'd been here about six hours now. If I didn't get out before dark, I'd have to spend the night out here in the open. I looked up at the mass of dirt above me, wondering if I could clear that before darkness descended.

I started digging again. Dirt covered me from head to toe. My biggest problem was trying to keep it out of my eyes. Then the overhead collapsed. Some dirt slid down the ramp, but most of it fell on my head and chest. Buried, I struggled, trying to push the dirt away, trying to move my head to make space and get air. If I'd had use of my legs, I could have used them for leverage. But here, on my back, I had one arm pinned under the dirt and only my knife arm sticking out of the pile. I couldn't let go of the knife, but in my near panic, I would have to remember I had the knife and not to stab or slice myself with it.

I finally got a hole opened around my mouth and thought I could inhale. But the weight of the dirt on my chest pushed the remaining air out and I didn't have the strength to inhale against it. Broken legs or not, I was going to die here if I didn't get this dirt off me. I wiggled my legs, trying to dislodge the dirt and let it slide down the ramp. Pain shot up both legs into my spine. I thought my head might explode. My knife arm flailed at the dirt, trying to push it away down the ramp.

Like an avalanche, the dirt suddenly gave way, taking me, the ramp, and the remaining overhead dirt with it. I flailed both arms, trying to swim to the surface of the dirt before it settled in the river with me buried under it.

When it stopped, I was in the water on my left side facing upriver. The dirt made a little jetty out into the stream, trapping some of the water against the shore. I got my hands free and clawed my way out of the mud. The current was making a little pool here, a pool several feet deep, over my head. I sat up and by pushing up on my hands, could barely break the surface and grab a breath of air. I gulped it in and clawed my way toward the shore. It took several cycles of this to get me to the point where my upper body was half out of the water. The little shoreline next to the embankment was now under water. I'd come as far as I could. But I no longer had anywhere to go to get out of the water. And I'd lost the knife.

I looked up at the embankment. Where I'd dug out the ramp was as vertical as ever, now just an indentation in the wall. Mother nature at work.

Panting, I put my head down on a rock and lay there. For some reason, the Gleaner came to mind. Then Daddy's head lying in the wheat bin. I saw the cotter pin with one unbent leg. I saw Momma standing on the front porch, looking out across the south pasture as a freight train rolled by in the distance.

I wasn't going to make it out of here. All the advice against this journey had been good advice I just didn't take. No, that wasn't true. If I was going to die, I was going to die trying to be who I wanted to be. No regrets at not becoming someone others wanted me to be. I was strong, chasing my own dreams and trying to be the best for me, and for what I'd hoped to do for mankind.

I thought of Sam. The only boy I would ever kiss. His wolf eyes twinkling. His goofy grin. I could hear Susie admonishing me for not have sex with him. My only chance, lost. This would be my grave, buried in the embankment, my flesh rotting away in wet sandy soil.

I was shivering again. The water was cold, drawing out what heat I had left. There was nowhere to get out of the water now. I'd given it my best. But I'd lost. I put my head back down on a rock. I knew my core temperature was dropping. The sunlight was getting dim, too. I wondered what death would be like on the other side. Would it be as horrific as it was on this side?

CHAPTER 38

My nose twitched. An antiseptic smell replaced the stench of wet riverbank. I tried to open my eyes, but everything was a glaring bright white. I wondered if this was heaven or hell. It was clean, bright, and white. Likely not hell.

A beeping sound caught my attention. Why did they have pagers in heaven? I drifted back to sleep.

The next time I woke up, the smell, bright lights, and beeping were still there. I cracked one eye open. Pain knifed into my head. I closed the eye. By squinting a little at a time, I was able to finally get my right eye open. I realized my left eye was open, too, but it seemed to be covered up with something. Dirt. My head was still buried in the riverbank. I tried to move my head, but I couldn't do it. It wasn't dirt. It didn't smell like dirt here.

I glanced around with one eye. Nothing much to see. White ceiling, white walls. The beeping continued. I wondered why they didn't shut that off. Maybe I was in hell, and this was to be my forever torture.

Something clicked in my head. The beeping was in time to my heartbeat. I tried to look behind me but couldn't turn my head. Still, I caught sight of several tubes and cables. And there was a bag hanging on a pole next to my bed. I was in a hospital.

I began to cry. Tears leaked out of my right eye and down my cheek. I wasn't sure why I was crying, but I needed to figure it out. Nevertheless, I drifted back to sleep, congratulating myself because I wasn't dead after all.

#####

Sometime later, I woke up again. This time I was immediately aware of being in a hospital. I lay there looking around. Both of my legs were encased in casts that were elevated by a series of ropes and pulleys attached to a bar over the foot of my bed.

With some effort, I was able to raise my right hand to my face and feel the bandage over my left eye. I blinked. Both eyes seemed to work. I thought about peeling the bandage off but decided that someone thought it was necessary for some reason. If I'd lost my eyesight, I'd never be an astronaut. My legs would heal. But my eye was a deal breaker.

A middle-aged nurse walked into the room. She was a very tan woman with black hair and dark eyes. Her mouth flew open when she realized I was awake.

"Hello, Trudy."

I tried to protest at the use of my given name, but all I could do was open and close my mouth.

She produced a cup of water with a straw. "Here. Sip a little of this."

I took a sip. It felt glorious. It didn't smell of rotting wood or riverbank. I whispered, "More."

She obliged. "Trudy, you're in a hospital and you're going to be okay."

"Hate my name. Call me Tink. Please."

"Okay, Tink. I'll make a note of it on your chart, too."

"How'd I get here?"

"Ambulance is all I know."

"When?"

"Three days ago."

"What's wrong with my eye?"

"You have a corneal abrasion. Lot of dirt in it, but it's going to be fine."

I felt a tear trickle out of my right eye. I could still have my dream. And that's what I did for the next few hours. I dreamed about being an astronaut. But in my dreams, I was a pirate astronaut with a patch over one eye.

CHAPTER 39

I think it was the next day when I fully woke up. It wasn't clear whether I had just been out of it or they had been sedating me. But when the sun rose, my brain awakened. Or maybe it was the odd noise that woke me.

I looked around the room. Someone sat in a chair near the foot of my bed. A man. His head was leaning on the footrail of my bed, long hair hanging down, covering his face. He was snoring. I snagged the water cup from the stand and took a couple of lubricating sips.

"Hello."

The snoring continued.

I called a little louder. "Hello."

Nothing. Still snoring.

There was a call button hanging from the side of my bed rail. I pushed it. In a few minutes, a nurse, the same middle-aged lady from yesterday, came in. She glanced at the snoring figure and walked over to my bedside.

"How are you feeling today?"

"I'm much better, thanks." I pointed to the snoring person at the foot of my bed. "Who is that?"

She smiled. "He hasn't left the hospital since they brought you in. I couldn't make him sleep in the lobby again, so I snuck him in here last night."

My heart took off like a drag racer. Was this one of the hobos who'd cornered me on the train. How had they tracked me down?

And why were they at the hospital? They probably planned to kill me anyhow.

Before I could say anything to the nurse, the snoring stopped and the head raised. Pale wolf eyes peered at me.

I screamed and tried to roll out of bed. My casts were attached, so all I really did was roll my shoulders into the nurse. She grabbed me. "Dear, what's wrong? Are you okay?"

The door to the room burst open. Another nurse and a man in green scrubs came running in.

The person at the bottom of the bed jumped up. "Tink. It's me. It's okay."

I was crying, at least from my right eye. I was trying to scramble behind the nurse who was holding me. And then his voice registered. Sam. No, it couldn't be Sam. He was in Chicago. It had to be the hobo who just sounded like Sam. I peeked over the nurse's shoulder while I sobbed. It was Sam. Or I was hallucinating.

I pulled back from the nurse. "Am I hallucinating? Is there really someone standing there?"

The other nurse said to her, "Do you need help, Tsula? Sedative?"

"We're good. Aren't we, Tink? Just settle down. You're not hallucinating. There really is a man standing at the foot of your bed. I thought he was your friend. Does he frighten you?" She glared in his direction.

It seemed like forever before my brain could process what was actually going on. I felt foolish and pushed back in my bed, letting go of Tsula. I looked at Sam. "Is it really you?"

He smiled. A tear dribbled down his cheek. "It's me, Tink. I found you. And you're gonna be okay."

I nodded, unable to speak because tears were streaming down my face. I could feel that the patch on my left eye had tears under it, too. I ripped it off and just lay there leaking tears in bewilderment. After a moment, I reached out my arms toward Sam. He came around the bed tand hugged me. We stayed like that for a long time, I think. When I was finally cried out and let go, the hospital folks were gone.

Sam sat on the edge of the bed and smoothed my hair back. "You're going to be okay, Tink."

CHAPTER 40

Before we could really get started with our stories, a white-coated man came in and introduced himself as Doctor Yellowtail. Sam stood up and moved away from my bed as he approached.

"Hello, Tink. How are you feeling today?"

"Overwhelmed. My friend Sam was about to fill me in on how I got here. I guess I'm missing a few days."

"You had quite a contusion above your right eye. Blunt trauma of some sort. We assumed it might have been from your fall."

I ran my hand over my forehead. There was a sore lump above my right eye. "I wasn't aware." It was from Raspy's fist, but I wasn't going to tell them that right now. It would just complicate the situation and maybe delay me even more.

"There was no intracerebral hemorrhage, but you were definitely concussed. Do you remember us talking yesterday?"

"Yesterday? No, this is the first time I've met you."

He made a note on his clipboard.

I looked at Sam, and then at Tsula. "Isn't it?"

Sam took my hand. "It's okay. He was here yesterday and the day before. You were groggy."

"Sam is correct, Tink. But don't worry about it. It's perfectly normal for a blow like that. And I think you're going to remember today." He scribbled some more on his clipboard. "Who removed your eye patch?"

"I did."

He chuckled. "It was coming off today anyhow." He moved closer and shined a small flashlight into my eyes. He asked me to follow his finger back and forth, up and down. "Does your left eye feel okay? Feel like there's anything in it?"

"No. Feels fine."

"How about vision? Clear?"

"Yes." He had me do some one-eye tests by covering my other eye. That seemed to go okay, and he scribbled some more.

"Okay. About your legs. In my opinion, you are extremely lucky to have both tibia's broken like that and not have a compound fracture nor any serious underlying tissue damage." He waved his hand. "I didn't put that very well. Breaking your legs isn't lucky. But the damage was minimal, given the nature of the breaks."

"Will they heal okay?"

"Yes. I think you'll be fine. Dr. Germann pinned each one. They are percutaneous pins—went right through your skin into your bones. You probably won't even have a scar."

"How long?"

"They'll come out when the healing is adequate. Maybe three to four weeks. After that, you can start to bear weight. Six weeks to walking with a cane or walker. Full recovery—maybe ten weeks."

"I have to be in Missoula on the thirty-first."

"I heard about that." He glanced at Sam, and then back to me. "You'll probably be here another few days and then you can make your way to Missoula. You can do follow-up there. Take out the pins. Physical therapy. I suggest you go in a car, though."

My head was starting to throb. I just realized I had a headache.

"We'll pull your IV shortly and get you started on solid food. Are you feeling hungry?"

My stomach growled in response.

He laughed. "I'll take that as a yes. Any questions for me?"

"Not right now. Thank you for taking care of me."

"My pleasure. I'll see you tomorrow morning." He left.

Tsula stepped forward and disconnected the IV. "We'll keep the cannula in your arm until you're discharged. We don't want to stick you over and over if we need you back on IV. How about some breakfast? We don't have much selection. Omelet or oatmeal?"

"Both?"

She smiled. "Sure. I'll be back shortly."

Sam resumed his seat on the bed and held my hand. That goofy grin with those wolf eyes was a psycho combination.

He said, "Maybe you need a nap before we start on the stories. I can wake you when breakfast shows up."

I nodded. He must have seen my droopy eyelids struggling to stay open. "Sorry. But I'll get better."

"Yes. I know." He kissed my hand and laid it across my chest as I drifted off.

#####

When I woke, the sun was bright. Sam sat in the chair at the foot of my bed reading a paperback.

"Hey. What are you reading?"

He came around to the bedside and took my hand. It's called *The Falling Astronauts*. Tsula gave it to me. Someone had left it at the hospital."

"Is it about me?"

"No, Tink. It's about astronauts who go mad on the moon."

"Maybe I can get a head start."

Sam grinned. "You slept through breakfast. They have burgers for lunch. Are you good with that?"

"Yeah. I'm starving."

"I'll tell Tsula."

When Sam came back, he raised the head of my bed so I could sit up. I recounted the story of Raspy and Squeaky, my fall from the boxcar, and my attempts to get off the riverbank. As I finished, Tsula brought in a tray of food. Pepsi, cheeseburger, and fries. How much better could it get? I bit into the cheeseburger and motioned towards Sam. "Your turn."

He pulled the chair around to the side of the bed and sat down. "After you hopped that train in Denver, I watched until it pulled out. Just as it started moving, two guys came out of the bushes and hopped a boxcar a few behind you. From what you'd told me about the guys you saw in Pueblo, I thought they might be the same ones. If they were, I thought they might be trying to follow you.

"Your train was gone, though. I was too late to get on it. But there was another in two hours. Remember, I told you the ticket lady had said that?"

I nodded as I chewed more cheeseburger. I realized I wasn't going to be able to eat all of this right now.

"The guys were only a few cars behind you, but I didn't think they'd try to get to your car in the dark. Cheyenne yard is too big and well lit. Not there. Casper was where they'd try to get to your car. Given the timing, it would be dark until after Sheridan. They'd wait until they had some light before moving in.

"I worked this out while I was riding the train behind you. There was no way I could catch up and that drove me crazy. All I could do was hope you got out of the car and I could find you along the way. So, after Sheridan, I hung at the door of my boxcar, scanning along the track and in the adjacent weeds."

I put the cheeseburger down, my stomach cramping at being so full. "You were looking for my body."

"Maybe. I was afraid of that. But I knew you were strong and resourceful. I figured you would outsmart those two."

"I should have knifed the guy in front of me first, and then jumped. I could probably have taken him before the other guy got back up." I looked at Sam. "So, how did you find me?"

"Luck. Providence. I don't know. I spotted something bright orange next to the weeds. It seemed to take a long time for me to figure out what it was. I'd already passed it when I realized it was your backpack.

"I jumped off and ran back to it. The top was open, so the orange underside was sticking out. That's what caught my eye. Even when I was five feet away, I couldn't have spotted it if the orange wasn't showing. Your mom's phone number was on the top flap.

"Was it empty?"

"Almost. They only thing in it was some notebooks. They stole everything else, Tink."

My heart leaped. "My notebooks? You got my notebooks?"

Sam smiled at me. "Yup. There's three.

I reached out both arms toward Sam. He jumped up and hugged me. "Thank you, Sam. Thank you so much. I can never repay you. You're such a good person. Thank you, thank you, thank you."

"Hey, I haven't even gotten to the good part yet."

"Yes, you did. My life. This journey. It's all in those notebooks."

"Okay. I'm glad you got them back."

I sniffed and sat back. "Okay. Continue. Before I fall asleep again."

"Boring story?"

"No, but I have a full stomach and I'm tired for some reason." I sipped the Pepsi.

Sam began to pace alongside my bed. "The guys had obviously found you, so I was right to follow. They'd dumped your backpack so there'd be no evidence of their encounter with you. They'd either keep what was in the backpack as theirs or sell it to some other hobo.

"I didn't think they'd take the time to sort out the backpack if they still had you. That meant they'd dumped you somewhere back down the track. Someplace I'd passed. Someplace I didn't spot you. I panicked."

"You thought I was dead."

Sam wrinkled up his face. "If you were injured, you'd know to stay near the tracks so a train engineer might spot you and send help. Either you walked away, or, yes, you were dead. Didn't matter. I had to find you.

"I ran back down the track, scouring the weeds alongside. I was frantic. But I found nothing. Just old trash, weeds, bushes, and trees all the way to the fence. After a couple of miles, I wasn't sure you were there anymore. And I was exhausted from running, searching, and worrying.

"And then I heard a noise. An engine. Down the track. Maybe another mile. I resumed my search in the weeds, working my way towards the engine. Halfway there, I decided the noise was a tractor. I thought maybe someone there could have seen you if you walked out.

"On the other side of the tracks, there was a state highway and next to that was a freeway. If you walked out, you could have hitched a ride and been long gone.

"Just before I found the tractor, the freeway split away and headed east. At the same time, a creek curved alongside the tracks. I started looking closer, thinking you might have tried to make it to water. Finally, the creek turned away and there was an open field with no bushes or fence on either side of the track. There was a tractor pulling some farm equipment behind it. I ran out into the field and flagged it down. The guy, his name was James, was planting spring wheat but he'd been there for several hours and hadn't seen anyone. He didn't remember the train. They went by all the time.

"He told me he had a barn across the highway. It had a well and I could get water there. I was sweating from running and decided to slow down and think while I got some water. I made my way across the tracks and highway and up the short road to his barn. The entrance was on the opposite side, so I had to walk around the barn to get in."

I could see Sam starting to tear up. I reached out a hand and he took it. He stared at the floor. "Tink. When I turned the corner and looked in the barn, there was a combine sitting in there."

He was almost fully crying now.

"It's okay, Sam."

He looked at me. "It was a Gleaner." He grabbed me and hugged while he sobbed. "I knew I'd found you, Tink. You were there, somehow, someplace."

He wiped his nose and resumed pacing. "I searched the barn and everywhere around it. Nothing. I knew you were there, Tink. I could feel it in my heart. You were right there. I started widening my search. I went back to the highway, up and down the ditches. I walked through the weeds between the highway and the track. I couldn't find you. Finally, I started yelling your name. I thought maybe you could give me a sign of where you were. Nothing. All I could hear was James' tractor and the rushing water in the stream. I was about to give up. I'd walked back up the track to where the stream turned away from the tracks. James's tractor stopped. I turned and saw him climb down from the tractor and start doing something with his equipment. The stream noise was all I could hear now. It occurred to me that maybe you fell into the stream. I started to climb over the fence and saw that the post was broken off. It was an old wooden post, half-rotted. But the top third was snapped over towards the stream, hanging there by one rusty wire. Recently. And the weeds on the other side were flattened all the way to the bank's edge.

"I think I jumped over the fence and landed right at the edge of the embankment. The creek had been eating out a lot of dirt and there was a recent slide the current hadn't yet carried downstream. I almost missed you, Tink. It was just your head and one arm sticking out, right up against the embankment. If the sun hadn't been from the west, you'd have been in shadow, and I'd have missed you for sure. You looked just like the other random rocks sticking out of the dirt.

"I waved my arms and yelled for James to come help me. I scrambled down there and waded through the water to you. You were still breathing so I started pushing the dirt away, into the water. By the time I had you uncovered, James was there. But we were afraid to move you. So he helped me built a kind of moat around you to get your body out of the water. He ran to call for help. I lay down next to you and tried to keep you warm without moving you.

"James got back in twenty minutes and the firemen got there ten minutes later. They saw your broken legs and splinted them right there in the mud and water. It took them a half-hour to get you onto their stretcher. I think it took six or eight of them to get you out of there.

"Fortunately, this little hospital serves a wide geography and has a serious emergency room. By the time James got me here in his truck, they already had you in surgery. All I could do was wait. I had your backpack and thought about calling your mom. But what would I tell her? It would just drive her crazy, so I waited. Maybe I went a little crazy. I'm sorry, but I was nuts. I read your notebooks."

"It's okay, Sam. It's okay. I'm not mad. It makes sense, after all you've been through." I yawned. "I think we have to stop here, though, before I fall asleep on you."

"Sure." He came to my bedside and stroked my hair. "We'll talk later, Tink. You rest and get better."

His touch was so soothing, I fell right to sleep.

#####

When I woke, I'd dreamed about Sam searching for me. I wouldn't be here if he hadn't. He saved my life. That was more important than my journals, but he'd saved those, too. We didn't even know each other. Two days together in Denver. That was it. And he'd turned his life upside down on a hunch that I might be in trouble.

I looked at him sitting in the chair reading that novel. His wolf eyes shifted back and forth from line to line. He turned a page and glanced up at me.

"Have you been playing possum?"

"Just woke up. Wondering why you're here at all."

He stood up and walked to the bedside. "Not really sure. Maybe I wanted you to finish that story about your nipples."

My face flashed hot-red. He stood there laughing at his own joke.

"I can guarantee you'll never hear about them again."

His face went serious. "I'm kidding, Tink. Just lightening the mood."

"Dug yourself a hole, I think."

He smirked. "We'll see." He sat down on the side of my bed. "I talked to your mom."

I felt my eyes tearing up. I bit my lip.

"She's relieved you're going to be okay, of course. Wanted to know when you'd be home. She'd like to talk to you."

"When?"

"When you're ready."

"What does she want to talk about?"

Sam shrugged. "Parent stuff, I guess."

I started fiddling with the corner of the sheet. Before I talked to Momma, I wanted to figure out where I was with Sam. She was going to ask a lot of questions about him. Questions I had, too.

"Maybe you should pull up a chair?"

He moved the chair next to the bed and sat down. "Guess we're having that talk now?"

"What talk?"

He smiled. "Elephant in the room, Tink. Pretty obvious. What now?"

My inexperience with men made me wonder if this was normal. Susie said boys never wanted to talk about their relationship or how they felt. They just wanted to have sex and a girlfriend when it was convenient for them. But Momma and Daddy weren't like that. I overheard them from time to time. They talked about their plans and expectations—more operational kinds of discussions about the farm, mortgage payments, and savings. Even though they whispered, I sometimes heard snippets of their conversations about their love for each other. They talked about how they felt, what made them mad, disappointed, or happy.

"Tink, I know you're quiet because you're thinking. Let's start with the easy part. Are you still going to Missoula?"

"Yes. But I don't know how I'm going to get there."

"This hospital is in an area known as the Crow Agency. It's like the headquarters of the Crow Indian reservation. We're about sixty miles from Billings. Dr. Yellowtail is driving to Billings on Saturday morning. He offered to let me ride with him. I'll rent a car there and drive back here to pick you up. Then we can make our way to Missoula."

"I don't have much money, Sam. Maybe forty dollars. The rest was in my pack."

"Don't worry about it. I can take care of the costs."

"What about the hospital? How will I pay them?"

"Your mother told them to send the bills to her."

There was plenty of money in the farm savings account. I'd put most of it there. Momma wasn't much of a money manager. That had always been Daddy. "Even if I had a checkbook, out-of-state checks take time to clear. Renting a car sounds expensive. We'll need to buy gas. Food. I can pay you back, but do you have that kind of cash?"

"I have a credit card. We can use that for most of it."

"You've already thought this through?"

He smiled. "Had lots of time waiting on you to wake up."

I studied those wolf eyes for a minute. "Why?"

"Why, what?"

"Why are you here? Why did you follow me? Why…" Something imploded inside me. I'd never felt kindness or caring like this. I couldn't think straight. I was happy, elated even, to be alive. I was astounded that he had found me, let alone decided to follow me. But rational thought stopped there, and a sea of swirling emotions swept over me. I covered my eyes with both hands as the tears slid down my cheeks.

He sat there, watching me while I wiped my face and blew my nose. After a moment, he said, "I guess this is where we have the hard part of the conversation."

I nodded.

He leaned forward in the chair and studied something on the floor. "Look, I've never had a real relationship. No high school girlfriend. I went off to 'Nam my junior year. When I came back, I was someone else. Angry. Unhappy. Confused. I didn't fit in my old shoes. Or my family. I had nothing in common with any of my old friends. So I started roaming. Looking for something."

He was quiet. I said, "What were you looking for?"

He sat back in the chair and looked at me. "I didn't know. Maybe I still don't. But when I'm with you, my anger goes away. I'm calm. Happy. You make me smile."

I could feel the heat from my flushed face. "Did you ever hear of the Florence Nightingale effect?"

He shook his head.

"It's where a caregiver falls in love with their patient."

He frowned. "You weren't a patient in Denver. Why do you think I followed you?"

He had a point. I sighed. My plans didn't include a relationship with a man—even one I adored. The little voice in my head was stunned at my thought. Did I just admit I adored him?

"Sam, I don't know what to say. I'm confused, lucky, and so very thankful. I loved our time together in Denver. It was the most fun I've had in years. But you know that—you read my notebooks."

He nodded.

"I need you right now. I can't do this by myself. That's hard for me to admit, but it's true. I don't have any experience to sort out my needs and gratitude from my emotions and the way I feel about you. I don't even know how to label what I feel. It's mostly confusion. But I like being with you. It's easy. It's fun. It makes me happy."

He stood and took my hand. "Tink, that's all we need right now. Let's just agree to get through this together and get you to Missoula. We'll figure out how to go from there. Deal?"

Cold chills ran up my back. Lying there on the muddy riverbank, I admitted Momma was right. I'd stopped living after Daddy died. Here it was now—an opportunity to go on living. Happily. With someone who made me laugh and treated me so kindly. He'd already saved my life in more ways than one.

I pulled his hand to my mouth and kissed it. "Deal."

#####

ACKNOWLEDGMENTS

As historical fiction, I tried to make this book as accurate as possible. However, there were some things that I knowingly fudged to make it work for the story.

The moon phases and moonrise/moonset times, for example, are inaccurate for April/May of 1971. The area around Second Creek near Altamont, Illinois, in 1971, was in the process of being turned into the Old Altamont Reservoir at the time of Tink's snake bite there. The reservoir was completed in 1972. The Open Door Diner was a gas station in 1971. The Crow/Northern Cheyenne Hospital wasn't built until 1995. I'm sure there are other inaccuracies, intended or mistaken.

For those who might think we didn't have hobos or train hopping in 1971, I invite you to visit the Hobo Museum in Britt, Iowa or visit Britt Hobo Days. They host a National Hobo Convention annually (August 10-13, 2023). The highlight of the festival is the election of the King and Queen of the Hobos. The hobos come to town and set up a hobo jungle. Don't miss the Hobo Memorial Cemetery where many steam-era hobos have been laid to rest.

To my knowledge, the Rolling Stones never played at Tulagi in Boulder, Colorado. But top headliner stars and groups of the rock era frequented the little bar as a warm-up for their recording sessions nearby. The last I read, the building that housed Tulagi is now a yoga studio and pizza parlor. Thanks to Rodney Mitchell for sharing his personal Tulagi stories when he was a student at the University of Colorado.

Thanks to Cathy Hull for the Packard inspiration and for editing this book.

The incident at the bridge with Tink's friend, Paul, was inspired by a real-life incident from my childhood with a real-life Paul.

As my family knows, throughout my life I always looked at open boxcars as doorways to adventure, but never stepped through.

Thanks to the ladies I met in the Open Door Diner when I was visiting Altamont. They provided me with accurate information for the timeline because they were in high school there in 1971.

Thanks to my late father for teaching me to tell the difference between the smell of cow manure and pig manure.

Thanks to my wife, Theresa, for putting up with my hours and hours in front of my computer.

Thanks to my beta readers, Carolyn Schwartz, Debbie Thomson, and Ashley Dorros.

You can find more information about my writing on my website at www.terryrcooper.com. My first foray into the mystery genre, *Lethal Lettuce,* is coming in December 2023. Also, my follow up to the middle grade book, *Orange Detention,* will be available on November 24, 2023, just in time for your holiday list.